Garfield ®

THE MONDAY THAT WOULDN'T END

BY JIM DAVIS

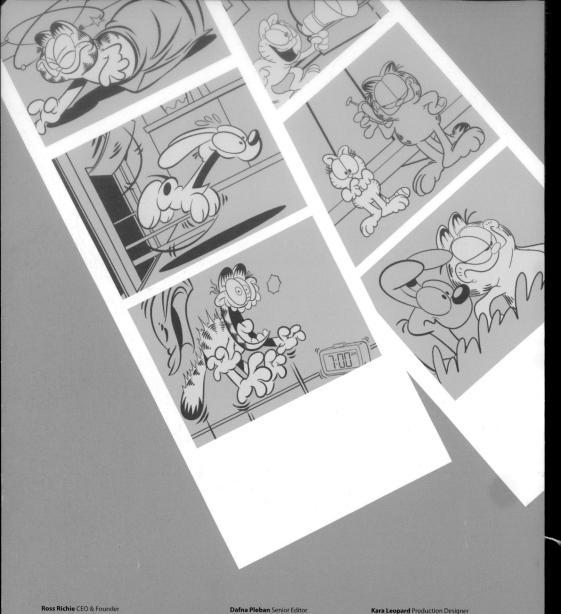

GARFIELD: THE MONDAY THAT WOULDN'T END, April 2019. Published by KaBOOM!, a division of Boom Entertainment, Inc. Garfield is © 2019 PAWS, INCORPORATED. ALL RIGHTS RESERVED. "GARFIELD" and the GARFIELD characters are registered and unregistered trademarks of Paws, Inc. KaBOOM!™ and the KaBOOM! logo are trademarks of Boom Entertainment, Inc., registered in various countries and categories. All characters, events, and institutions depicted herein are fictional. Any similarity between any of the names, characters, persons, events, and/or institutions in this publication to actual names, characters, persons, whether living or dead, events, and/or institutions is unintended and purely coincidental. KaBOOM! does not read or accept unsolicited submissions of ideas, stories, or artwork.

BOOM! Studios, 5670 Wilshire Boulevard, Suite 400, Los Angeles, CA 90036-5679. Printed in China. First Printing.

ISBN: 978-1-68415-342-8, eISBN: 978-1-64144-278-7

CONTENTS

LETTERED BY JIM CAMPBELL

COVER BY ANDY HIRSCH

DESIGNER JILLIAN CRAB
EDITOR CHRIS ROSA

GARFIELD CREATED BY
JIM DAVIS

SPECIAL THANKS TO JIM DAVIS AND THE ENTIRE PAWS, INC. TEAM.

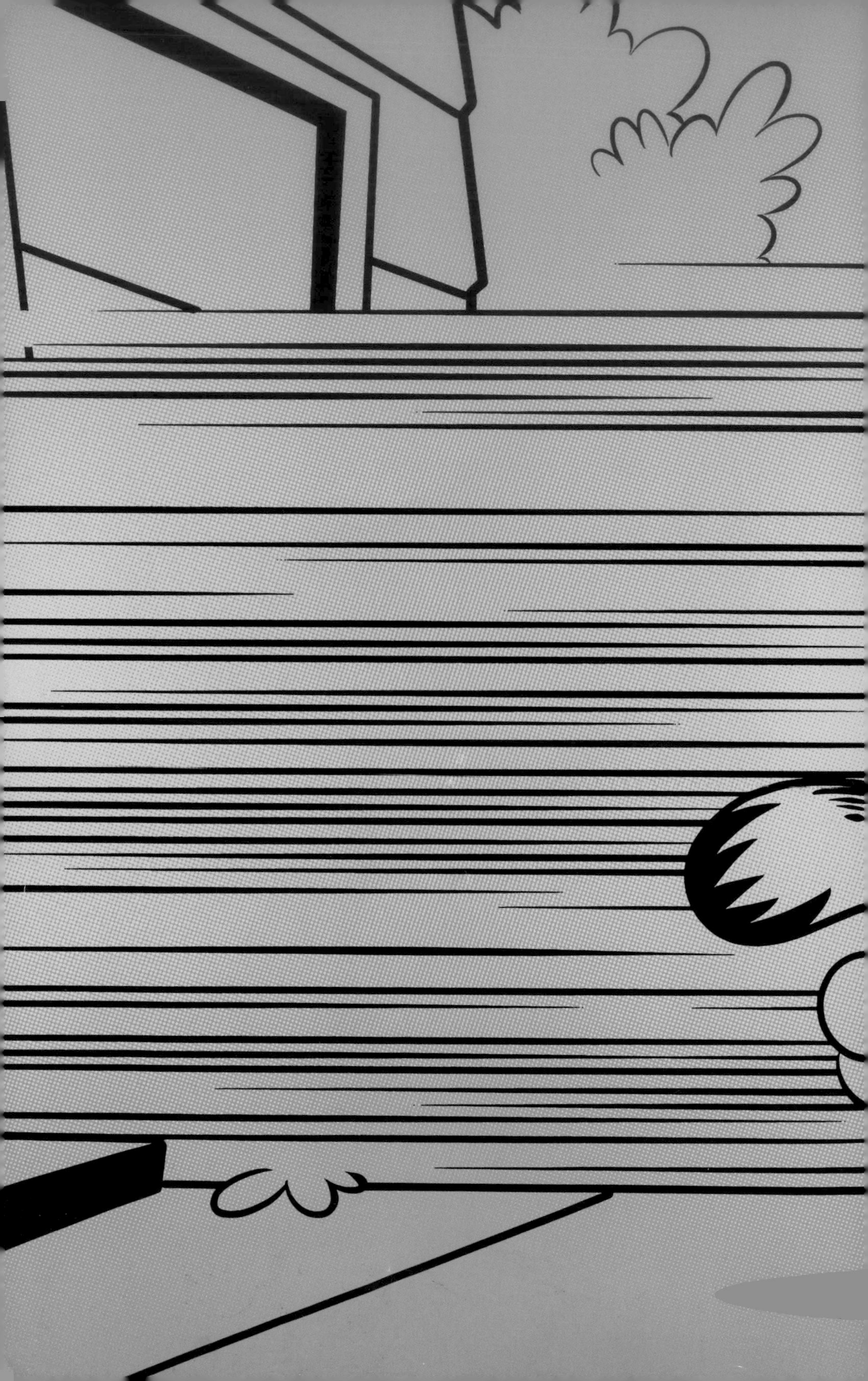

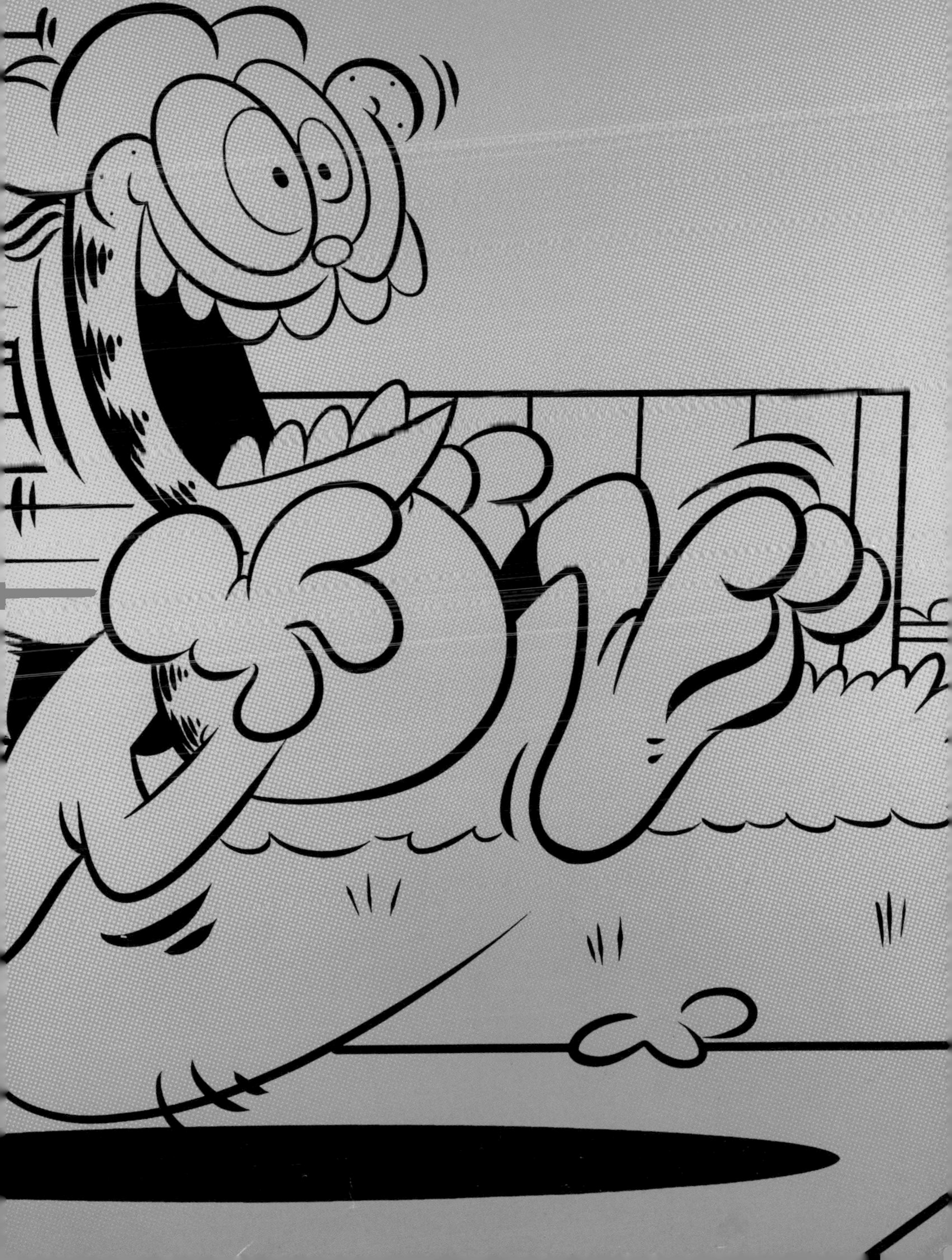

"THE MONDAY THAT WOULDN'T END"

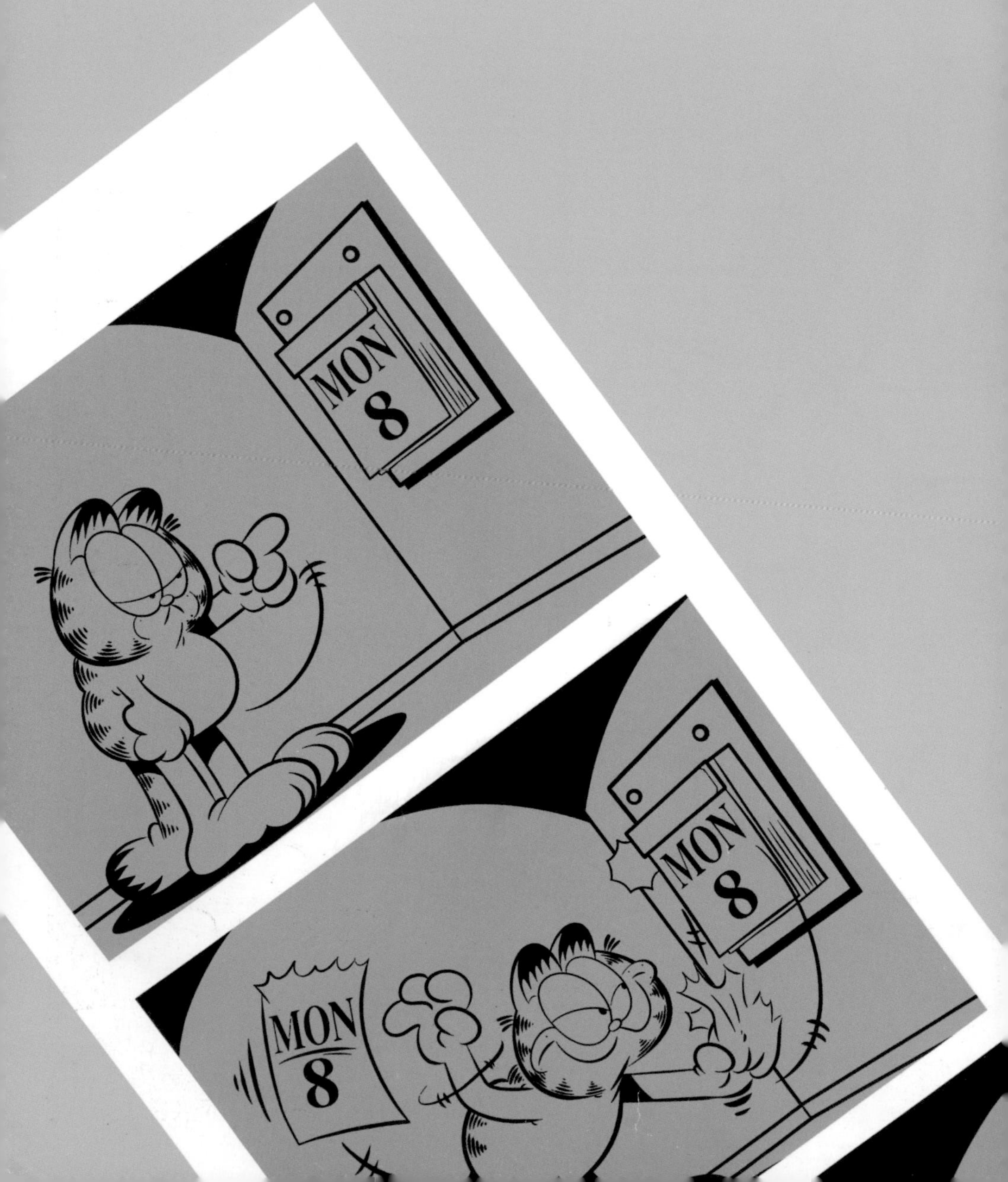

MON
8
MON
8
MON
8

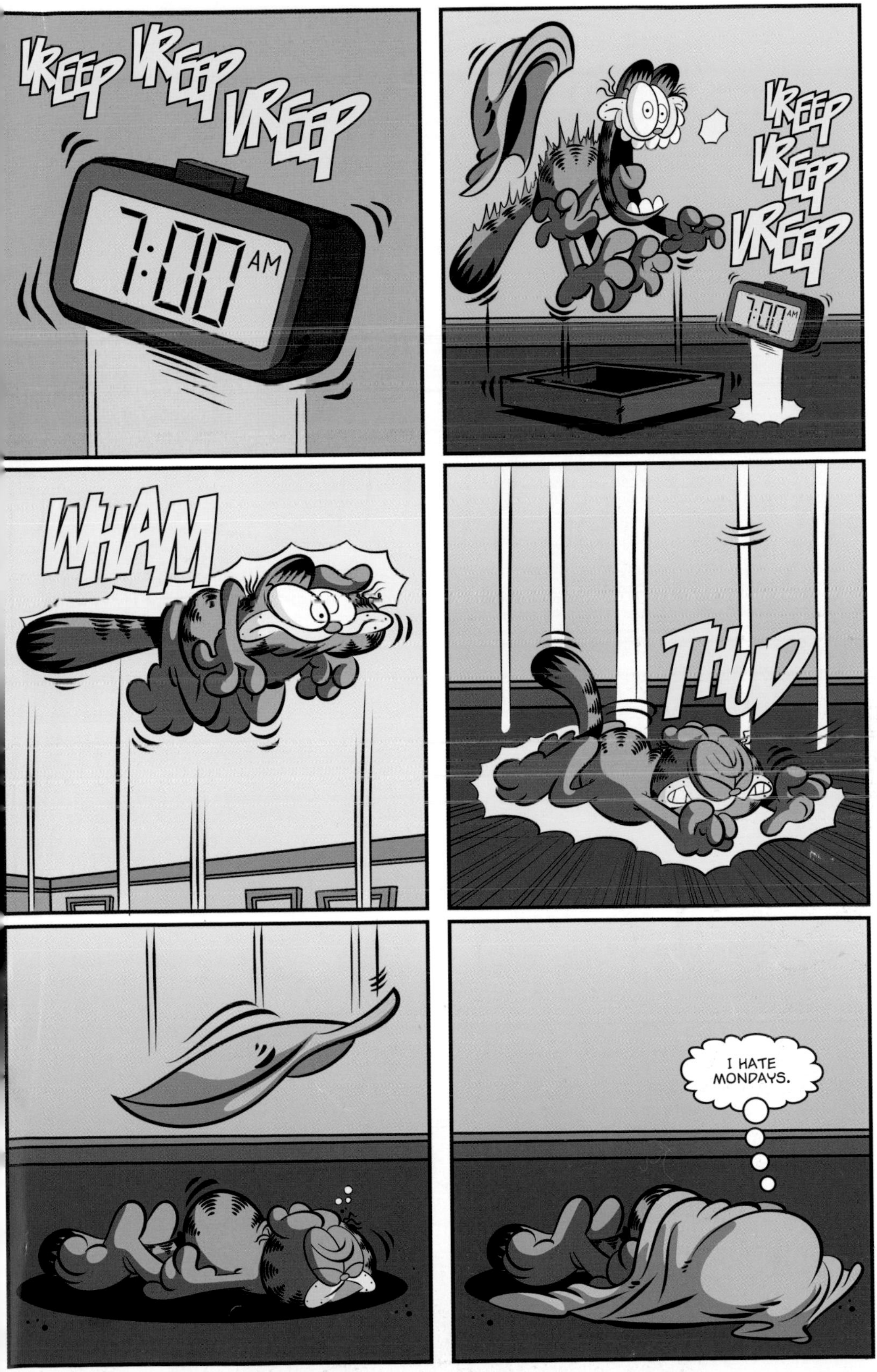
VREEP VREEP VREEP
7:00 AM
VREEP VREEP VREEP
7:00 AM
WHAM
THUD
I HATE MONDAYS.

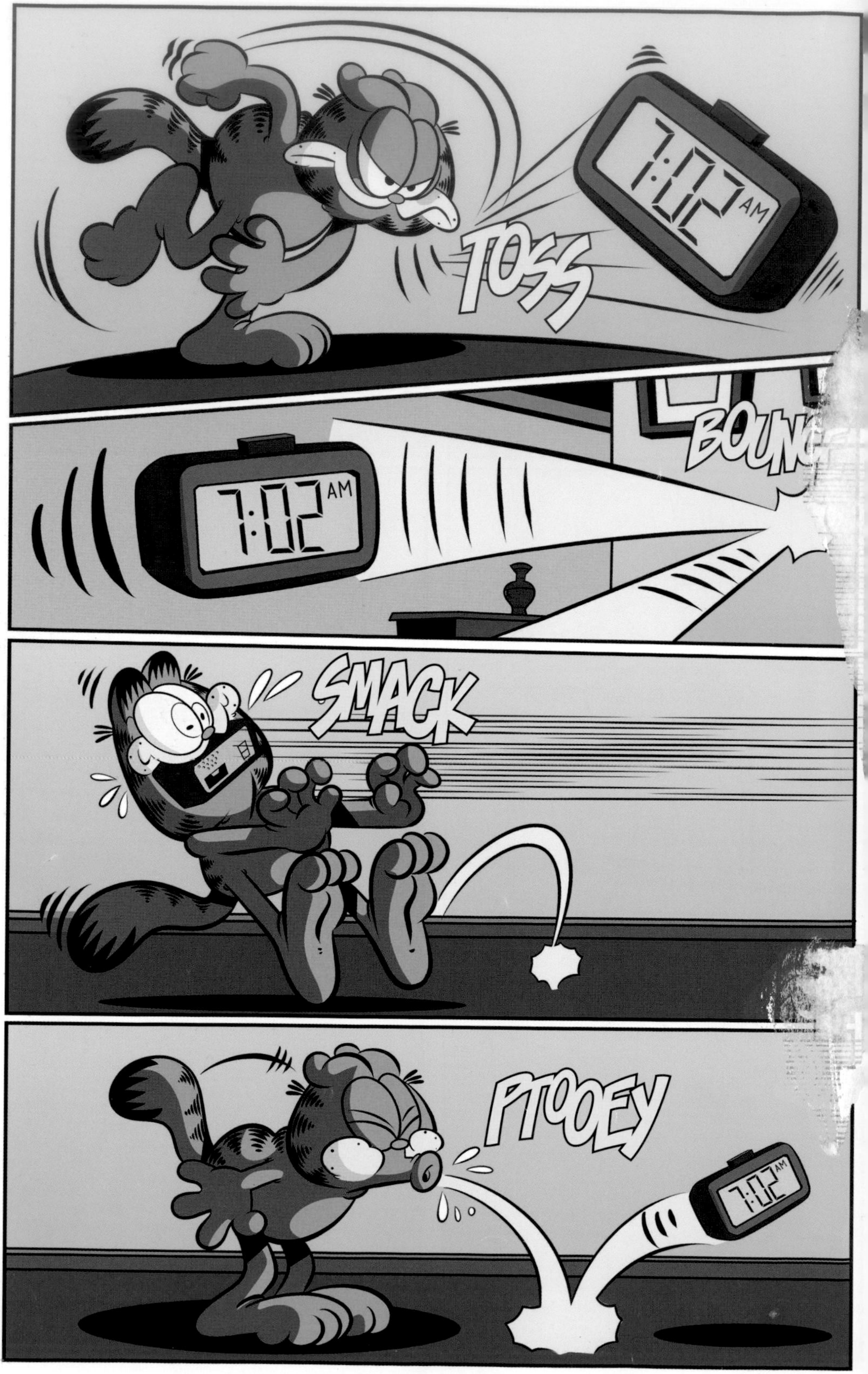
TOSS
7:02 AM
7:02 AM
SMACK
PTOOEY
7:02 AM

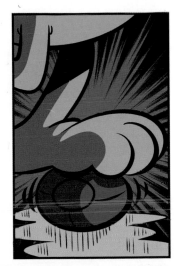

WHOA, WHOA, **WHOA!**

SPLASH

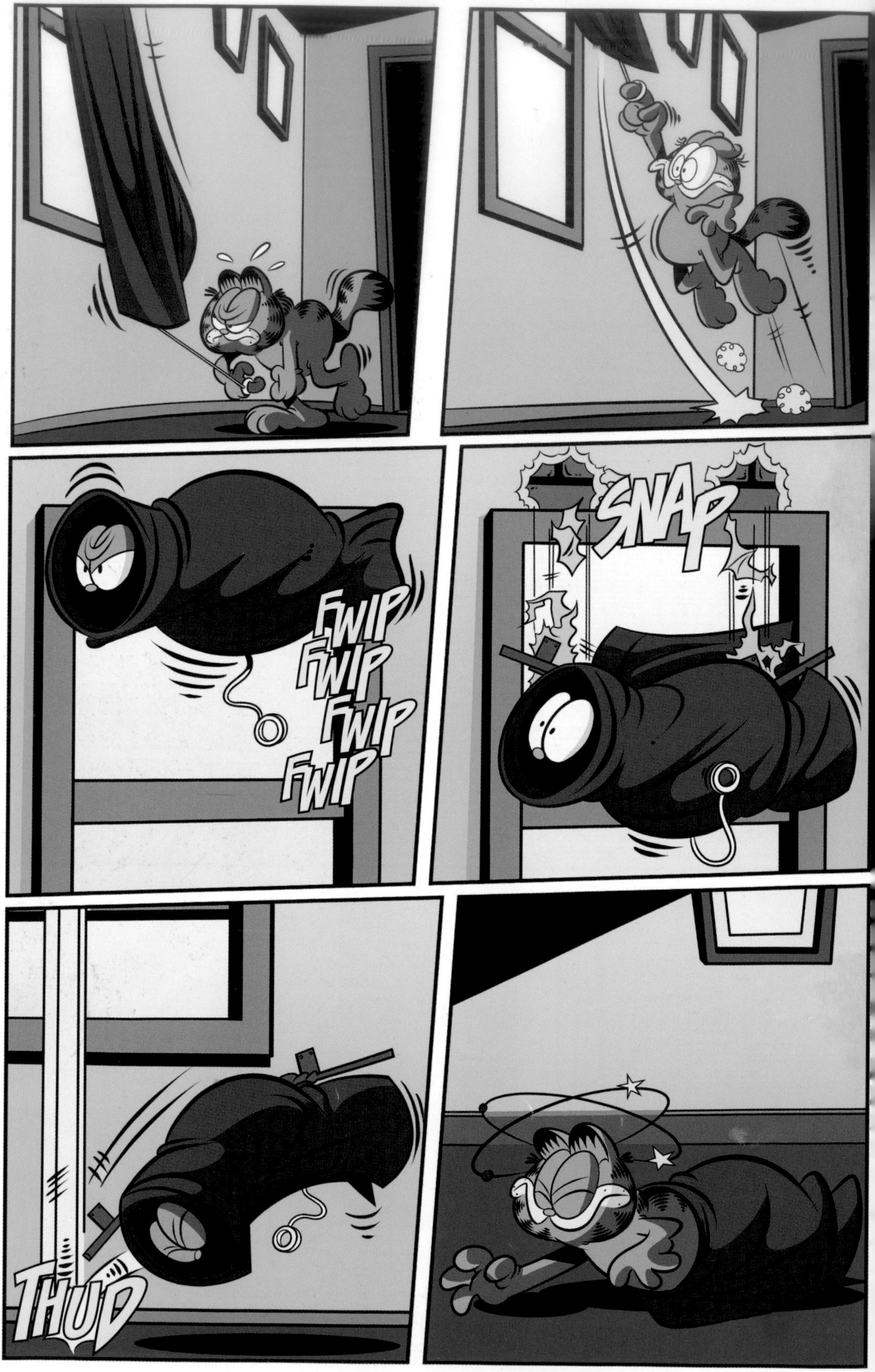
FWIP
FWIP
FWIP
FWIP
SNAP
THUD

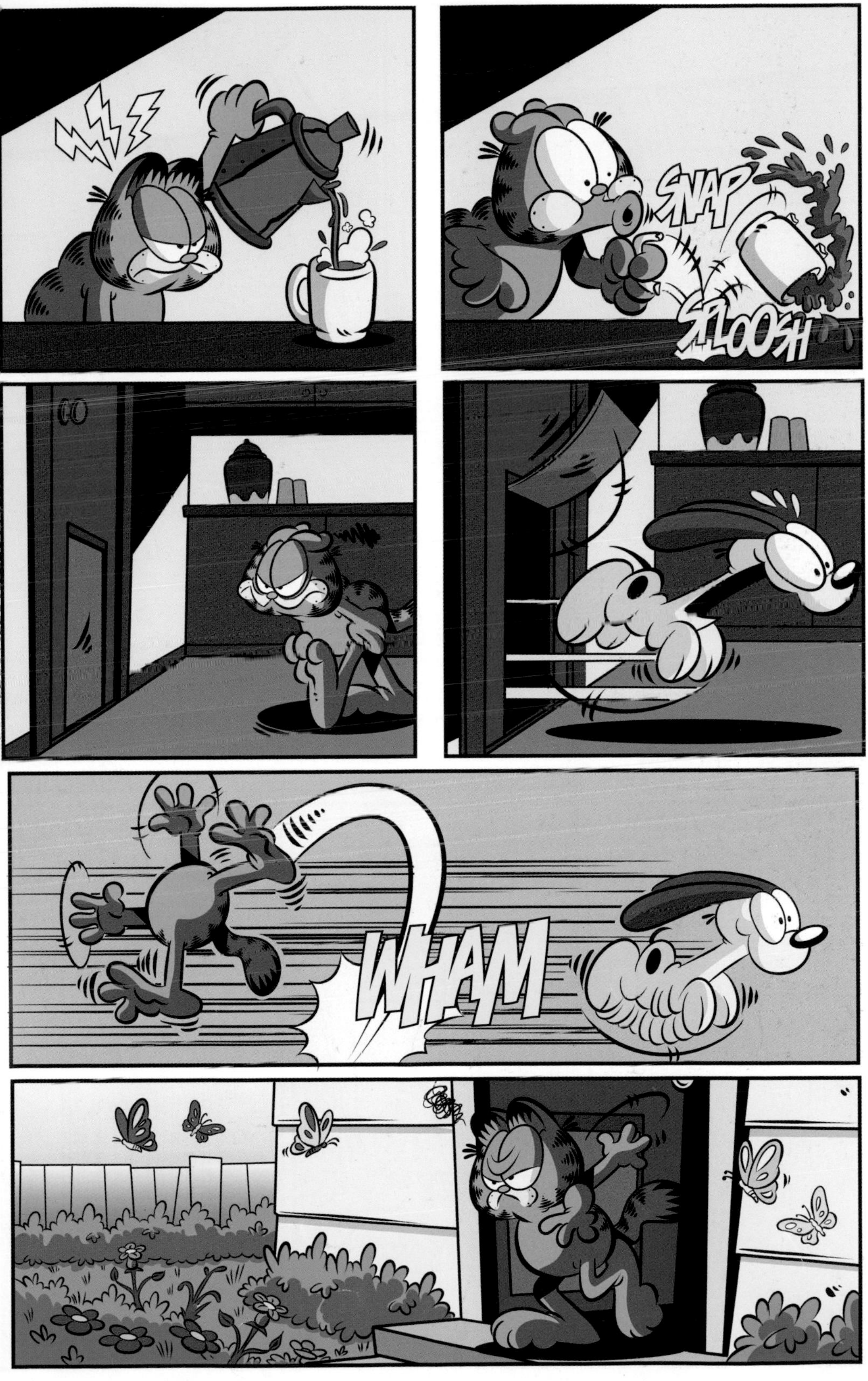
SNAP
SPLOOSH
WHAM

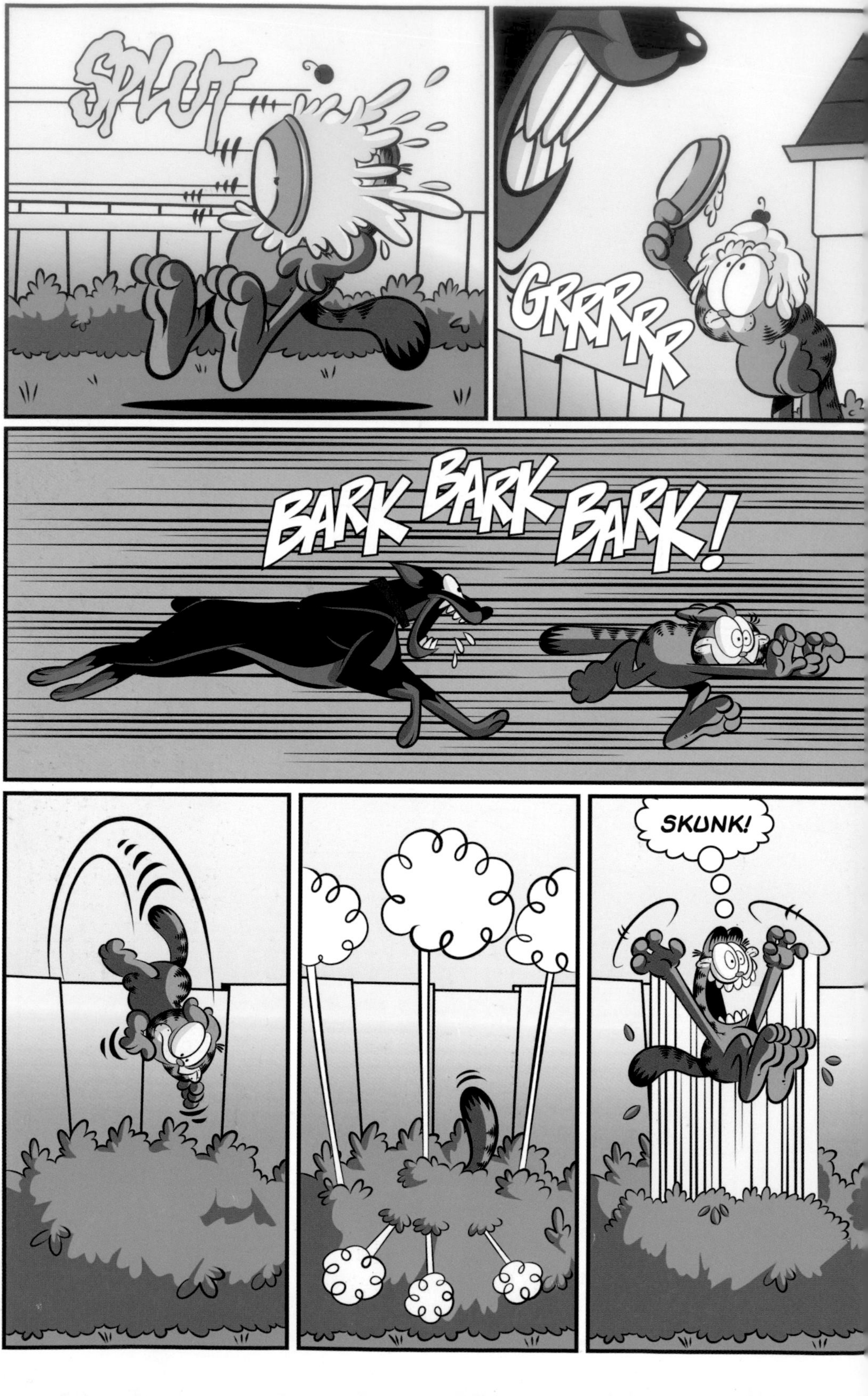
SPLUT
GRRRRRR
BARK BARK BARK!
SKUNK!

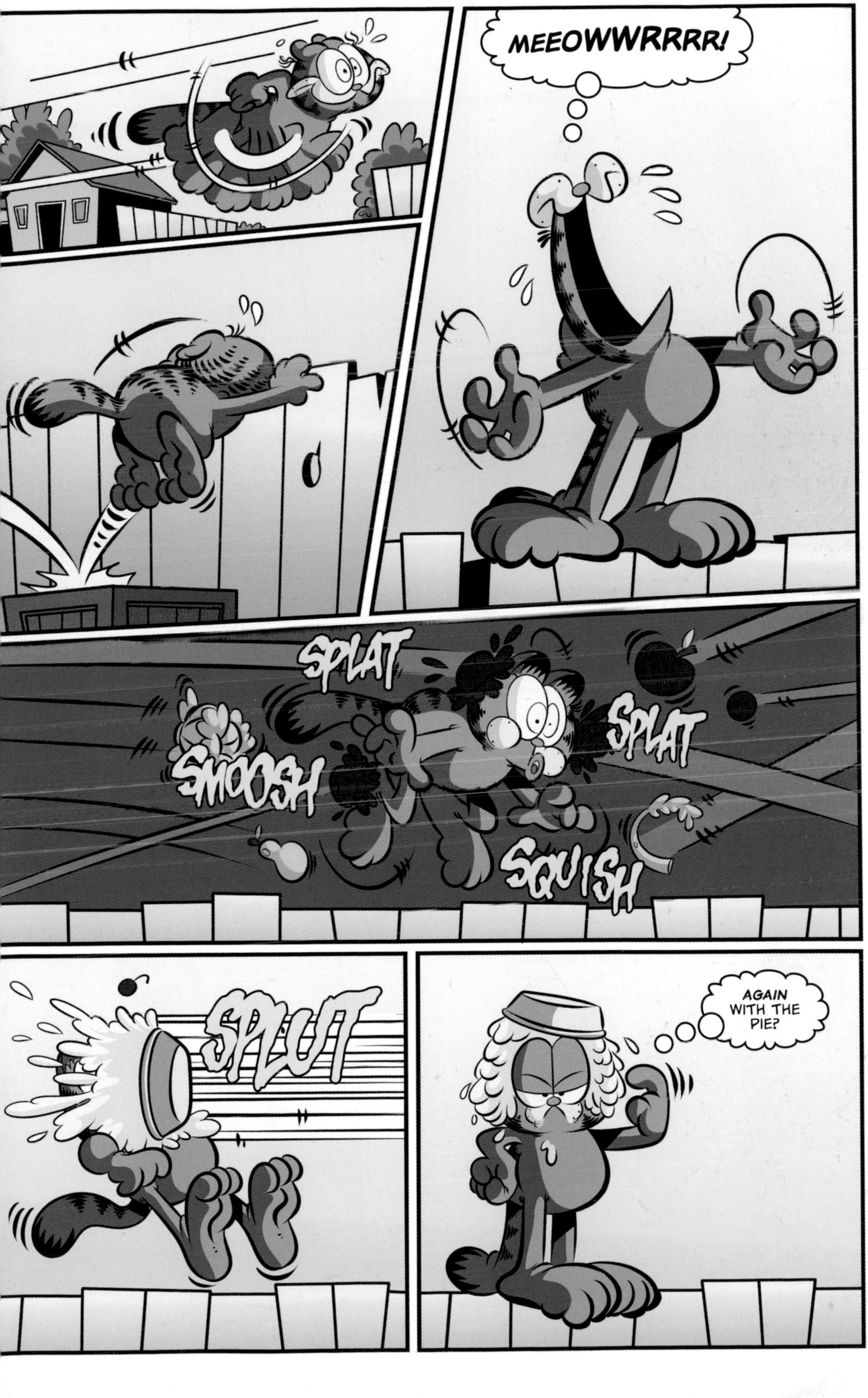
MEEOWWRRRR!
SPLAT
SPLAT
SMOOSH
SQUISH
SPLUT
AGAIN WITH THE PIE?

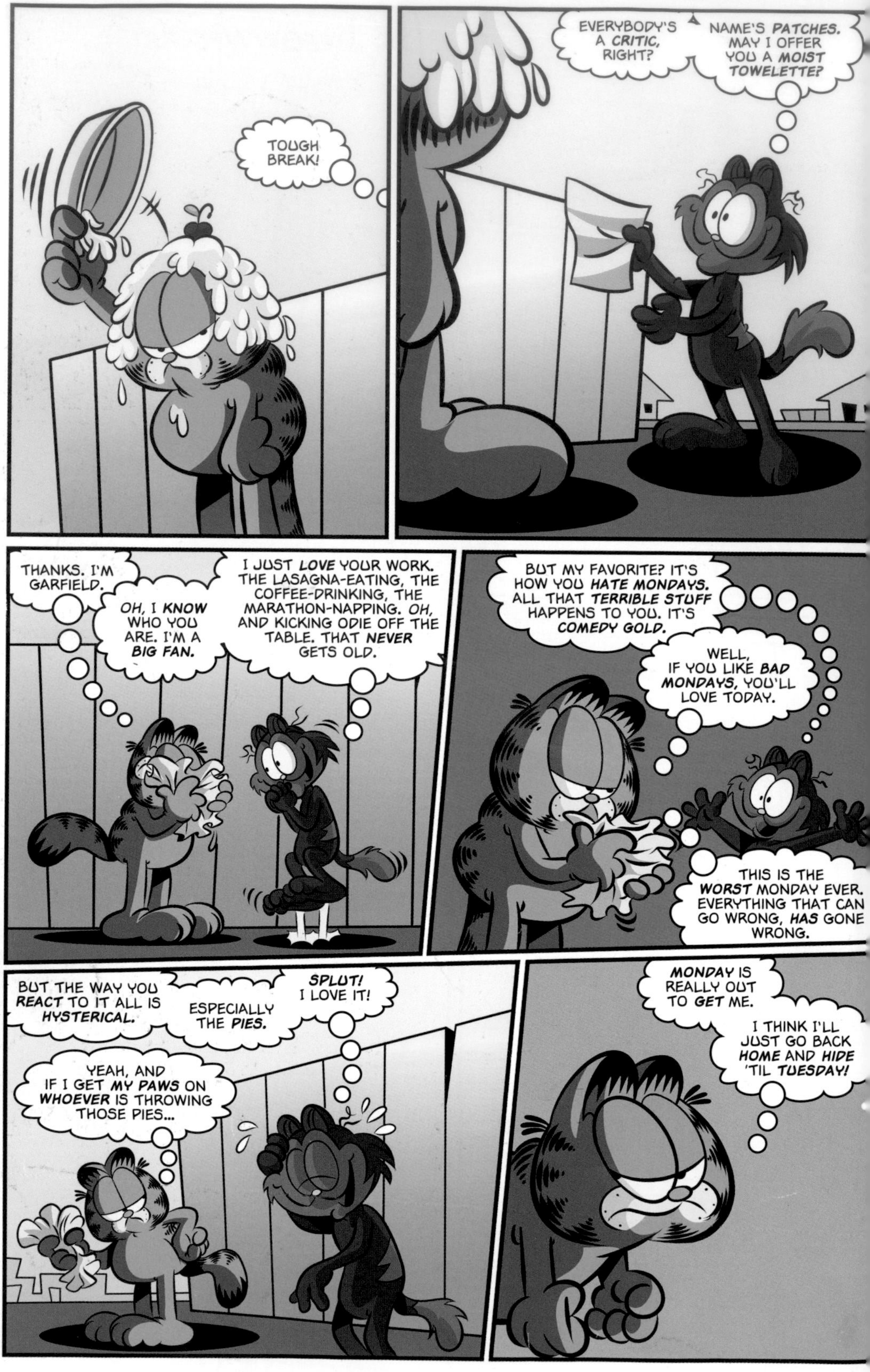
TOUGH BREAK!
EVERYBODY'S A CRITIC, RIGHT?
NAME'S PATCHES. MAY I OFFER YOU A MOIST TOWELETTE?
THANKS. I'M GARFIELD.
OH, I KNOW WHO YOU ARE. I'M A BIG FAN.
I JUST LOVE YOUR WORK. THE LASAGNA-EATING, THE COFFEE-DRINKING, THE MARATHON-NAPPING. OH, AND KICKING ODIE OFF THE TABLE. THAT NEVER GETS OLD.
BUT MY FAVORITE? IT'S HOW YOU HATE MONDAYS. ALL THAT TERRIBLE STUFF HAPPENS TO YOU. IT'S COMEDY GOLD.
WELL, IF YOU LIKE BAD MONDAYS, YOU'LL LOVE TODAY.
THIS IS THE WORST MONDAY EVER. EVERYTHING THAT CAN GO WRONG, HAS GONE WRONG.
BUT THE WAY YOU REACT TO IT ALL IS HYSTERICAL.
ESPECIALLY THE PIES.
SPLUT! I LOVE IT!
YEAH, AND IF I GET MY PAWS ON WHOEVER IS THROWING THOSE PIES...
MONDAY IS REALLY OUT TO GET ME.
I THINK I'LL JUST GO BACK HOME AND HIDE 'TIL TUESDAY!

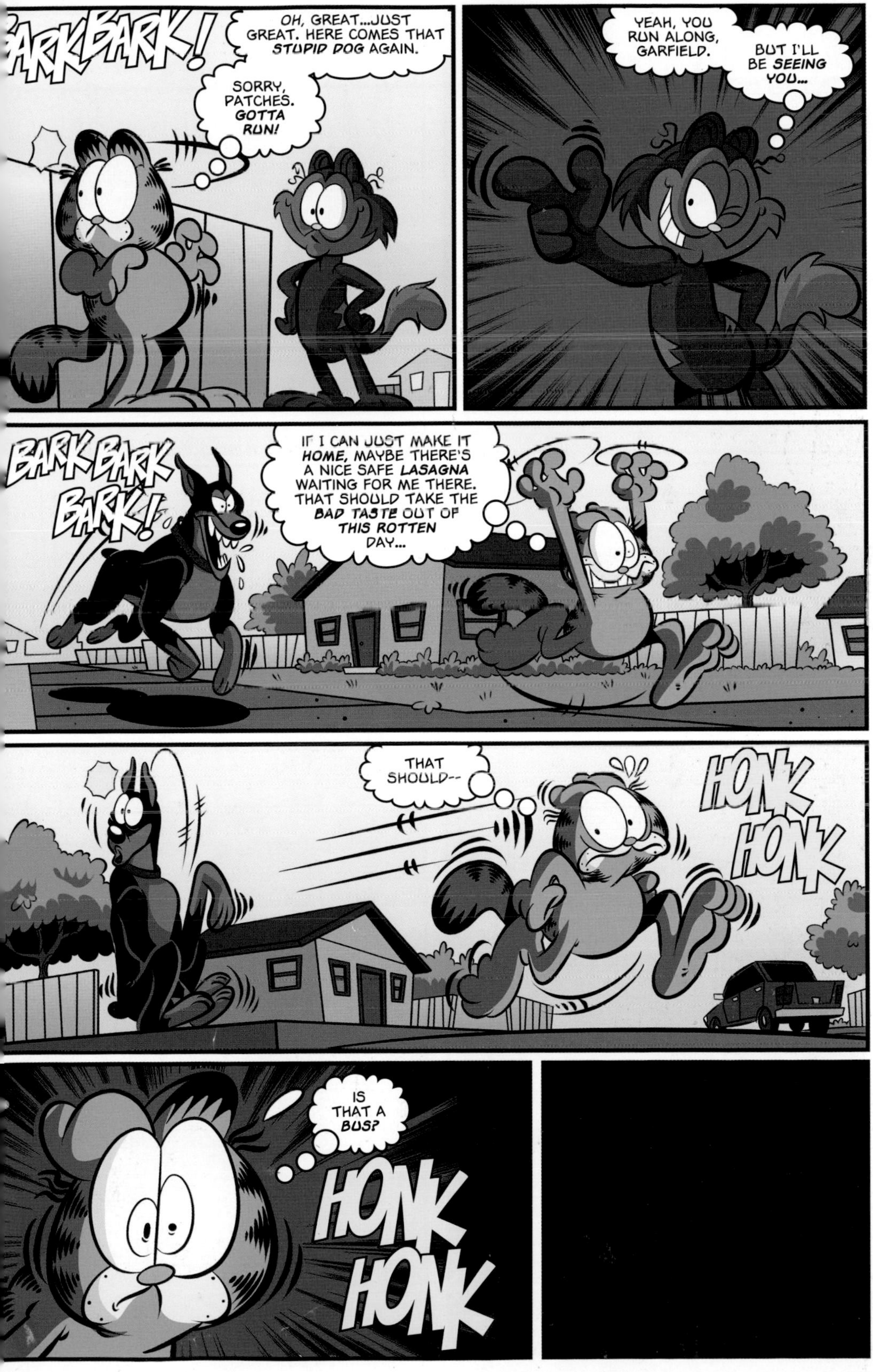
BARK BARK!
OH, GREAT...JUST GREAT. HERE COMES THAT STUPID DOG AGAIN.
SORRY, PATCHES. GOTTA RUN!
YEAH, YOU RUN ALONG, GARFIELD.
BUT I'LL BE SEEING YOU...
BARK BARK BARK!
IF I CAN JUST MAKE IT HOME, MAYBE THERE'S A NICE SAFE LASAGNA WAITING FOR ME THERE. THAT SHOULD TAKE THE BAD TASTE OUT OF THIS ROTTEN DAY...
THAT SHOULD--
HONK HONK
IS THAT A BUS?
HONK HONK

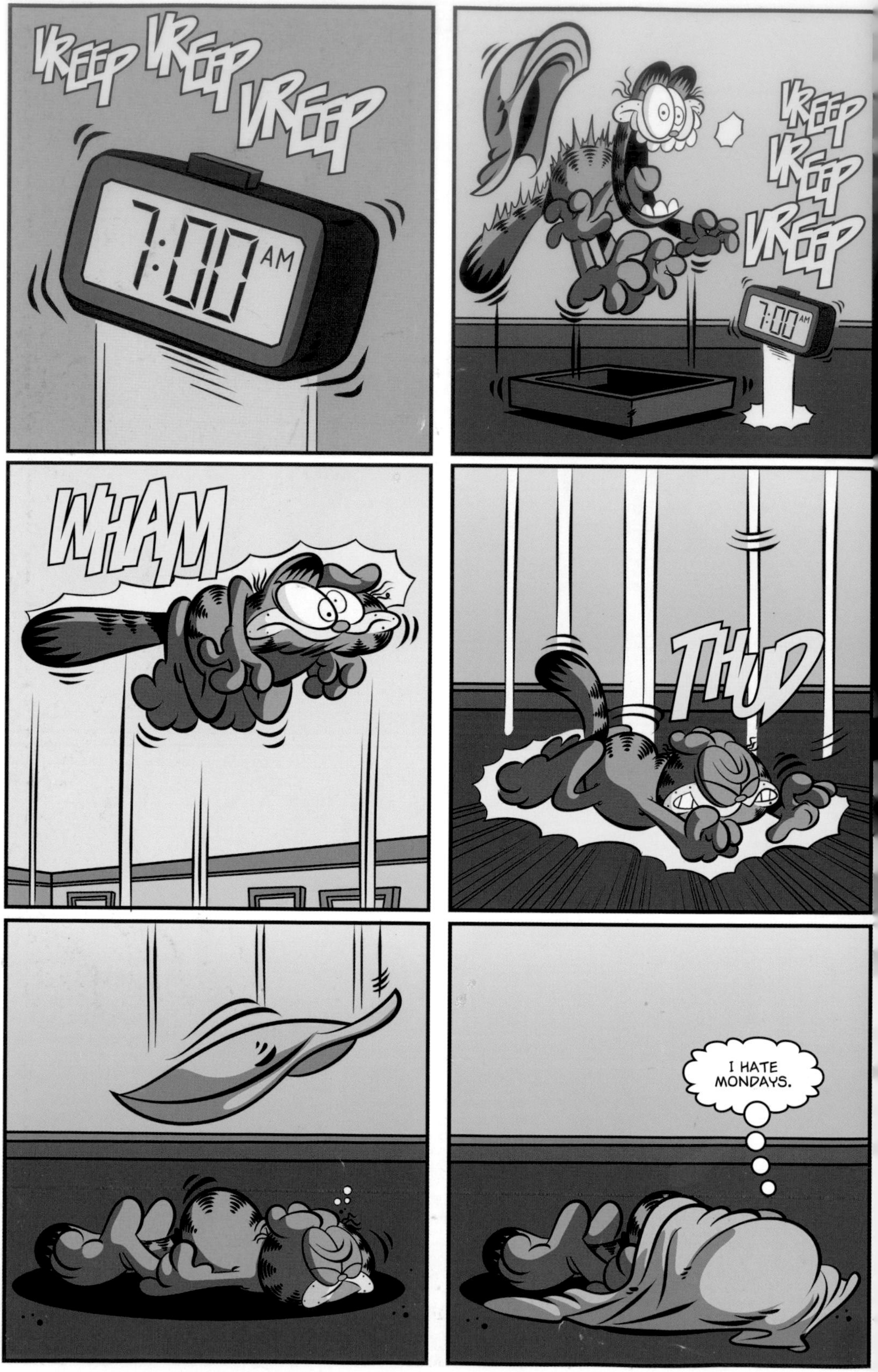
VREEP VREEP VREEP
7:00 AM
VREEP VREEP VREEP
7:00 AM
WHAM
THUD
I HATE MONDAYS.

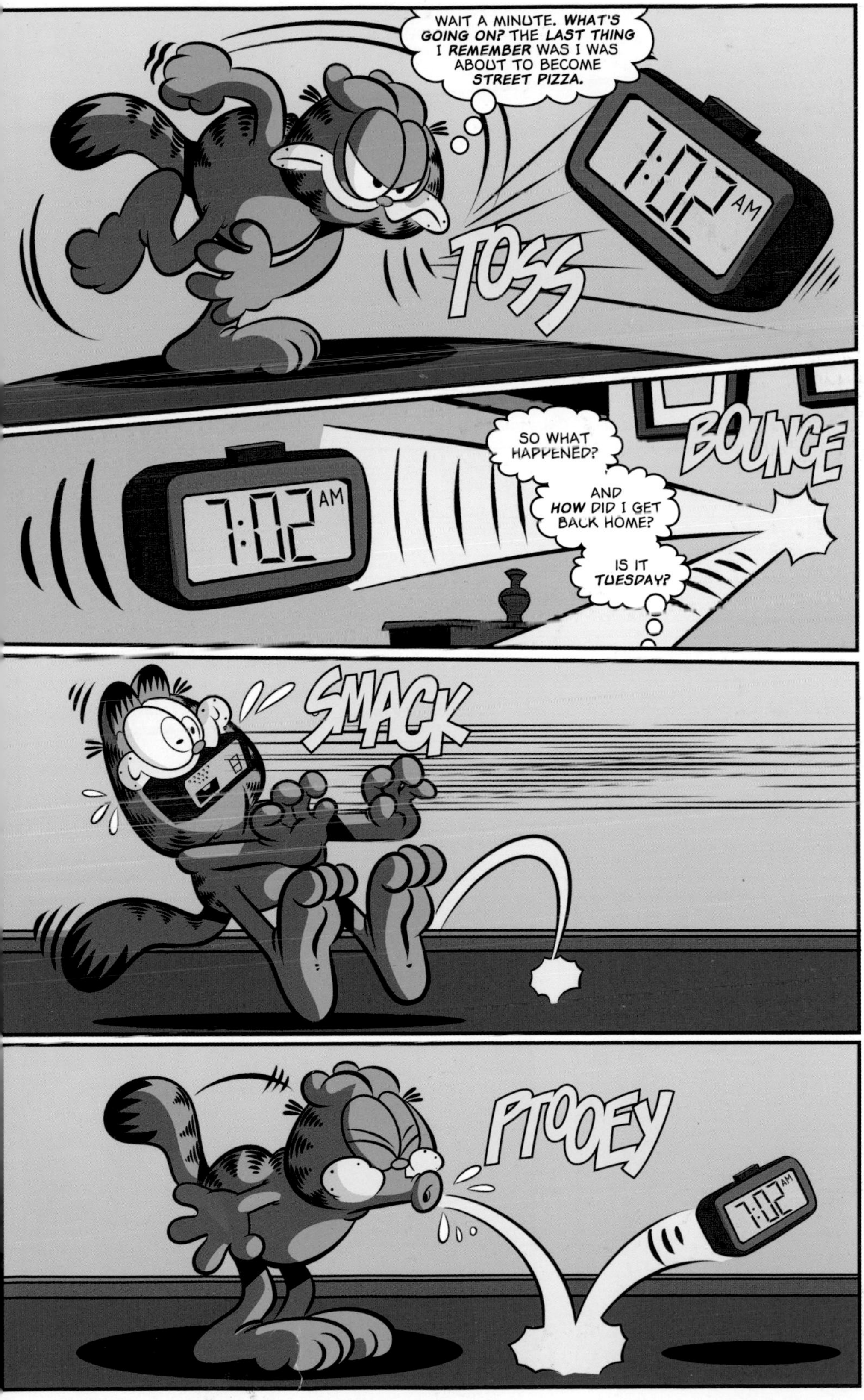
WAIT A MINUTE. WHAT'S GOING ON? THE LAST THING I REMEMBER WAS I WAS ABOUT TO BECOME STREET PIZZA.
7:02 AM
TOSS
SO WHAT HAPPENED?
AND HOW DID I GET BACK HOME?
IS IT TUESDAY?
BOUNCE
7:02 AM
SMACK
PTOOEY
7:02 AM

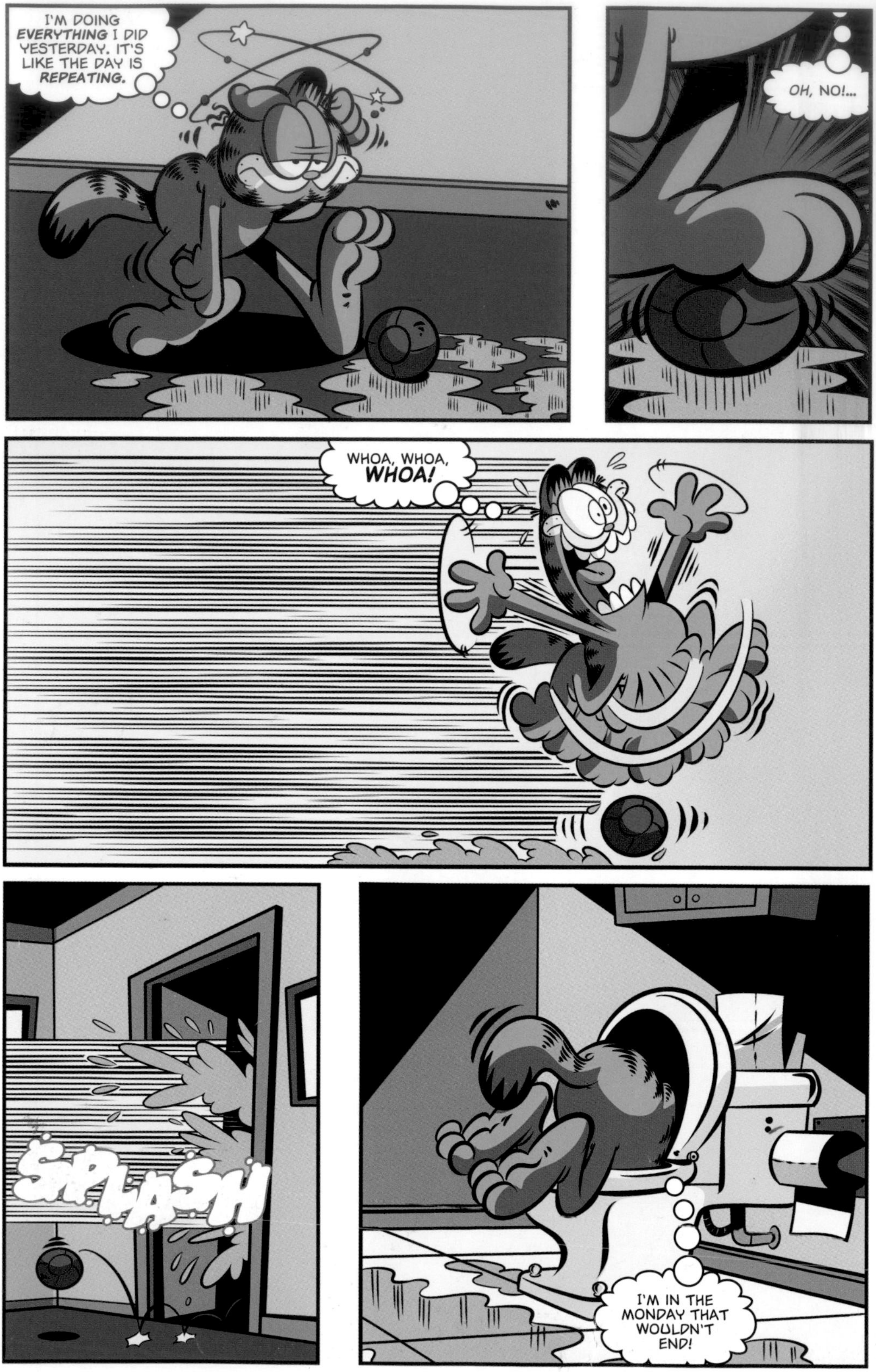
I'M DOING EVERYTHING I DID YESTERDAY. IT'S LIKE THE DAY IS REPEATING.
OH, NO!...
WHOA, WHOA, WHOA!
SPLASH
I'M IN THE MONDAY THAT WOULDN'T END!

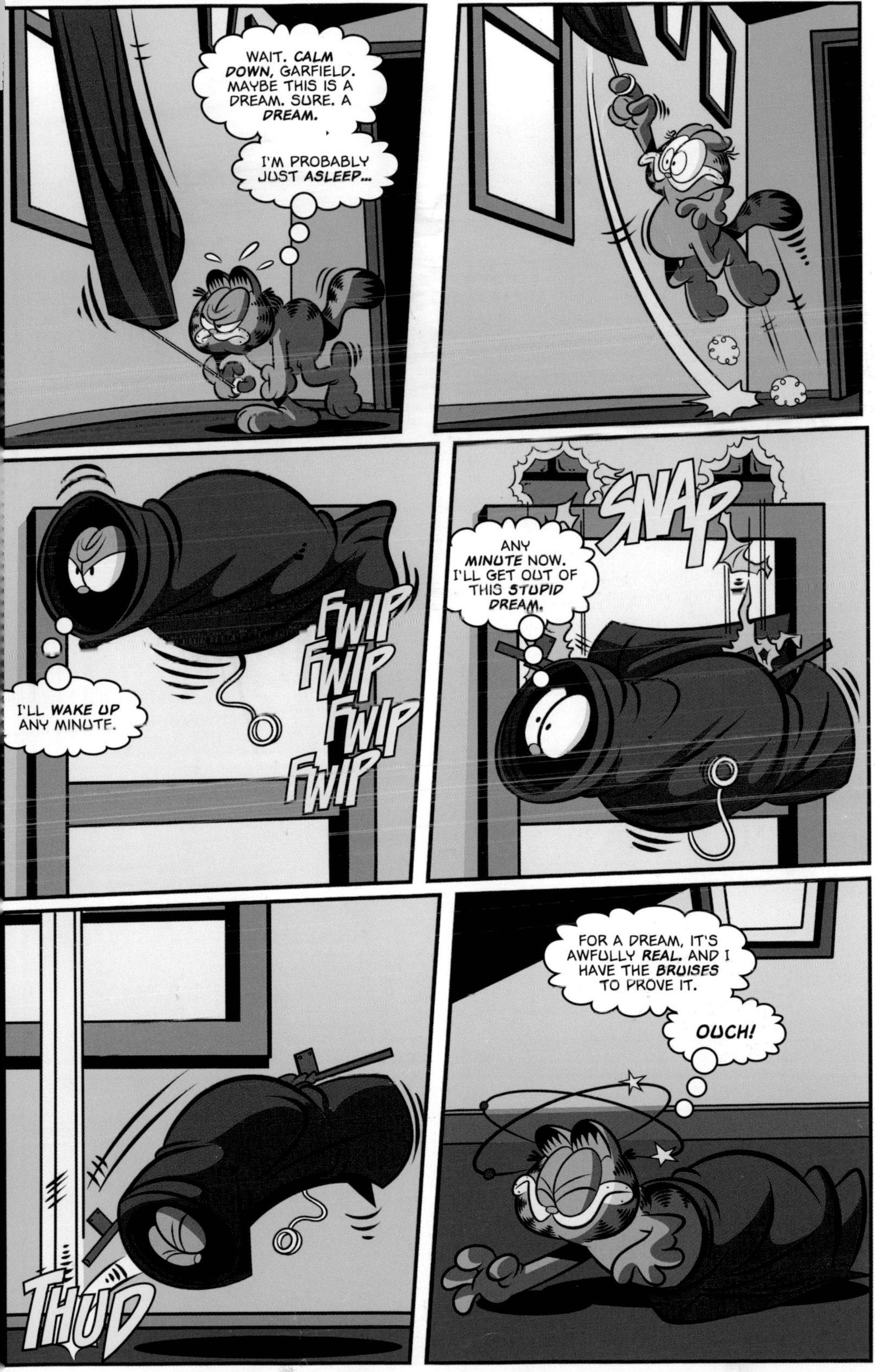
WAIT. CALM DOWN, GARFIELD. MAYBE THIS IS A DREAM. SURE. A DREAM.
I'M PROBABLY JUST ASLEEP...
I'LL WAKE UP ANY MINUTE.
FWIP FWIP FWIP FWIP
SNAP
ANY MINUTE NOW. I'LL GET OUT OF THIS STUPID DREAM.
THUD
FOR A DREAM, IT'S AWFULLY REAL. AND I HAVE THE BRUISES TO PROVE IT.
OUCH!

BUT IF THIS ISN'T A *DREAM*, WHAT IS IT?

IT'S LIKE I'M STUCK IN TIME...

SNAP

SPLOOSH

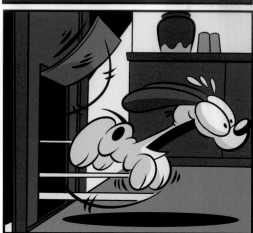

WHAM

AND I NEED TO GET *UNSTUCK*. BUT HOW?

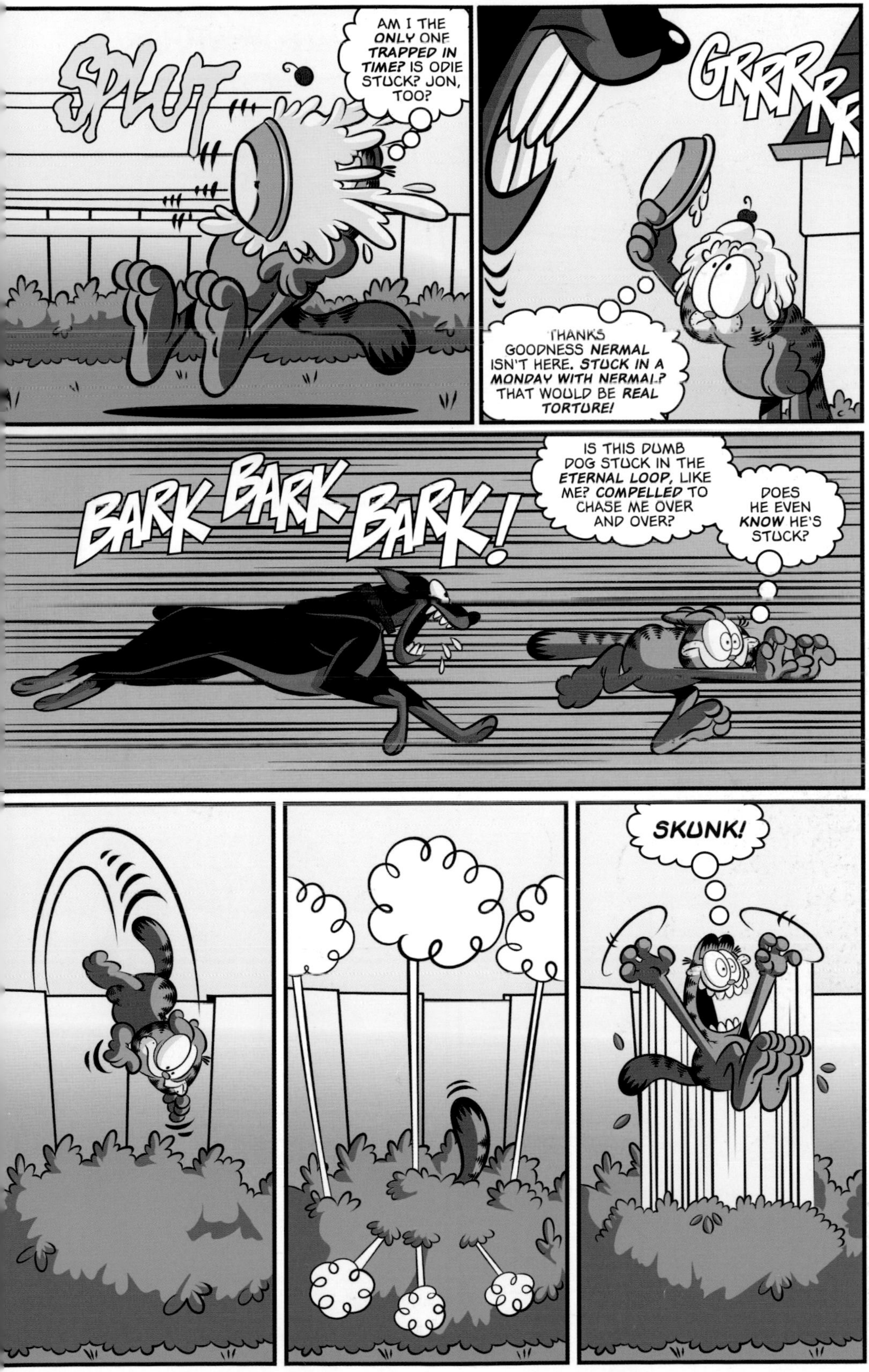
SPLUT
AM I THE ONLY ONE TRAPPED IN TIME? IS ODIE STUCK? JON, TOO?
GRRRRR
THANKS GOODNESS NERMAL ISN'T HERE. STUCK IN A MONDAY WITH NERMAL? THAT WOULD BE REAL TORTURE!
BARK BARK BARK!
IS THIS DUMB DOG STUCK IN THE ETERNAL LOOP, LIKE ME? COMPELLED TO CHASE ME OVER AND OVER?
DOES HE EVEN KNOW HE'S STUCK?
SKUNK!

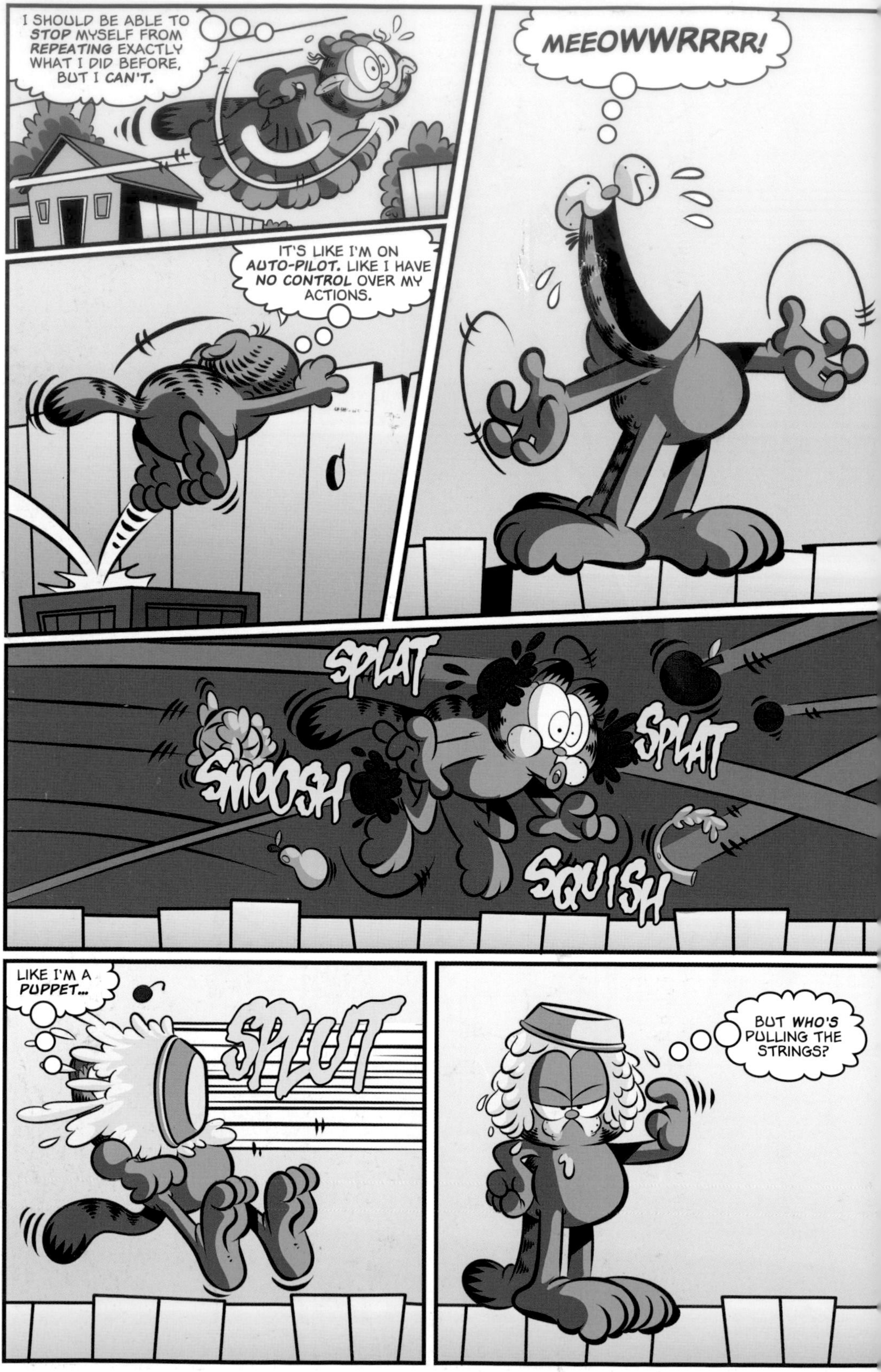
I SHOULD BE ABLE TO STOP MYSELF FROM REPEATING EXACTLY WHAT I DID BEFORE, BUT I CAN'T.
MEEOWWRRRR!
IT'S LIKE I'M ON AUTO-PILOT. LIKE I HAVE NO CONTROL OVER MY ACTIONS.
SPLAT
SPLAT
SMOOSH
SQUISH
LIKE I'M A PUPPET...
SPLUT
BUT WHO'S PULLING THE STRINGS?

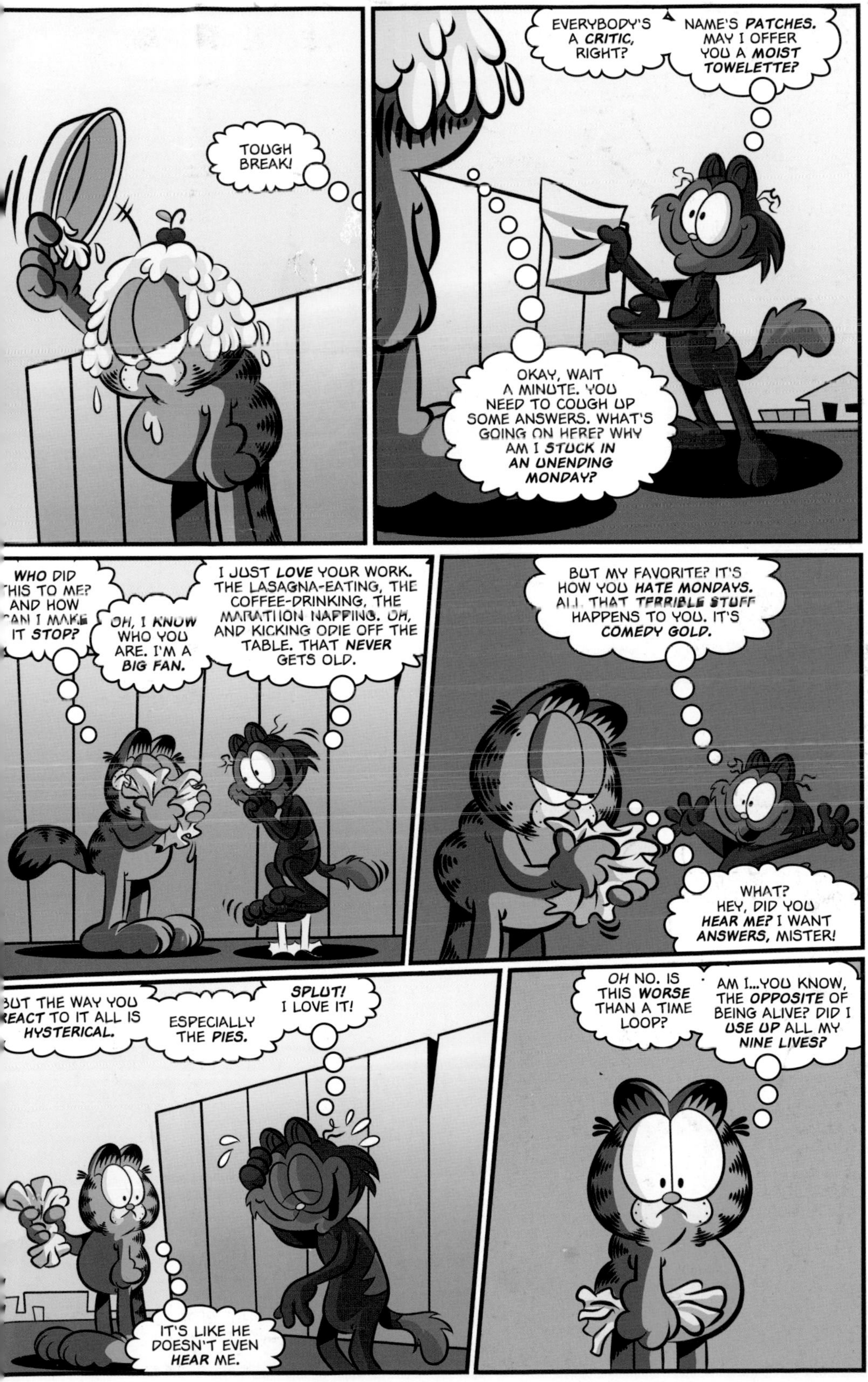
TOUGH BREAK!
EVERYBODY'S A CRITIC, RIGHT?
NAME'S PATCHES. MAY I OFFER YOU A MOIST TOWELETTE?
OKAY, WAIT A MINUTE. YOU NEED TO COUGH UP SOME ANSWERS. WHAT'S GOING ON HERE? WHY AM I STUCK IN AN UNENDING MONDAY?
WHO DID THIS TO ME? AND HOW CAN I MAKE IT STOP?
OH, I KNOW WHO YOU ARE. I'M A BIG FAN.
I JUST LOVE YOUR WORK. THE LASAGNA-EATING, THE COFFEE-DRINKING, THE MARATHON NAPPING. OH, AND KICKING ODIE OFF THE TABLE. THAT NEVER GETS OLD.
BUT MY FAVORITE? IT'S HOW YOU HATE MONDAYS. ALL THAT TERRIBLE STUFF HAPPENS TO YOU. IT'S COMEDY GOLD.
WHAT? HEY, DID YOU HEAR ME? I WANT ANSWERS, MISTER!
BUT THE WAY YOU REACT TO IT ALL IS HYSTERICAL.
ESPECIALLY THE PIES.
SPLUT! I LOVE IT!
IT'S LIKE HE DOESN'T EVEN HEAR ME.
OH NO. IS THIS WORSE THAN A TIME LOOP?
AM I...YOU KNOW, THE OPPOSITE OF BEING ALIVE? DID I USE UP ALL MY NINE LIVES?

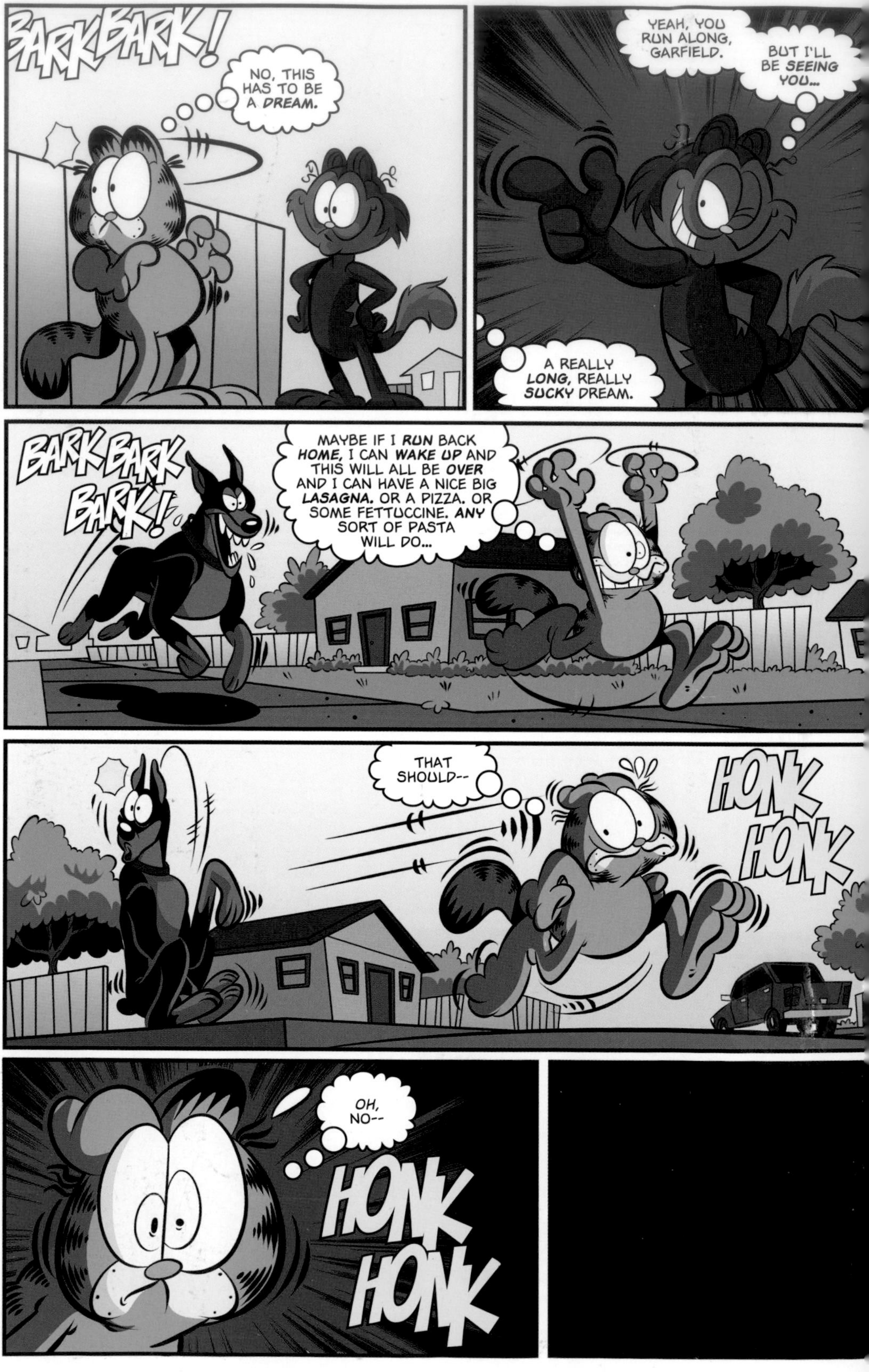
BARK BARK!
NO, THIS HAS TO BE A DREAM.
YEAH, YOU RUN ALONG, GARFIELD.
BUT I'LL BE SEEING YOU...
A REALLY LONG, REALLY SUCKY DREAM.
BARK BARK BARK!
MAYBE IF I RUN BACK HOME, I CAN WAKE UP AND THIS WILL ALL BE OVER AND I CAN HAVE A NICE BIG LASAGNA. OR A PIZZA. OR SOME FETTUCCINE. ANY SORT OF PASTA WILL DO...
THAT SHOULD--
HONK HONK
OH, NO--
HONK HONK

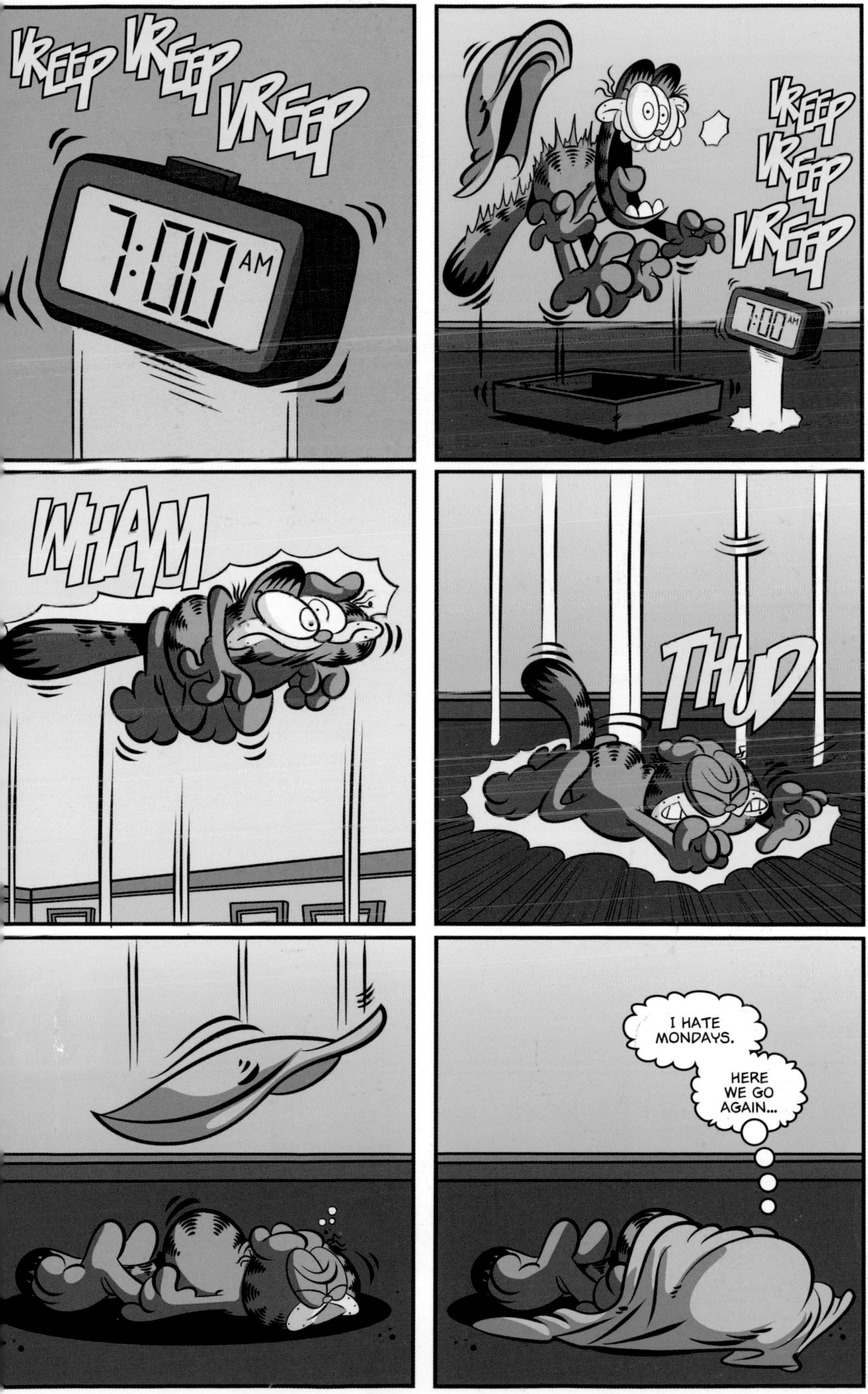
VREEP VREEP VREEP
7:00 AM
VREEP VREEP VREEP
7:00 AM
WHAM
THUD
I HATE MONDAYS.
HERE WE GO AGAIN...

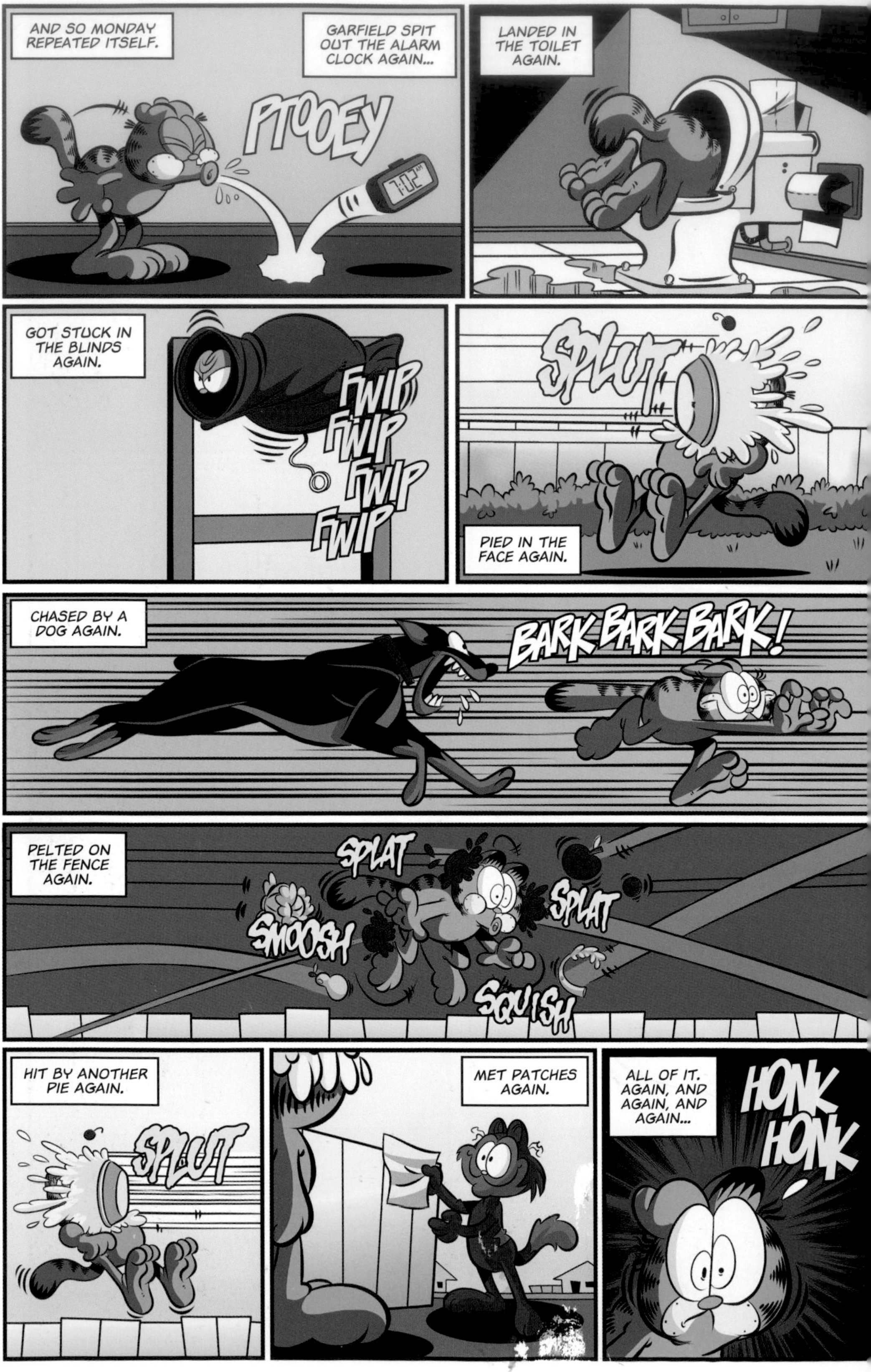
AND SO MONDAY REPEATED ITSELF.
GARFIELD SPIT OUT THE ALARM CLOCK AGAIN...
PTOOEY
7:02 AM
LANDED IN THE TOILET AGAIN.
GOT STUCK IN THE BLINDS AGAIN.
FWIP
FWIP
FWIP
FWIP
SPLUT
PIED IN THE FACE AGAIN.
CHASED BY A DOG AGAIN.
BARK BARK BARK!
PELTED ON THE FENCE AGAIN.
SPLAT
SPLAT
SMOOSH
SQUISH
HIT BY ANOTHER PIE AGAIN.
SPLUT
MET PATCHES AGAIN.
ALL OF IT. AGAIN, AND AGAIN, AND AGAIN...
HONK
HONK

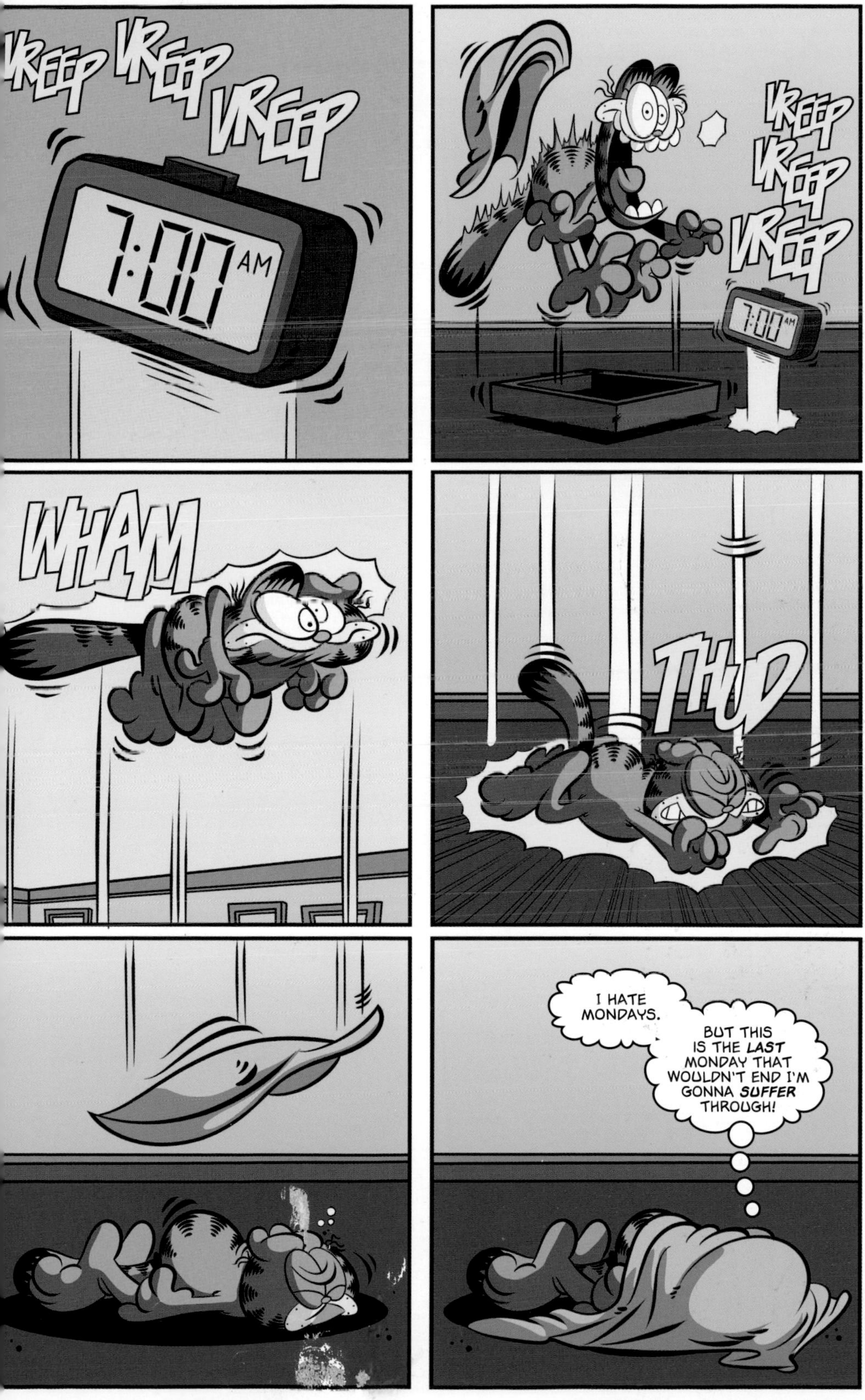

VREEP VREEP VREEP
7:00 AM
VREEP VREEP VREEP
7:00 AM
WHAM
THUD
I HATE MONDAYS.
BUT THIS IS THE LAST MONDAY THAT WOULDN'T END I'M GONNA SUFFER THROUGH!

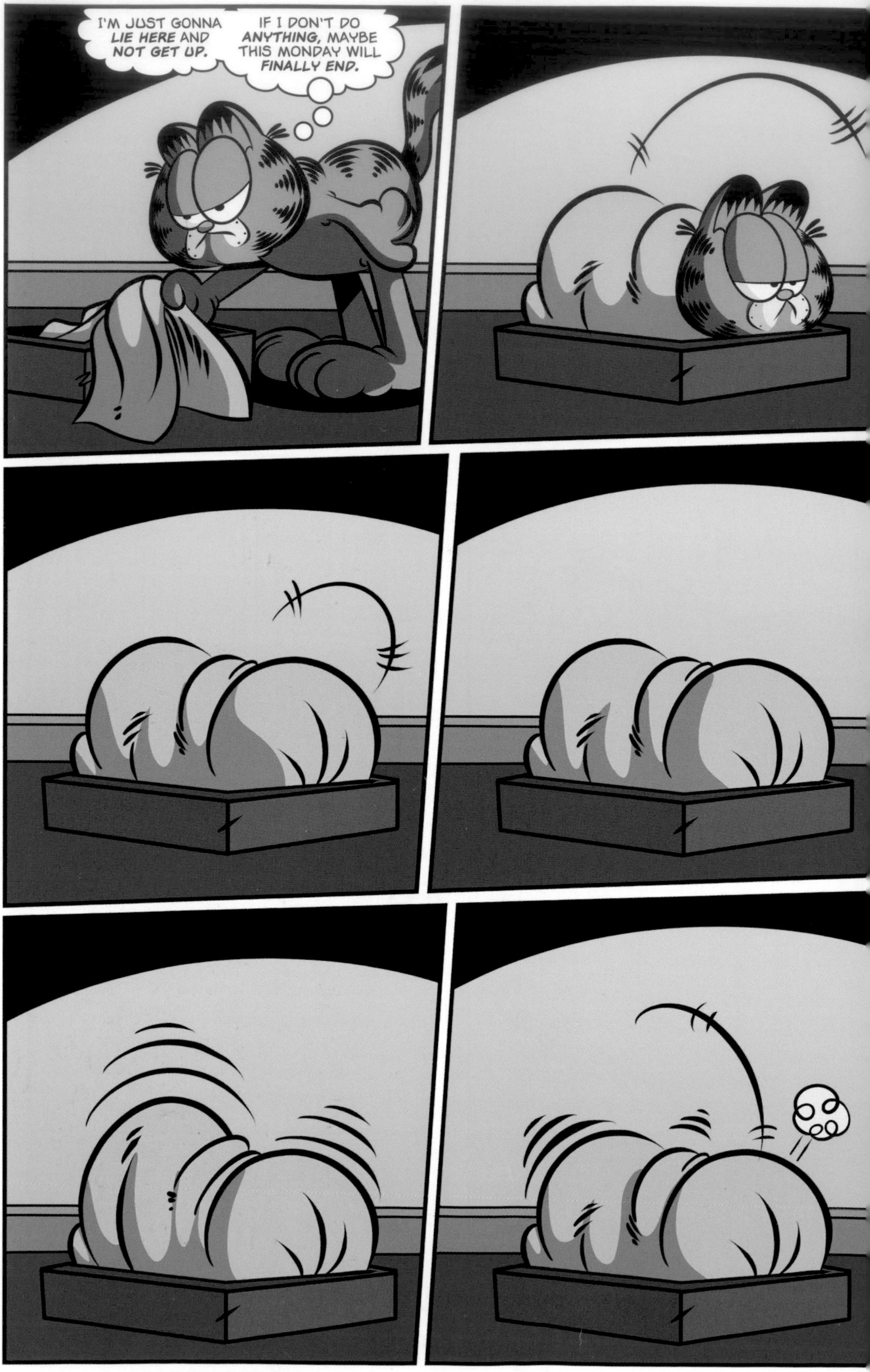
I'M JUST GONNA LIE HERE AND NOT GET UP.
IF I DON'T DO ANYTHING, MAYBE THIS MONDAY WILL FINALLY END.

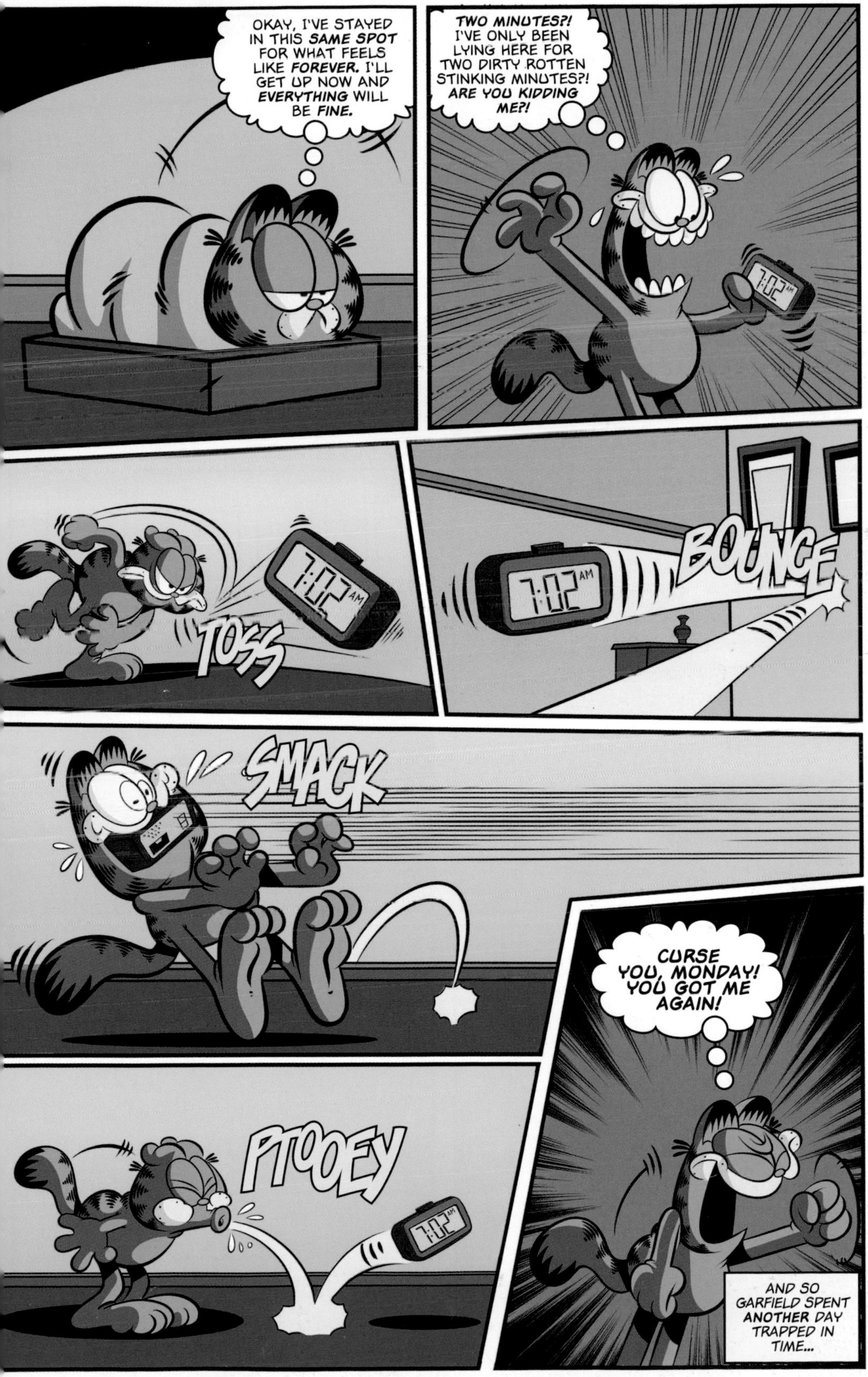
OKAY, I'VE STAYED IN THIS SAME SPOT FOR WHAT FEELS LIKE FOREVER. I'LL GET UP NOW AND EVERYTHING WILL BE FINE.
TWO MINUTES?! I'VE ONLY BEEN LYING HERE FOR TWO DIRTY ROTTEN STINKING MINUTES?! ARE YOU KIDDING ME?!
7:02 AM
TOSS
7:02 AM
BOUNCE
7:02 AM
SMACK
PTOOEY
7:02 AM
CURSE YOU, MONDAY! YOU GOT ME AGAIN!
AND SO GARFIELD SPENT ANOTHER DAY TRAPPED IN TIME...

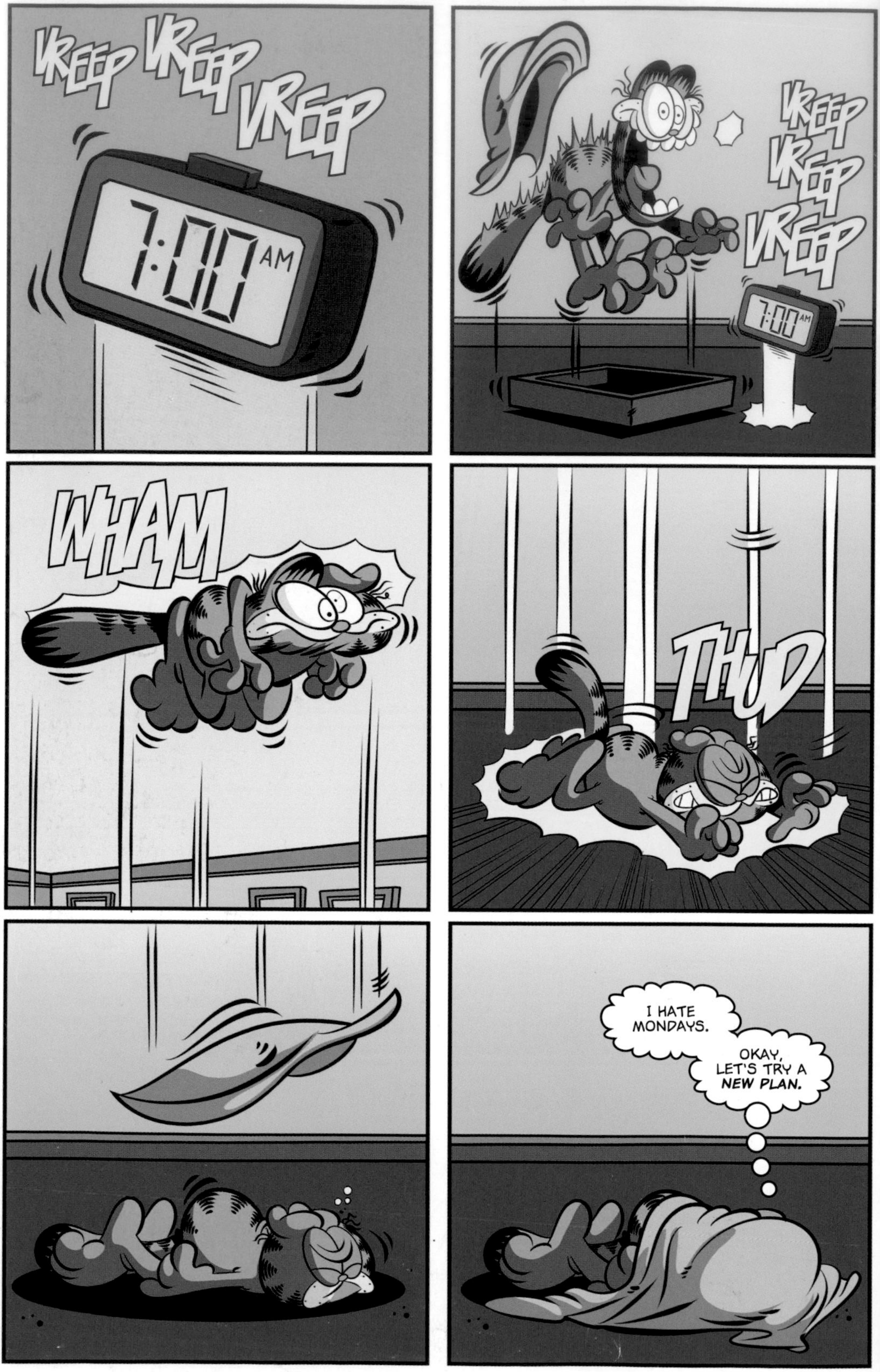

VREEP VREEP VREEP
VREEP VREEP VREEP
WHAM
THUD
I HATE MONDAYS.
OKAY, LET'S TRY A **NEW PLAN.**

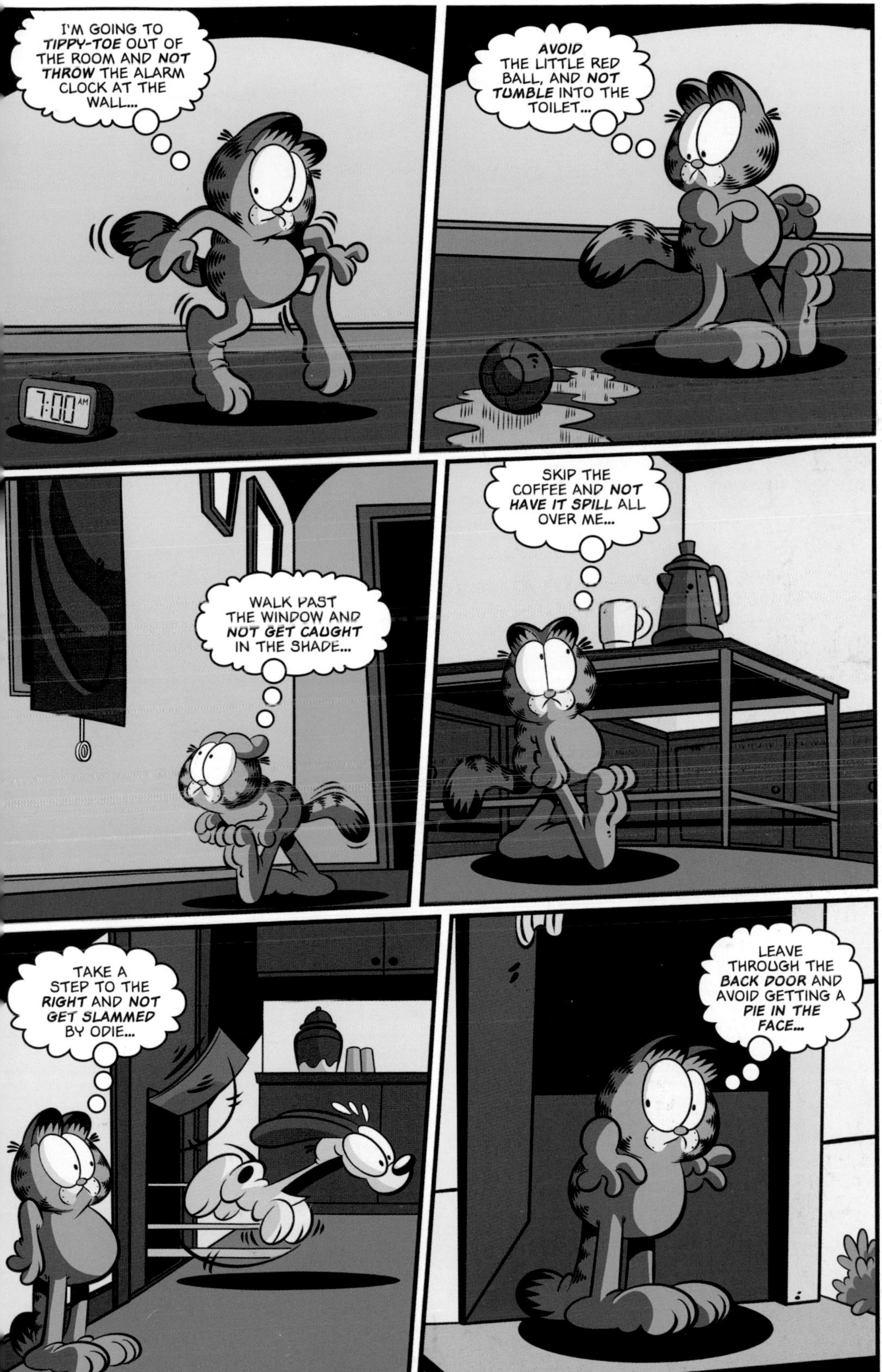
I'M GOING TO TIPPY-TOE OUT OF THE ROOM AND NOT THROW THE ALARM CLOCK AT THE WALL...
7:00 AM
AVOID THE LITTLE RED BALL, AND NOT TUMBLE INTO THE TOILET...
WALK PAST THE WINDOW AND NOT GET CAUGHT IN THE SHADE...
SKIP THE COFFEE AND NOT HAVE IT SPILL ALL OVER ME...
TAKE A STEP TO THE RIGHT AND NOT GET SLAMMED BY ODIE...
LEAVE THROUGH THE BACK DOOR AND AVOID GETTING A PIE IN THE FACE...

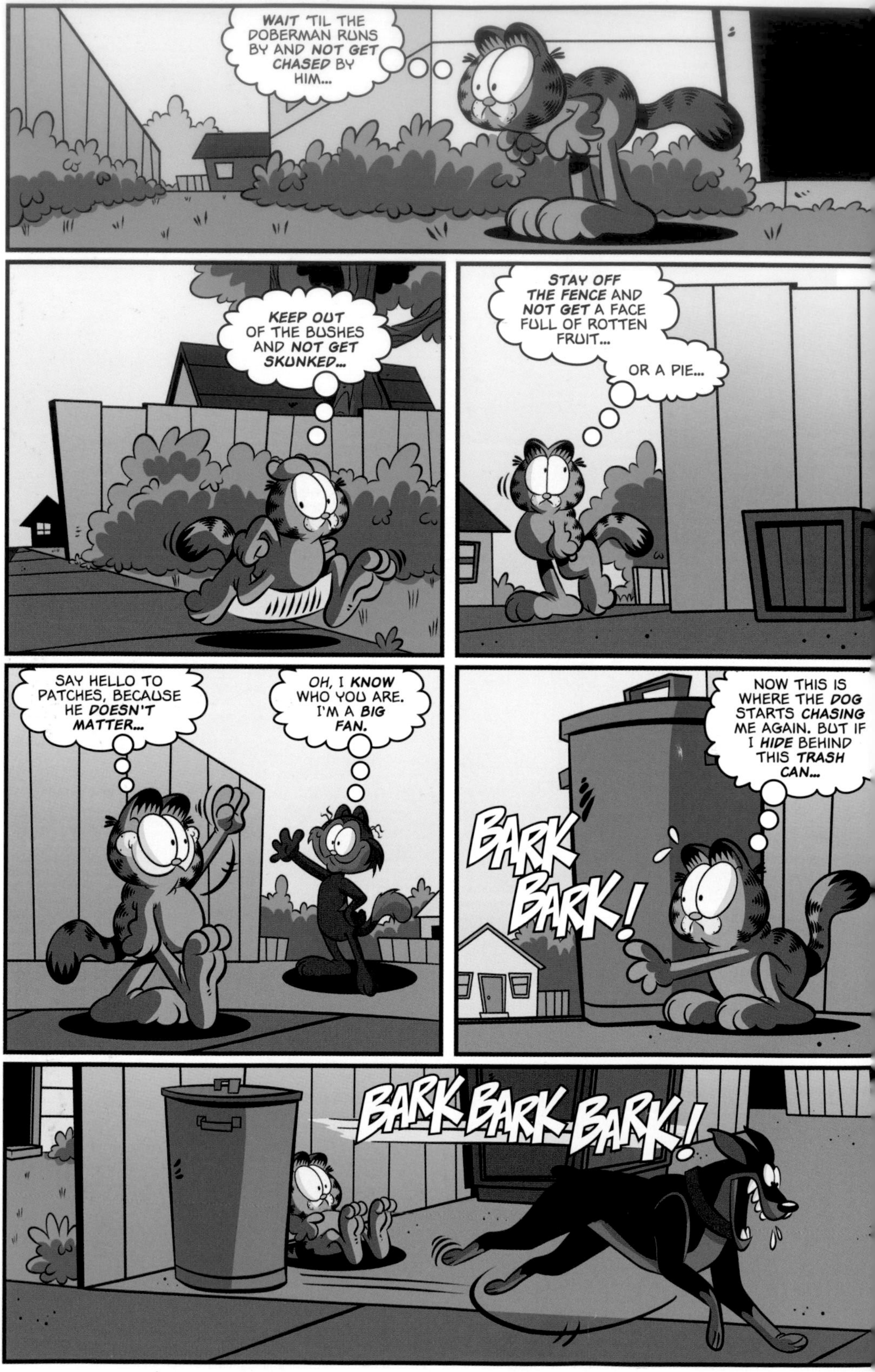
WAIT 'TIL THE DOBERMAN RUNS BY AND NOT GET CHASED BY HIM...
KEEP OUT OF THE BUSHES AND NOT GET SKUNKED...
STAY OFF THE FENCE AND NOT GET A FACE FULL OF ROTTEN FRUIT...
OR A PIE...
SAY HELLO TO PATCHES, BECAUSE HE DOESN'T MATTER...
OH, I KNOW WHO YOU ARE. I'M A BIG FAN.
NOW THIS IS WHERE THE DOG STARTS CHASING ME AGAIN. BUT IF I HIDE BEHIND THIS TRASH CAN...
BARK BARK!
BARK BARK BARK!

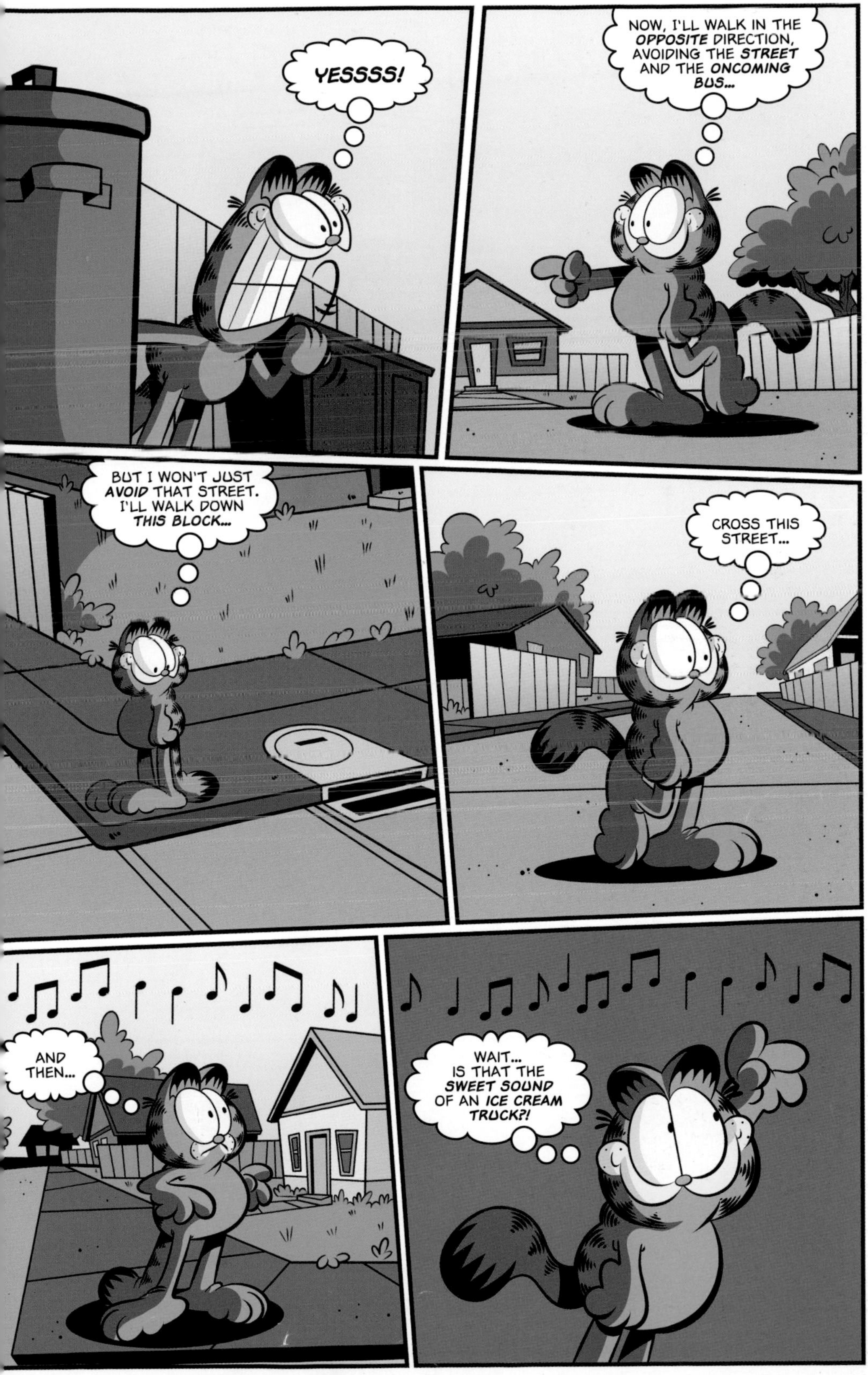
YESSSS!
NOW, I'LL WALK IN THE OPPOSITE DIRECTION, AVOIDING THE STREET AND THE ONCOMING BUS...
BUT I WON'T JUST AVOID THAT STREET. I'LL WALK DOWN THIS BLOCK...
CROSS THIS STREET...
AND THEN...
WAIT... IS THAT THE SWEET SOUND OF AN ICE CREAM TRUCK?!

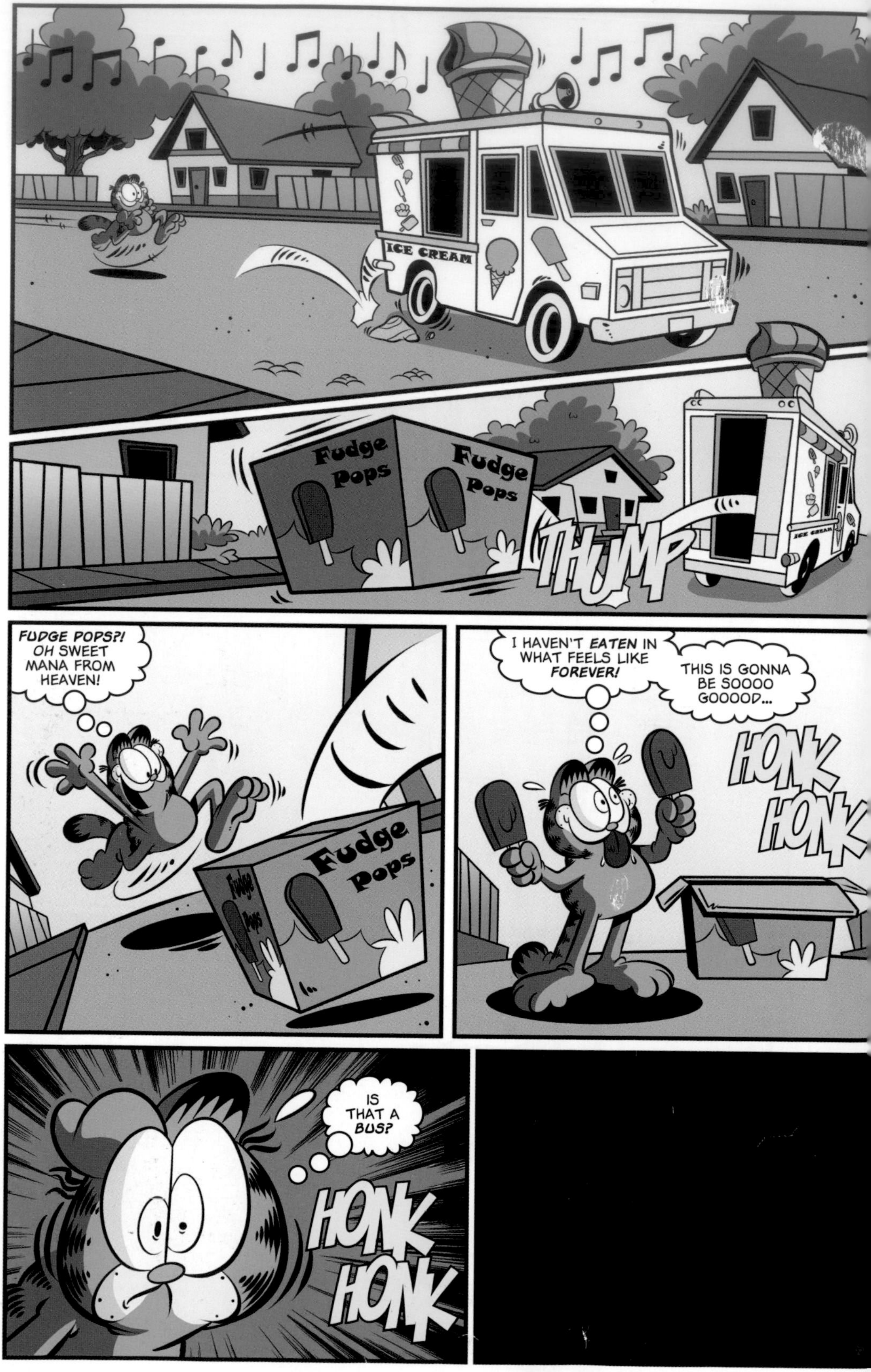
Fudge Pops
Fudge Pops
THUMP
FUDGE POPS?! OH SWEET MANA FROM HEAVEN!
Fudge Pops
I HAVEN'T EATEN IN WHAT FEELS LIKE FOREVER!
THIS IS GONNA BE SOOOO GOOOOD...
HONK HONK
IS THAT A BUS?
HONK HONK

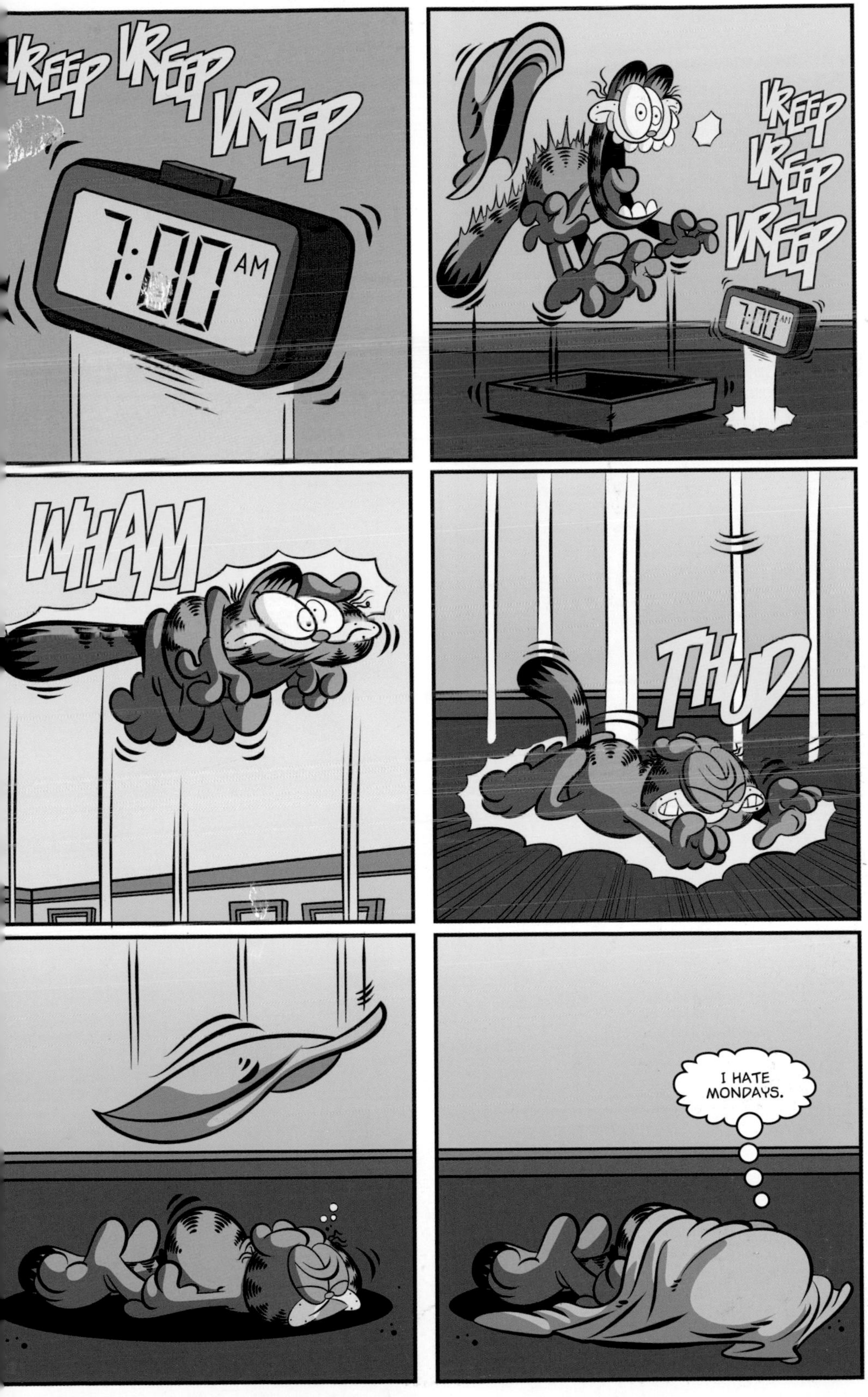
VREEP VREEP VREEP
7:00 AM
VREEP VREEP VREEP
7:00 AM
WHAM
THUD
I HATE MONDAYS.

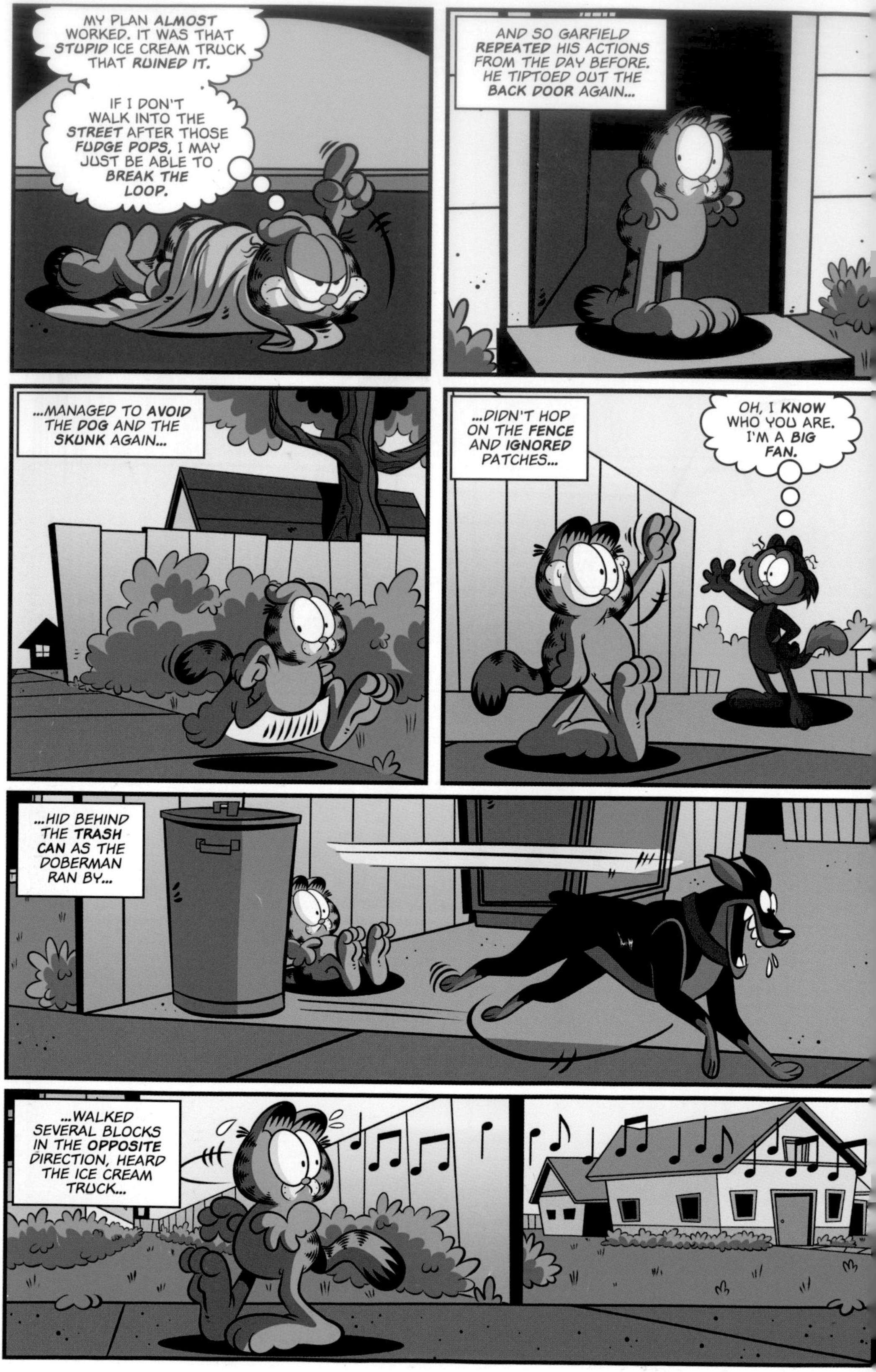
MY PLAN ALMOST WORKED. IT WAS THAT STUPID ICE CREAM TRUCK THAT RUINED IT.
IF I DON'T WALK INTO THE STREET AFTER THOSE FUDGE POPS, I MAY JUST BE ABLE TO BREAK THE LOOP.
AND SO GARFIELD REPEATED HIS ACTIONS FROM THE DAY BEFORE. HE TIPTOED OUT THE BACK DOOR AGAIN...
...MANAGED TO AVOID THE DOG AND THE SKUNK AGAIN...
...DIDN'T HOP ON THE FENCE AND IGNORED PATCHES...
OH, I KNOW WHO YOU ARE. I'M A BIG FAN.
...HID BEHIND THE TRASH CAN AS THE DOBERMAN RAN BY...
...WALKED SEVERAL BLOCKS IN THE OPPOSITE DIRECTION, HEARD THE ICE CREAM TRUCK...

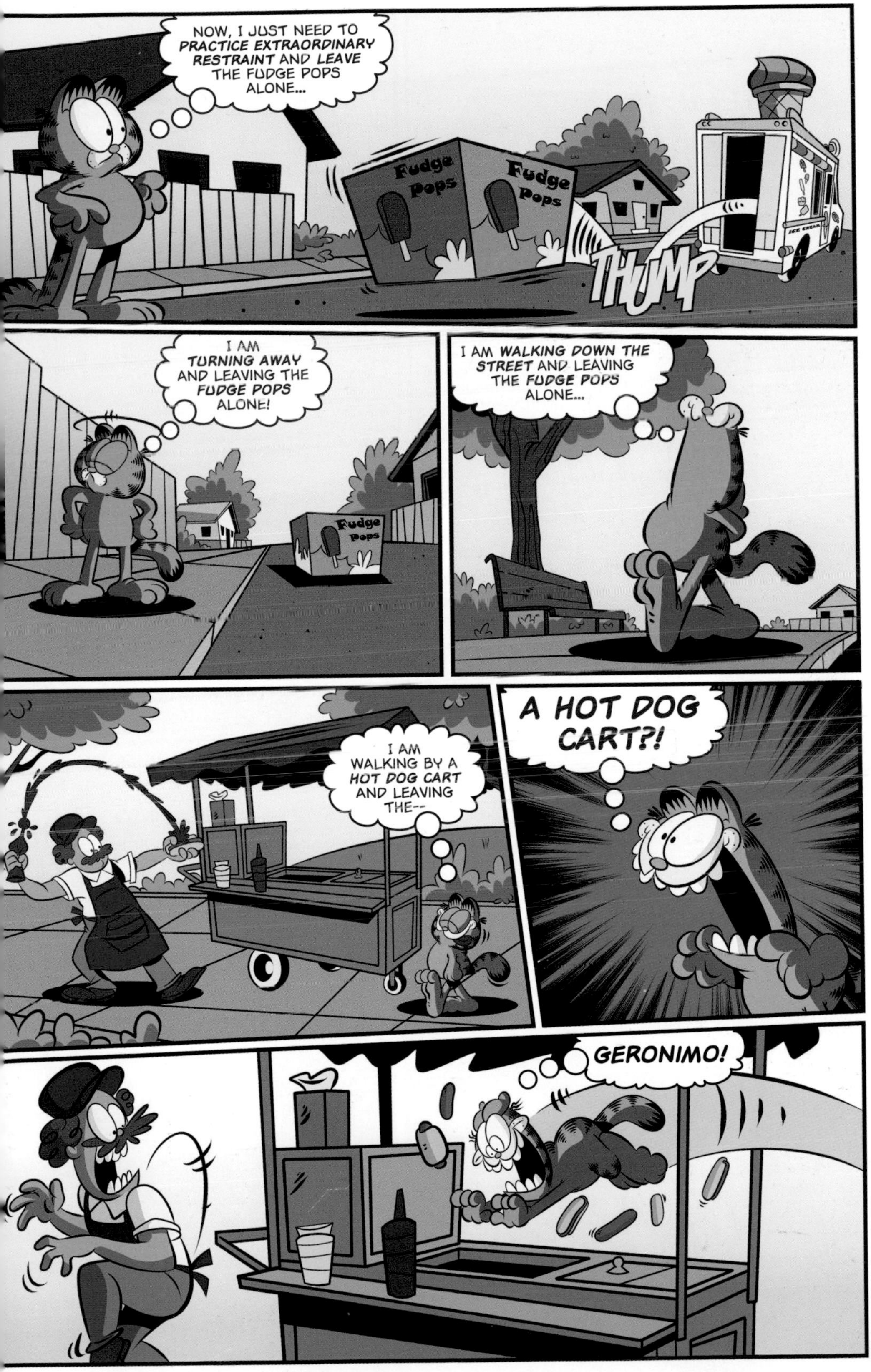
NOW, I JUST NEED TO PRACTICE EXTRAORDINARY RESTRAINT AND LEAVE THE FUDGE POPS ALONE...
Fudge Pops
Fudge Pops
THUMP
I AM TURNING AWAY AND LEAVING THE FUDGE POPS ALONE!
Fudge Pops
I AM WALKING DOWN THE STREET AND LEAVING THE FUDGE POPS ALONE...
I AM WALKING BY A HOT DOG CART AND LEAVING THE--
A HOT DOG CART?!
GERONIMO!

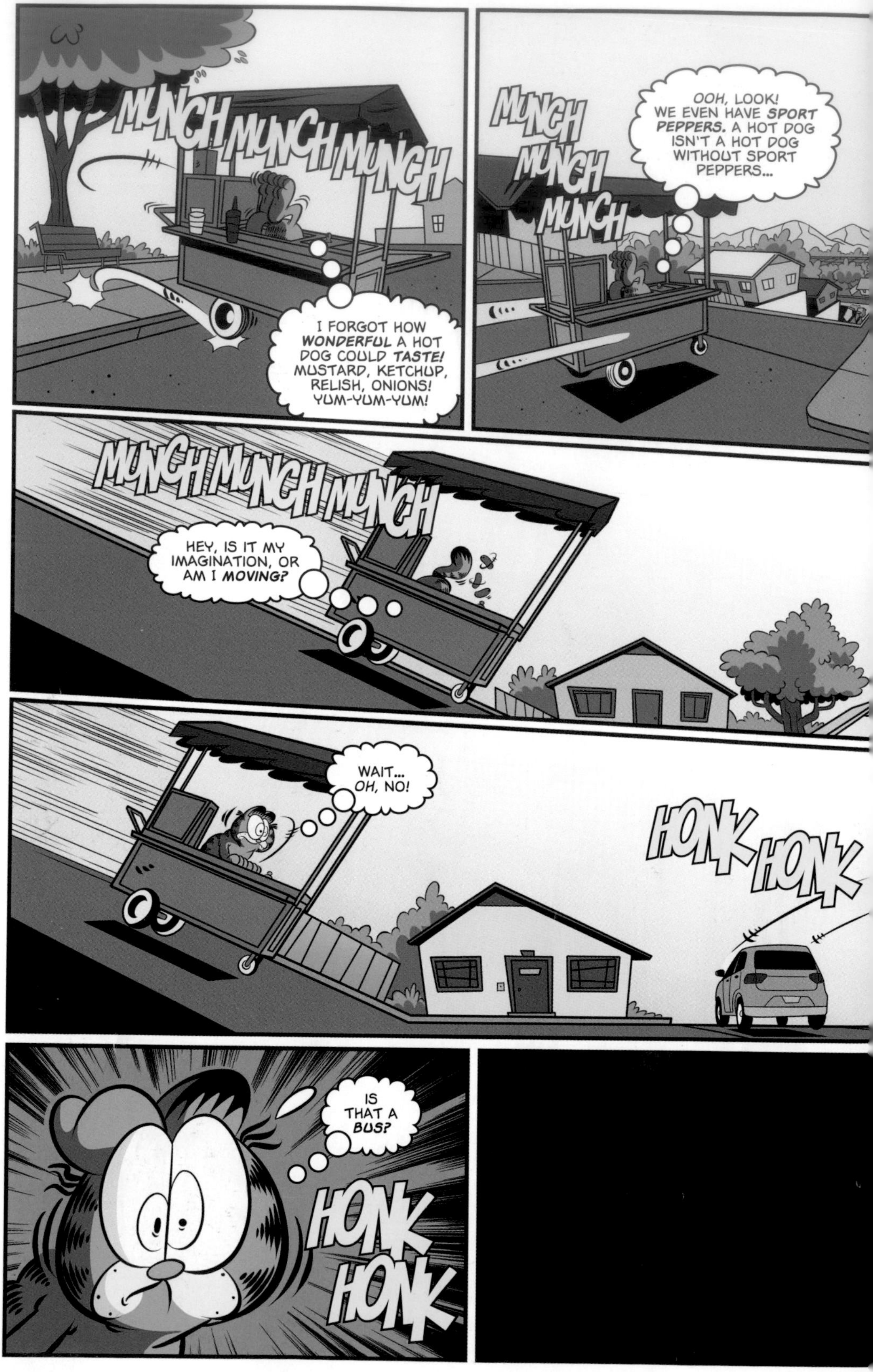
MUNCH MUNCH MUNCH
I FORGOT HOW WONDERFUL A HOT DOG COULD TASTE! MUSTARD, KETCHUP, RELISH, ONIONS! YUM-YUM-YUM!
MUNCH MUNCH MUNCH
OOH, LOOK! WE EVEN HAVE SPORT PEPPERS. A HOT DOG ISN'T A HOT DOG WITHOUT SPORT PEPPERS...
MUNCH MUNCH MUNCH
HEY, IS IT MY IMAGINATION, OR AM I MOVING?
WAIT... OH, NO!
HONK HONK
IS THAT A BUS?
HONK HONK

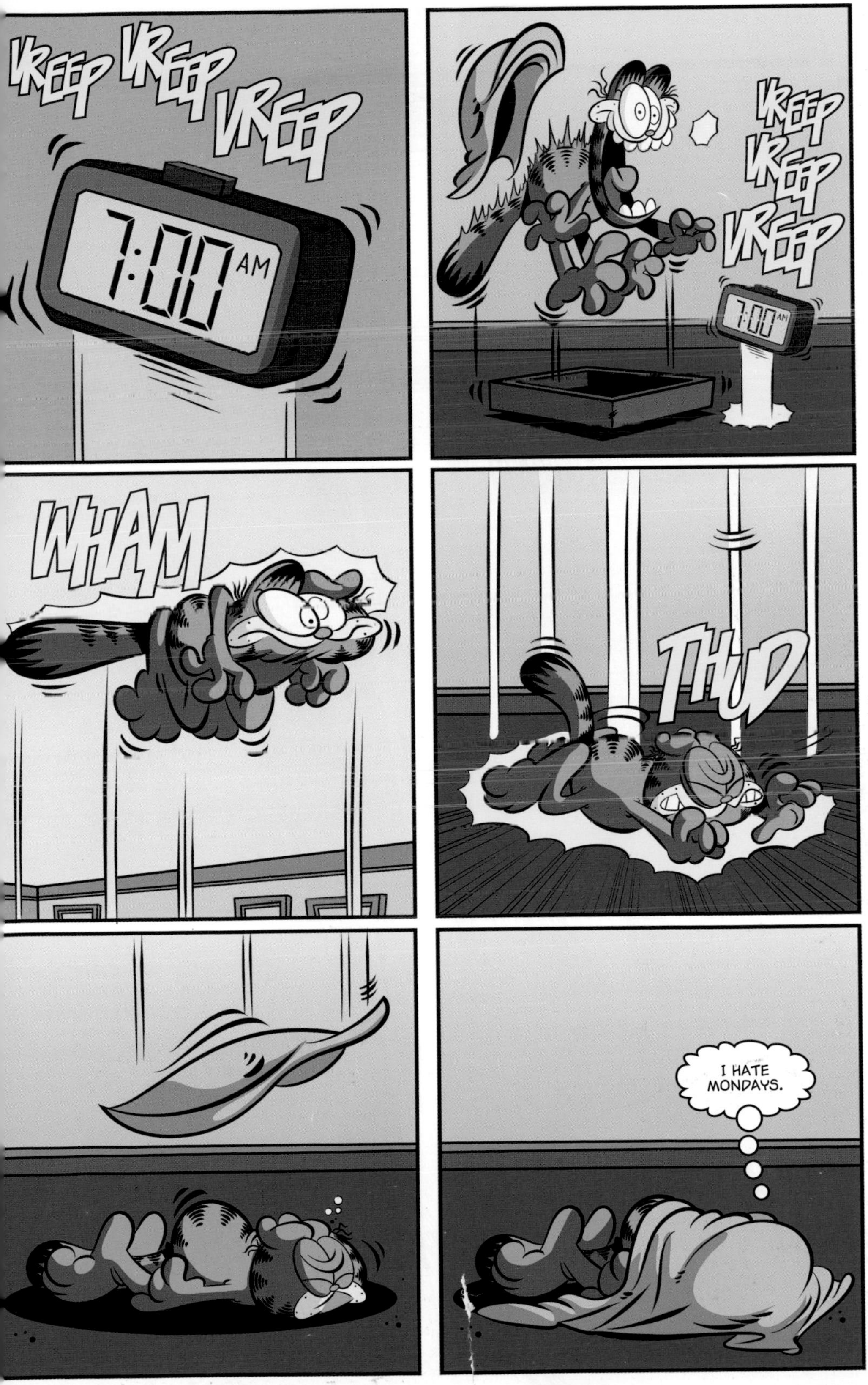
VREEP VREEP VREEP
7:00 AM
VREEP VREEP VREEP
7:00 AM
WHAM
THUD
I HATE MONDAYS.

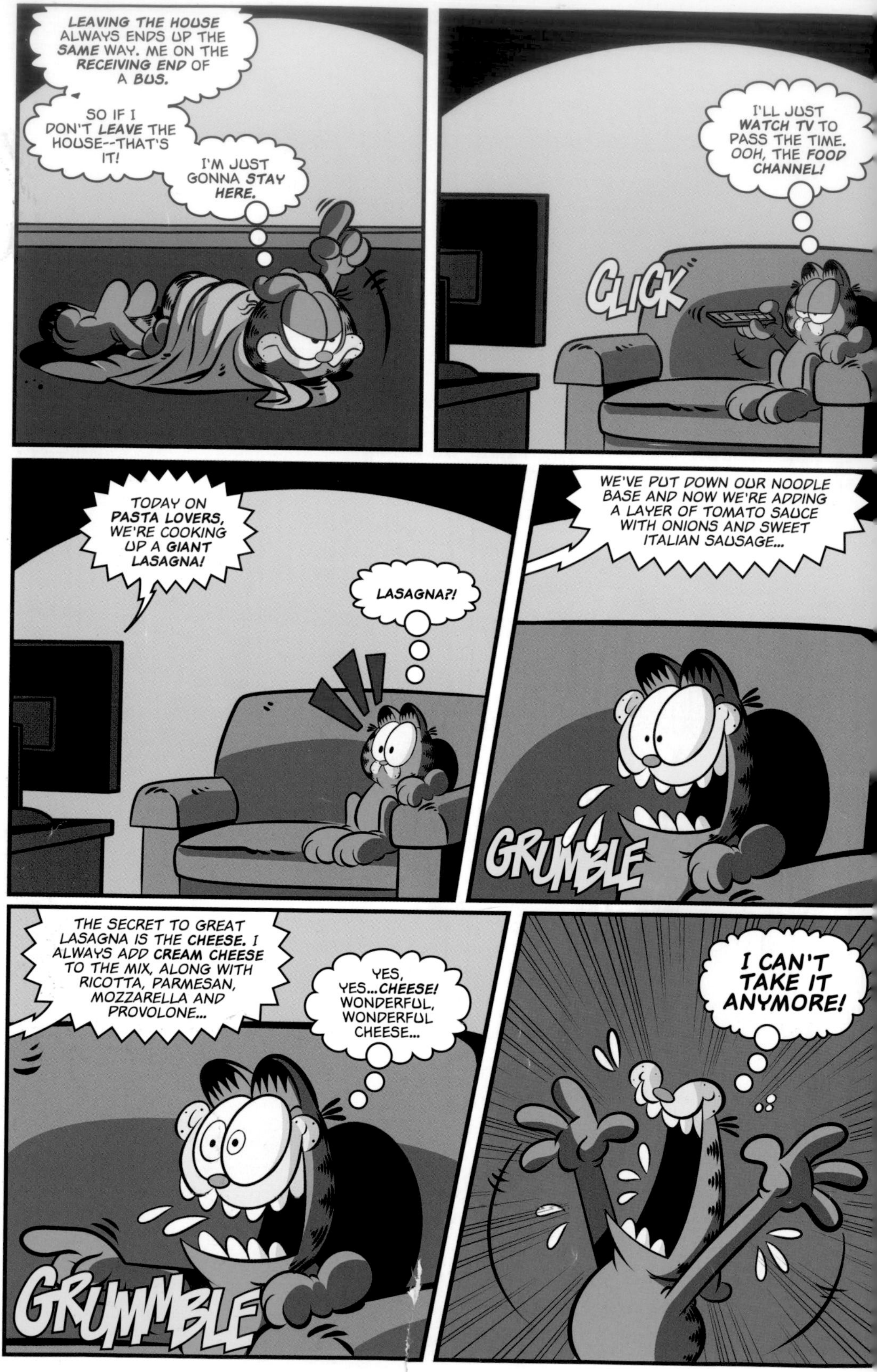

LEAVING THE HOUSE ALWAYS ENDS UP THE SAME WAY. ME ON THE RECEIVING END OF A BUS.
SO IF I DON'T LEAVE THE HOUSE--THAT'S IT!
I'M JUST GONNA STAY HERE.
I'LL JUST WATCH TV TO PASS THE TIME. OOH, THE FOOD CHANNEL!
CLICK
TODAY ON PASTA LOVERS, WE'RE COOKING UP A GIANT LASAGNA!
LASAGNA?!
WE'VE PUT DOWN OUR NOODLE BASE AND NOW WE'RE ADDING A LAYER OF TOMATO SAUCE WITH ONIONS AND SWEET ITALIAN SAUSAGE...
GRUMBLE
THE SECRET TO GREAT LASAGNA IS THE CHEESE. I ALWAYS ADD CREAM CHEESE TO THE MIX, ALONG WITH RICOTTA, PARMESAN, MOZZARELLA AND PROVOLONE...
YES, YES...CHEESE! WONDERFUL, WONDERFUL CHEESE...
GRUMMBLE
I CAN'T TAKE IT ANYMORE!

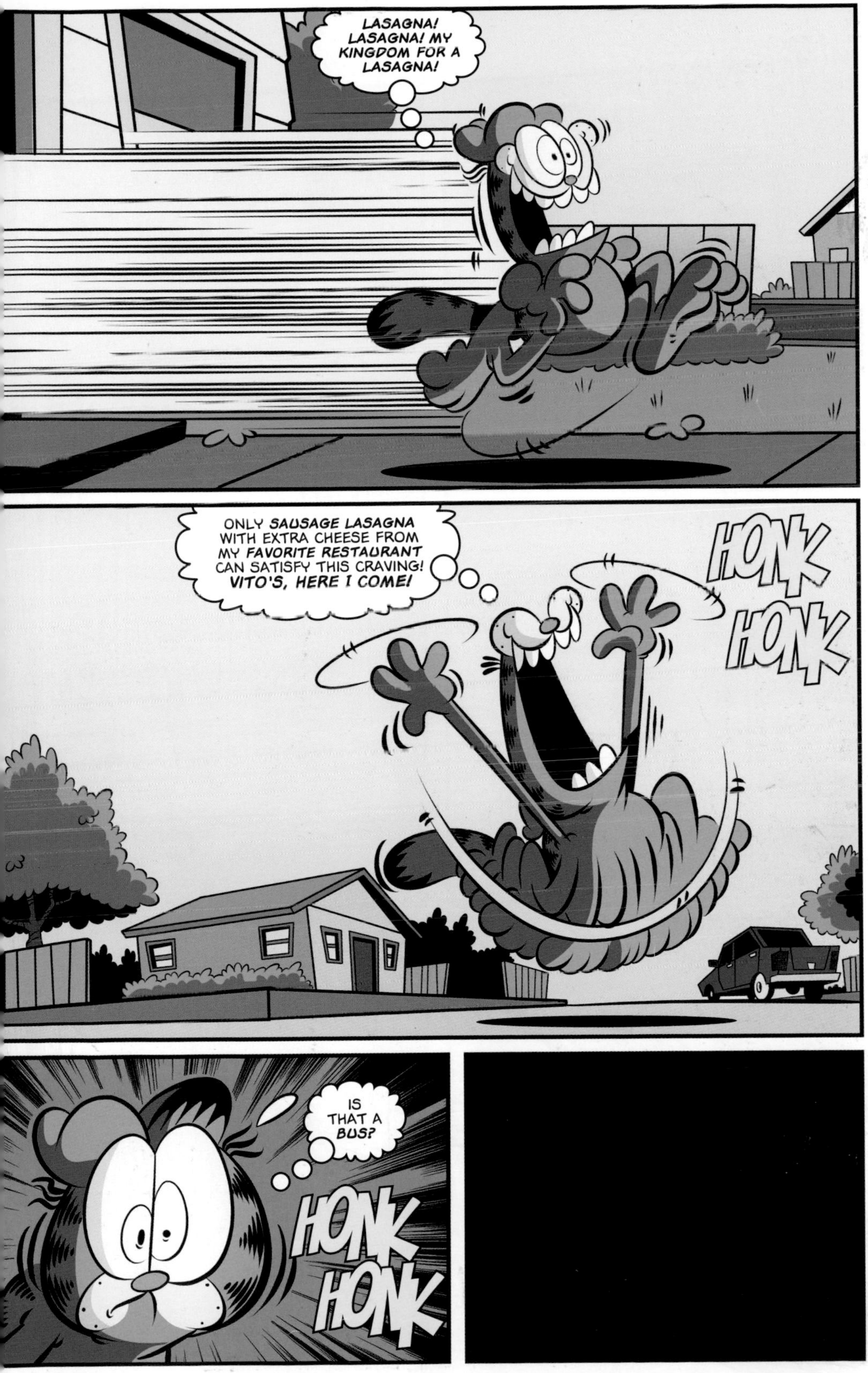
LASAGNA! LASAGNA! MY KINGDOM FOR A LASAGNA!
ONLY SAUSAGE LASAGNA WITH EXTRA CHEESE FROM MY FAVORITE RESTAURANT CAN SATISFY THIS CRAVING! VITO'S, HERE I COME!
HONK HONK
IS THAT A BUS?
HONK HONK

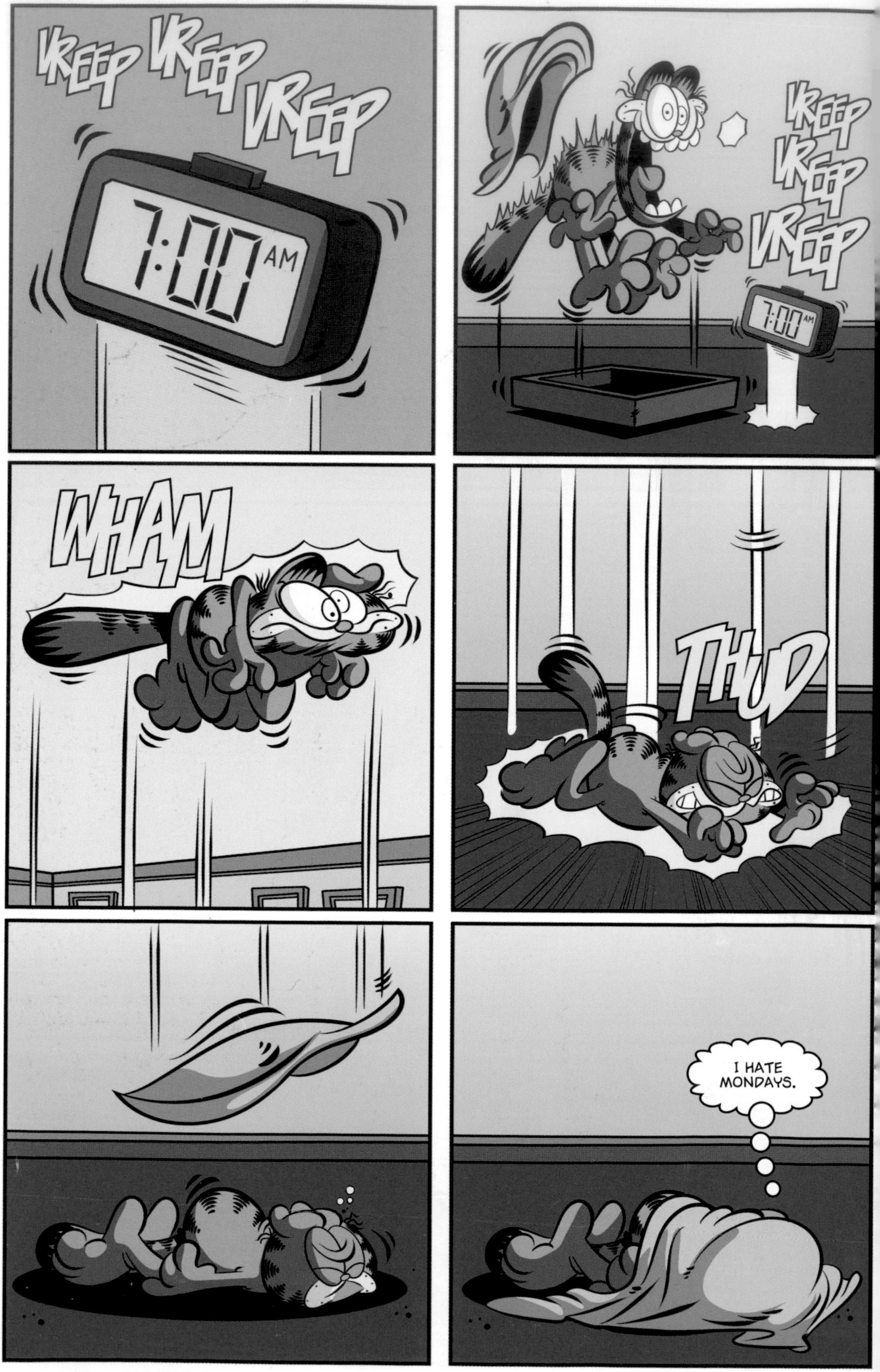
VREEP VREEP VREEP
7:00 AM
VREEP VREEP VREEP
7:00 AM
WHAM
THUD
I HATE MONDAYS.

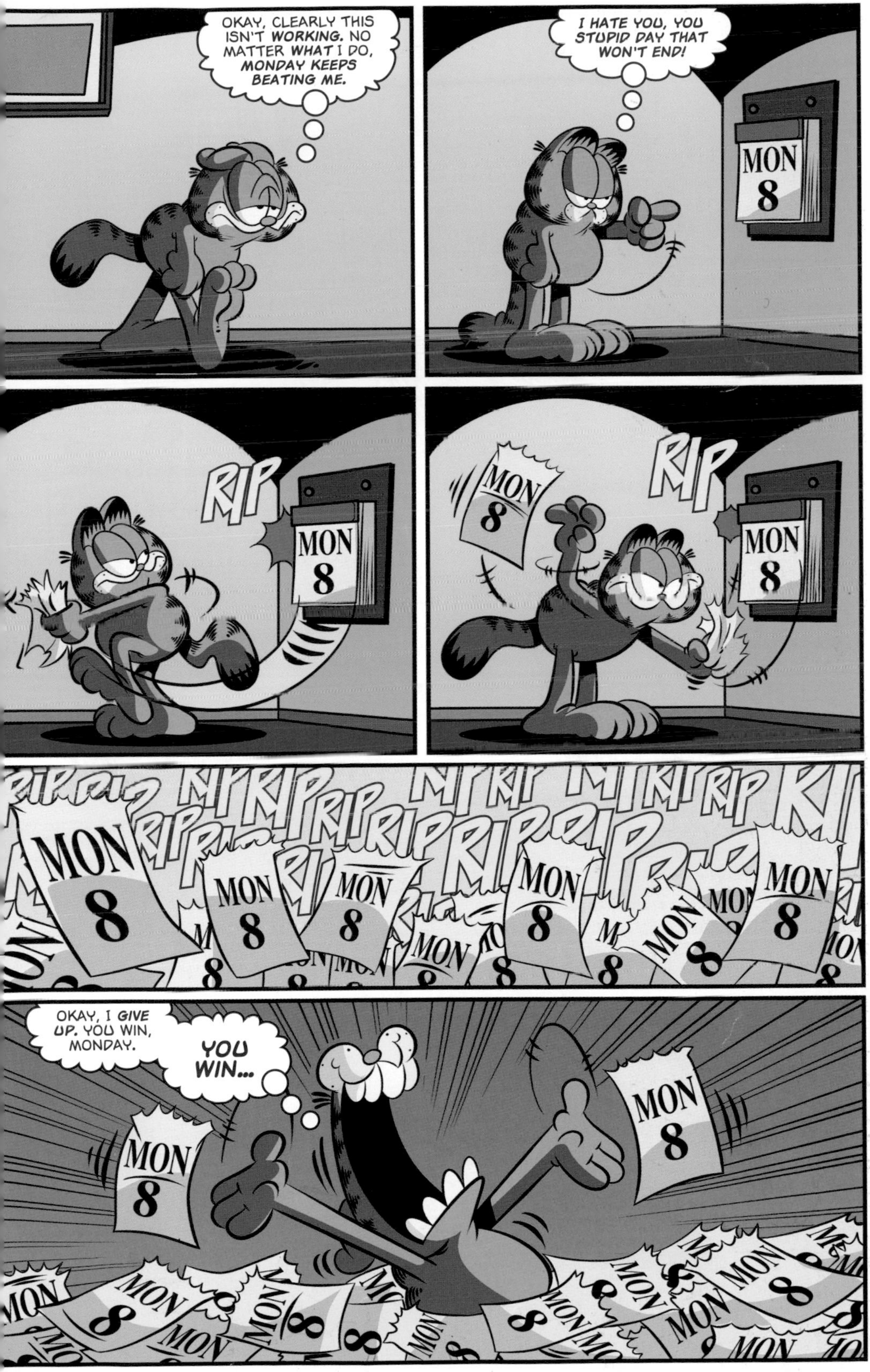
OKAY, CLEARLY THIS ISN'T WORKING. NO MATTER WHAT I DO, MONDAY KEEPS BEATING ME.
I HATE YOU, YOU STUPID DAY THAT WON'T END!
MON 8
RIP
MON 8
RIP
MON 8
OKAY, I GIVE UP. YOU WIN, MONDAY.
YOU WIN...

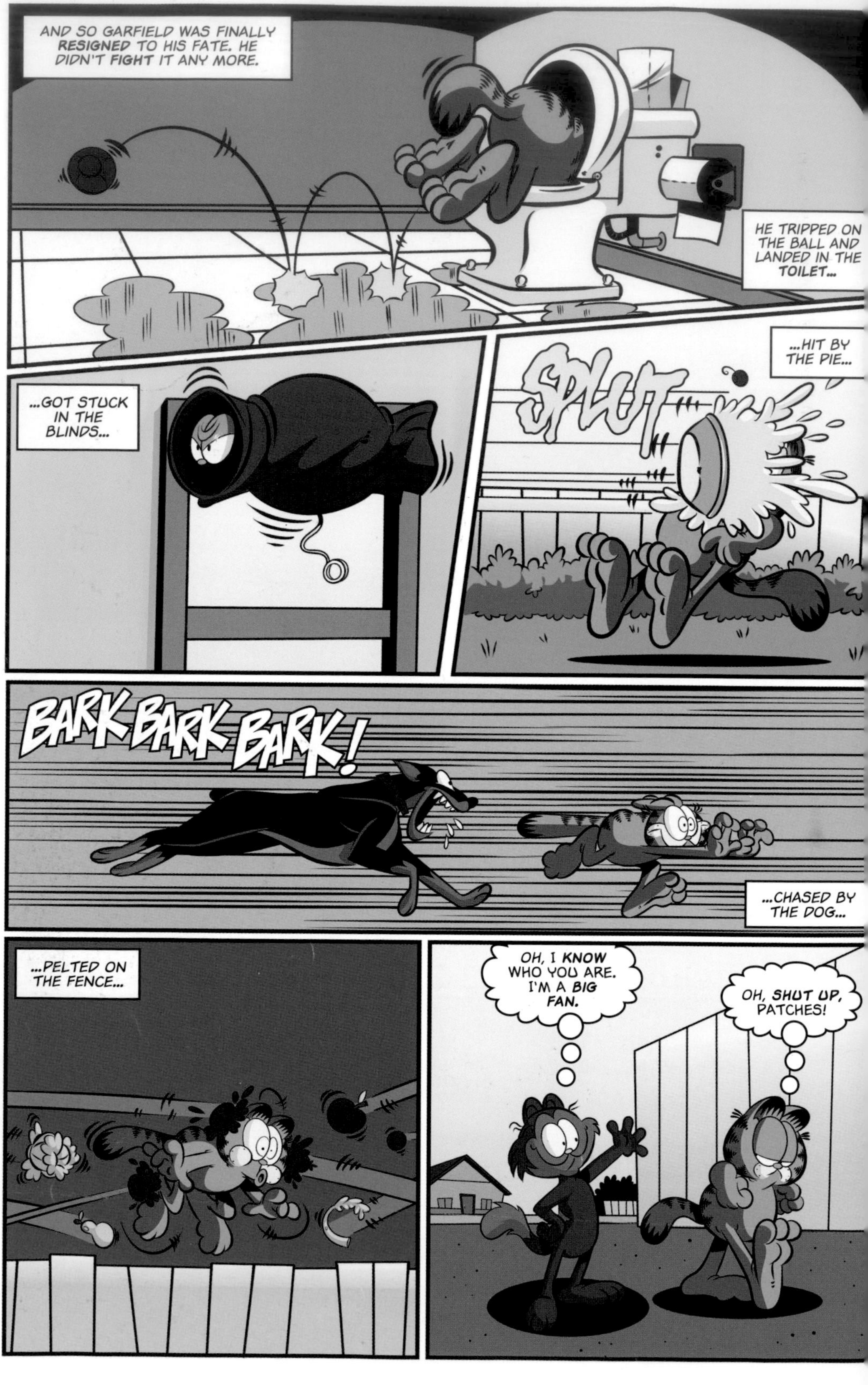
AND SO GARFIELD WAS FINALLY RESIGNED TO HIS FATE. HE DIDN'T FIGHT IT ANY MORE.
HE TRIPPED ON THE BALL AND LANDED IN THE TOILET...
...GOT STUCK IN THE BLINDS...
SPLUT
...HIT BY THE PIE...
BARK BARK BARK!
...CHASED BY THE DOG...
...PELTED ON THE FENCE...
OH, I KNOW WHO YOU ARE. I'M A BIG FAN.
OH, SHUT UP, PATCHES!

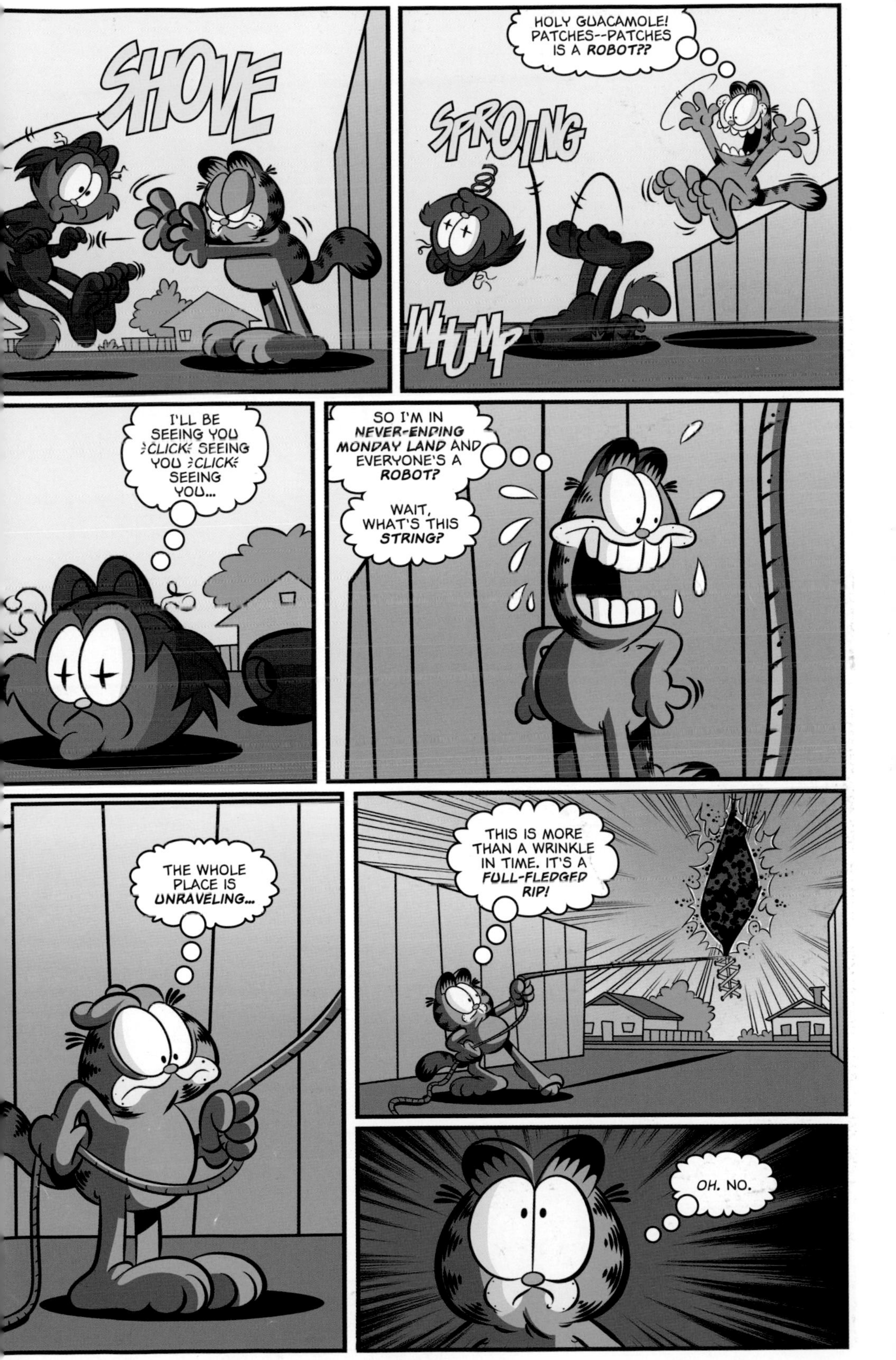
SHOVE
HOLY GUACAMOLE! PATCHES--PATCHES IS A ROBOT??
SPROING
WHUMP
I'LL BE SEEING YOU ≥CLICK≤ SEEING YOU ≥CLICK≤ SEEING YOU...
SO I'M IN NEVER-ENDING MONDAY LAND AND EVERYONE'S A ROBOT?
WAIT, WHAT'S THIS STRING?
THE WHOLE PLACE IS UNRAVELING...
THIS IS MORE THAN A WRINKLE IN TIME. IT'S A FULL-FLEDGED RIP!
OH. NO.

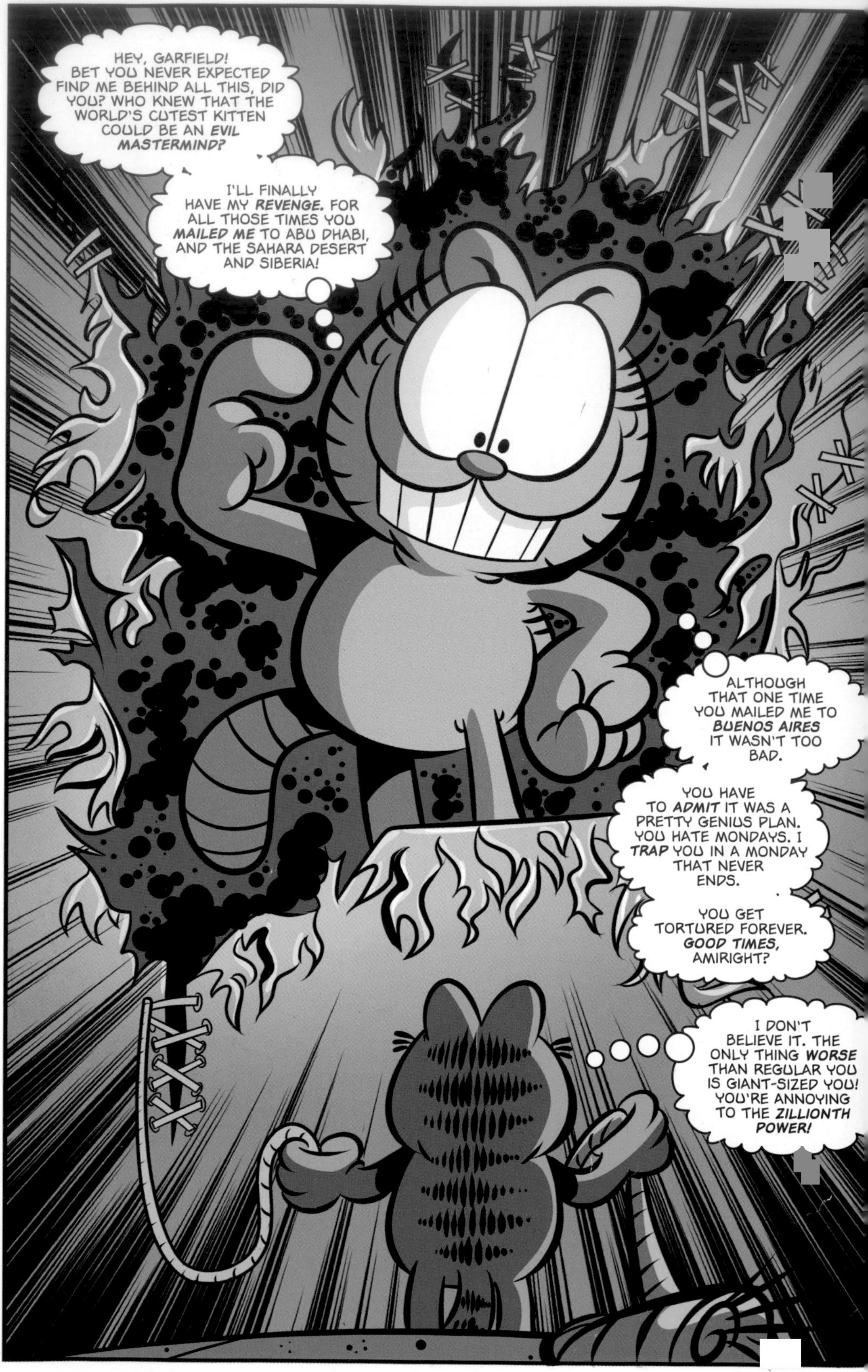
HEY, GARFIELD! BET YOU NEVER EXPECTED FIND ME BEHIND ALL THIS, DID YOU? WHO KNEW THAT THE WORLD'S CUTEST KITTEN COULD BE AN *EVIL MASTERMIND?*
I'LL FINALLY HAVE MY *REVENGE.* FOR ALL THOSE TIMES YOU *MAILED ME* TO ABU DHABI, AND THE SAHARA DESERT AND SIBERIA!
ALTHOUGH THAT ONE TIME YOU MAILED ME TO *BUENOS AIRES* IT WASN'T TOO BAD.
YOU HAVE TO *ADMIT* IT WAS A PRETTY GENIUS PLAN. YOU HATE MONDAYS. I *TRAP* YOU IN A MONDAY THAT NEVER ENDS.
YOU GET TORTURED FOREVER. *GOOD TIMES,* AMIRIGHT?
I DON'T BELIEVE IT. THE ONLY THING *WORSE* THAN REGULAR YOU IS GIANT-SIZED YOU! YOU'RE ANNOYING TO THE *ZILLIONTH POWER!*

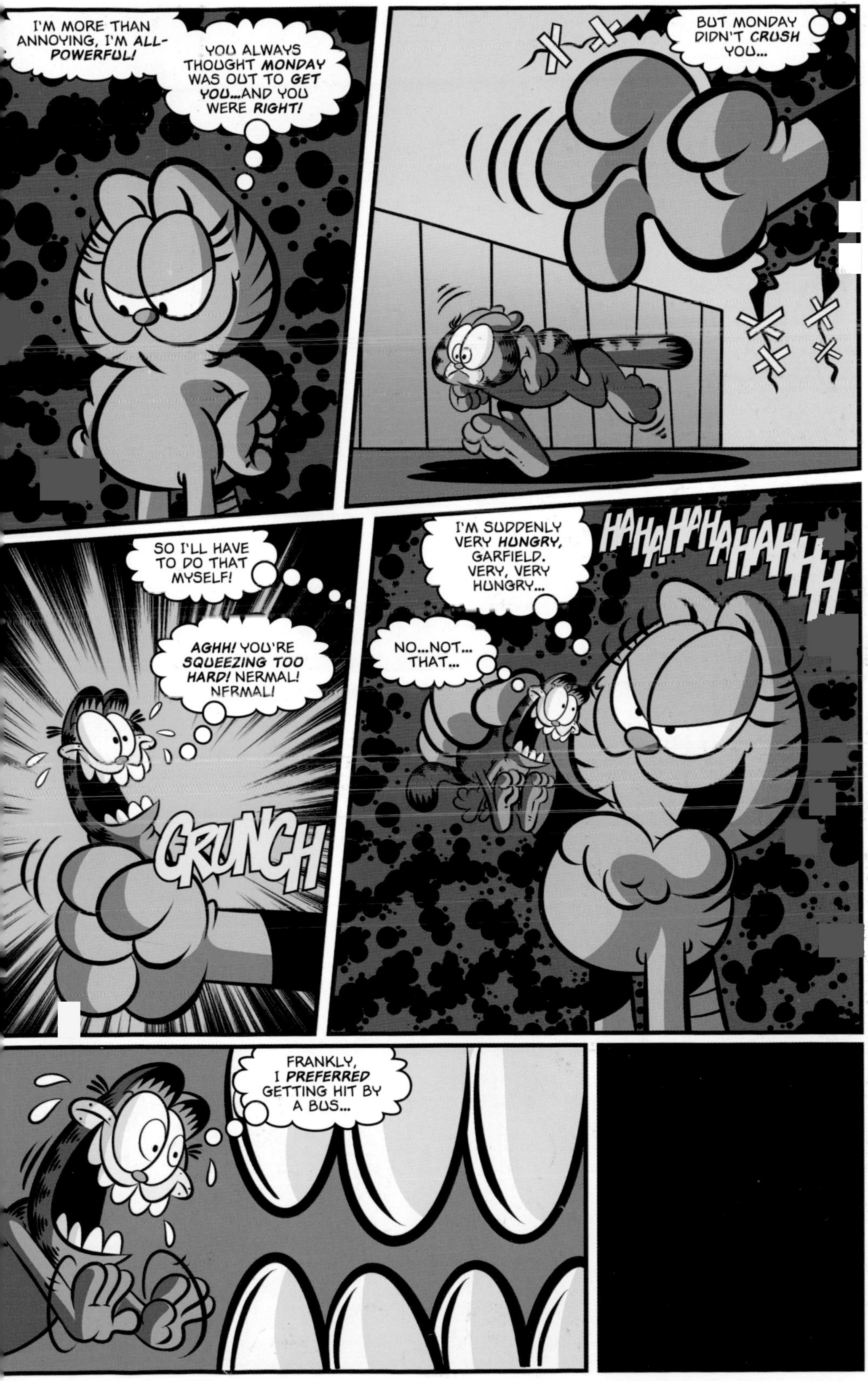

I'M MORE THAN ANNOYING, I'M ALL-POWERFUL!
YOU ALWAYS THOUGHT MONDAY WAS OUT TO GET YOU...AND YOU WERE RIGHT!
BUT MONDAY DIDN'T CRUSH YOU...
SO I'LL HAVE TO DO THAT MYSELF!
AGHH! YOU'RE SQUEEZING TOO HARD! NERMAL! NERMAL!
CRUNCH
I'M SUDDENLY VERY HUNGRY, GARFIELD. VERY, VERY HUNGRY...
HAHAHAHAHAHHH
NO...NOT... THAT...
FRANKLY, I PREFERRED GETTING HIT BY A BUS...

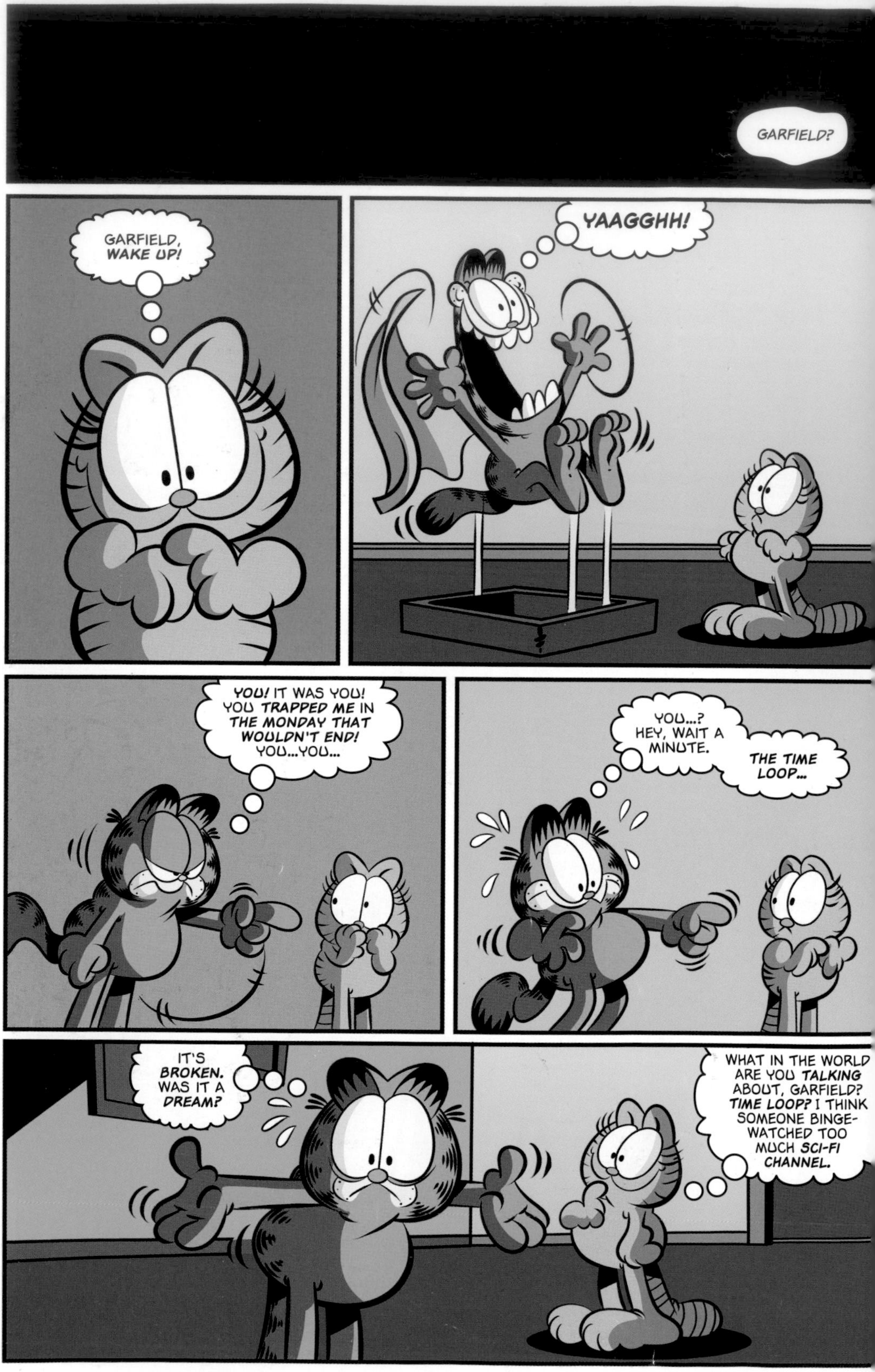
GARFIELD?
GARFIELD, WAKE UP!
YAAGGHH!
YOU! IT WAS YOU! YOU TRAPPED ME IN THE MONDAY THAT WOULDN'T END! YOU...YOU...
YOU...? HEY, WAIT A MINUTE.
THE TIME LOOP...
IT'S BROKEN. WAS IT A DREAM?
WHAT IN THE WORLD ARE YOU TALKING ABOUT, GARFIELD? TIME LOOP? I THINK SOMEONE BINGE-WATCHED TOO MUCH SCI-FI CHANNEL.

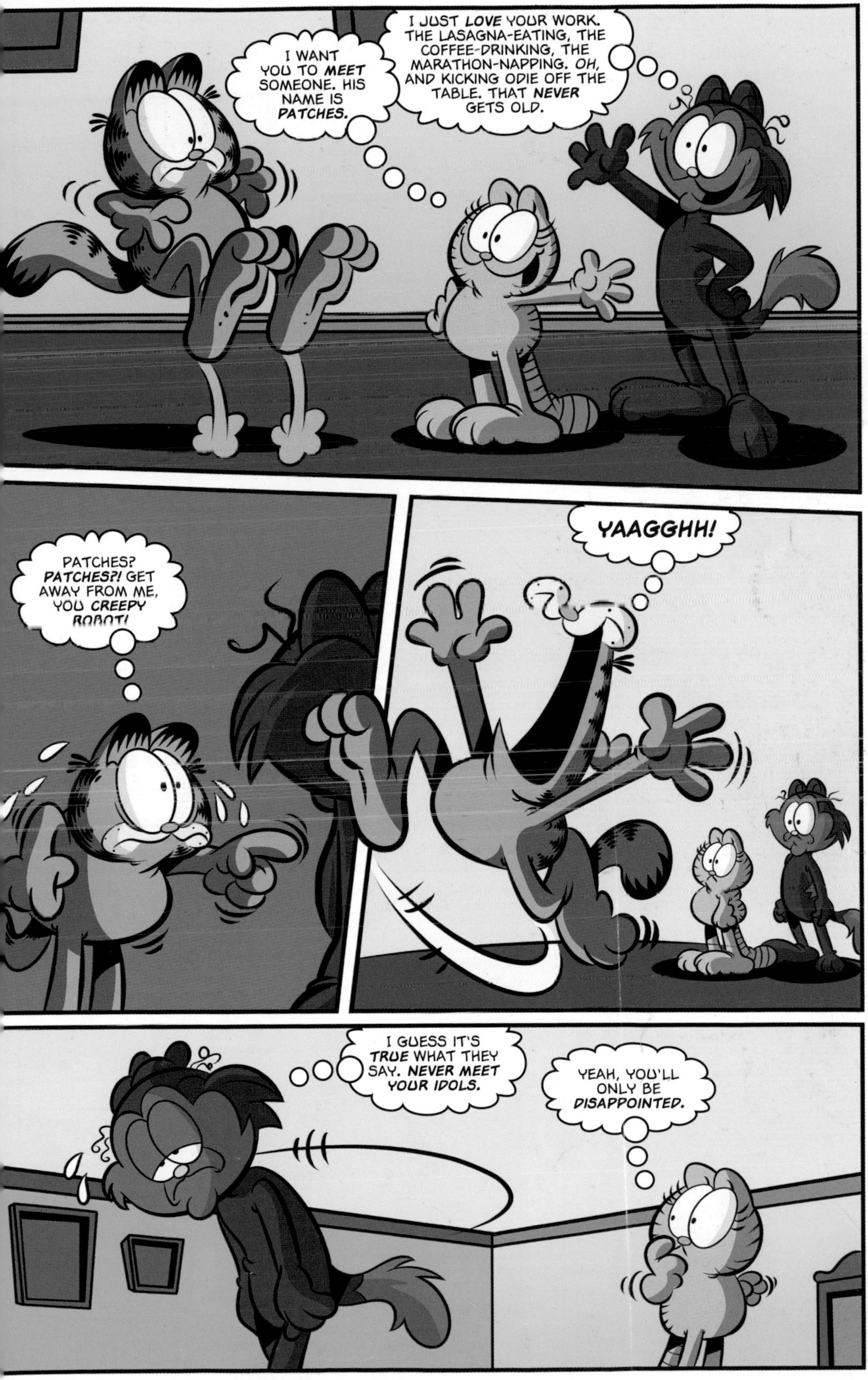
I WANT YOU TO MEET SOMEONE. HIS NAME IS PATCHES.
I JUST LOVE YOUR WORK. THE LASAGNA-EATING, THE COFFEE-DRINKING, THE MARATHON-NAPPING. OH, AND KICKING ODIE OFF THE TABLE. THAT NEVER GETS OLD.
PATCHES? PATCHES?! GET AWAY FROM ME, YOU CREEPY ROBOT!
YAAGGHH!
I GUESS IT'S TRUE WHAT THEY SAY. NEVER MEET YOUR IDOLS.
YEAH, YOU'LL ONLY BE DISAPPOINTED.

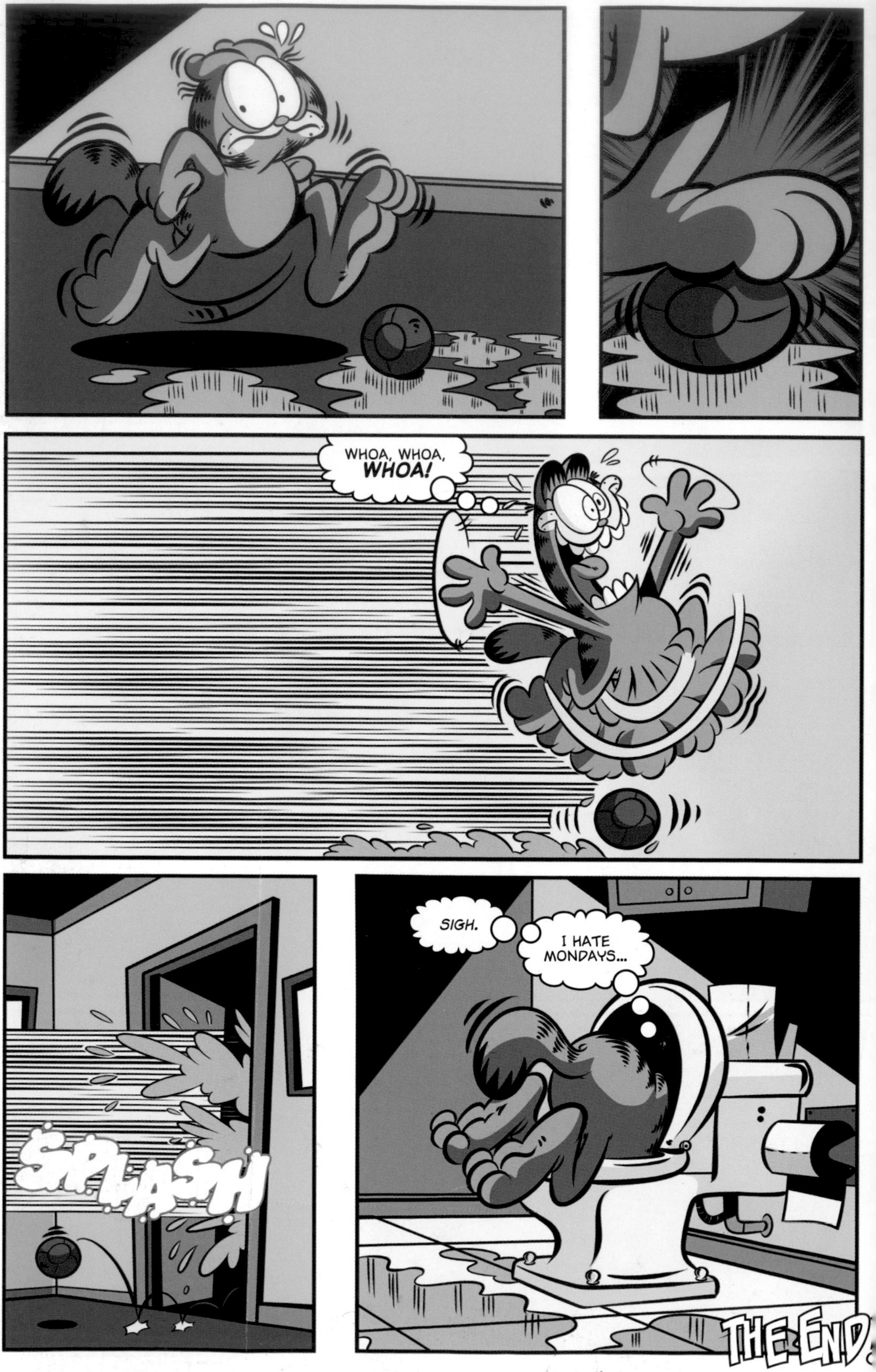
WHOA, WHOA, WHOA!
SPLASH
SIGH.
I HATE MONDAYS...
THE END

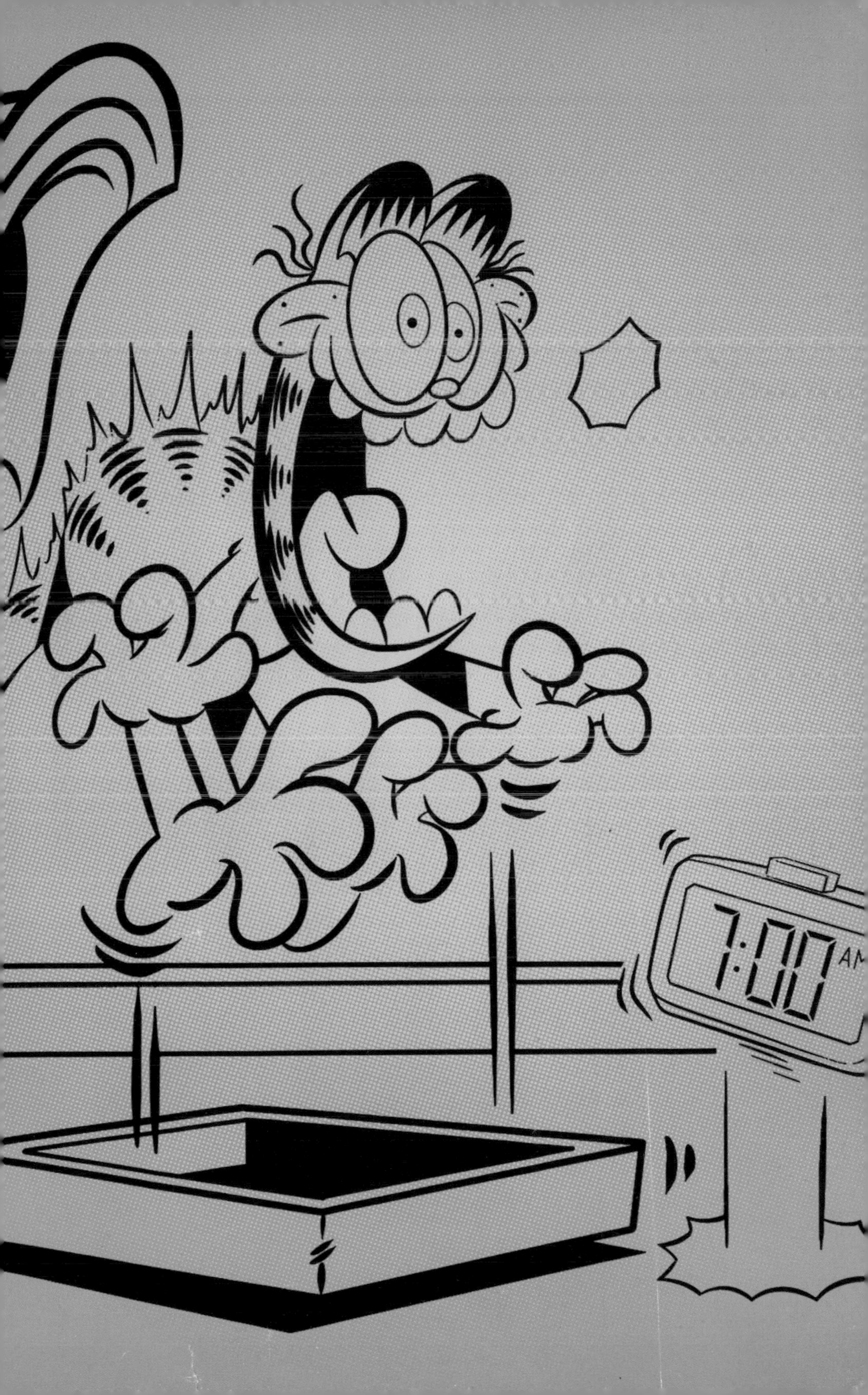
7:00 A

"NERMAL TAKES OVER"

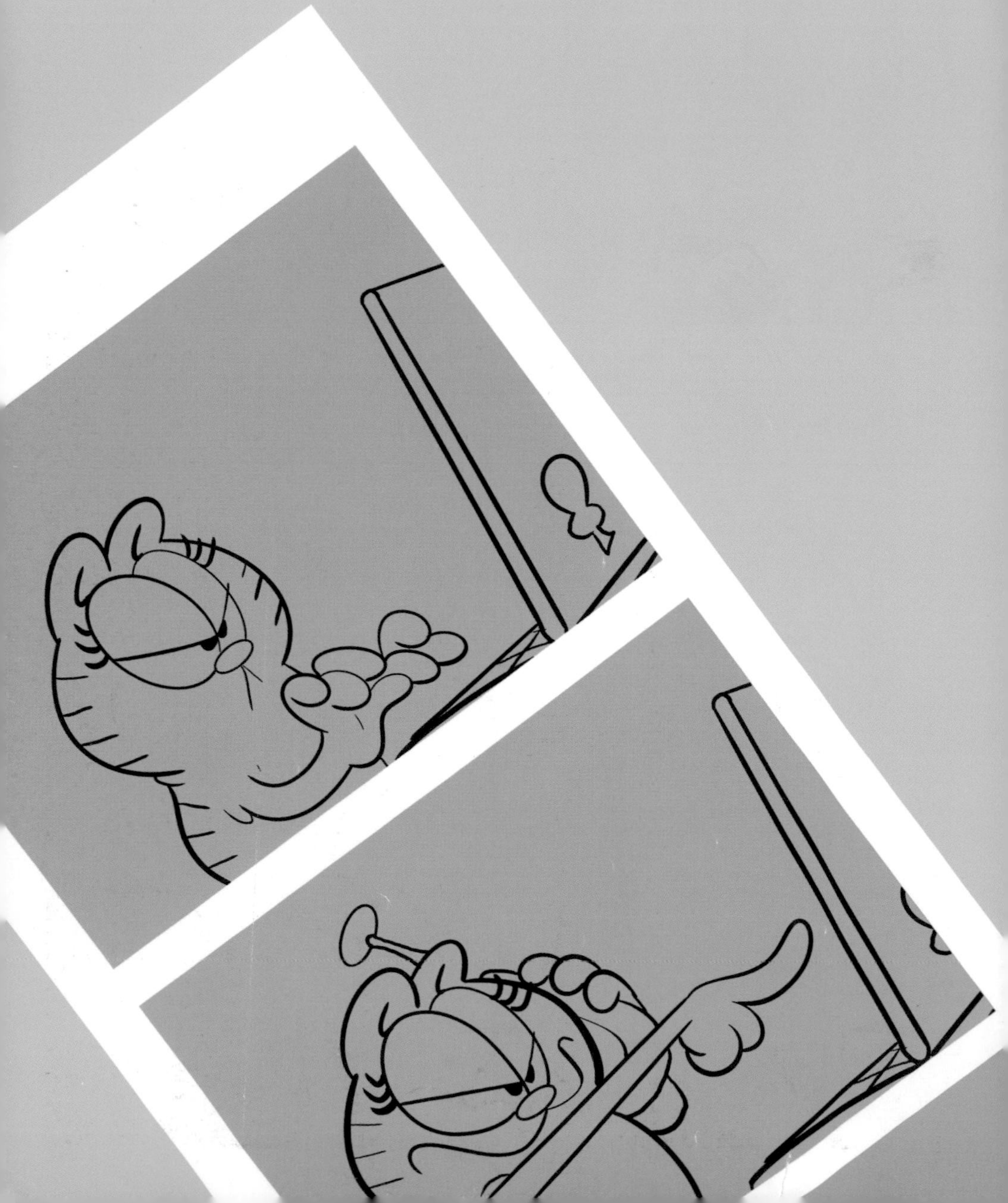

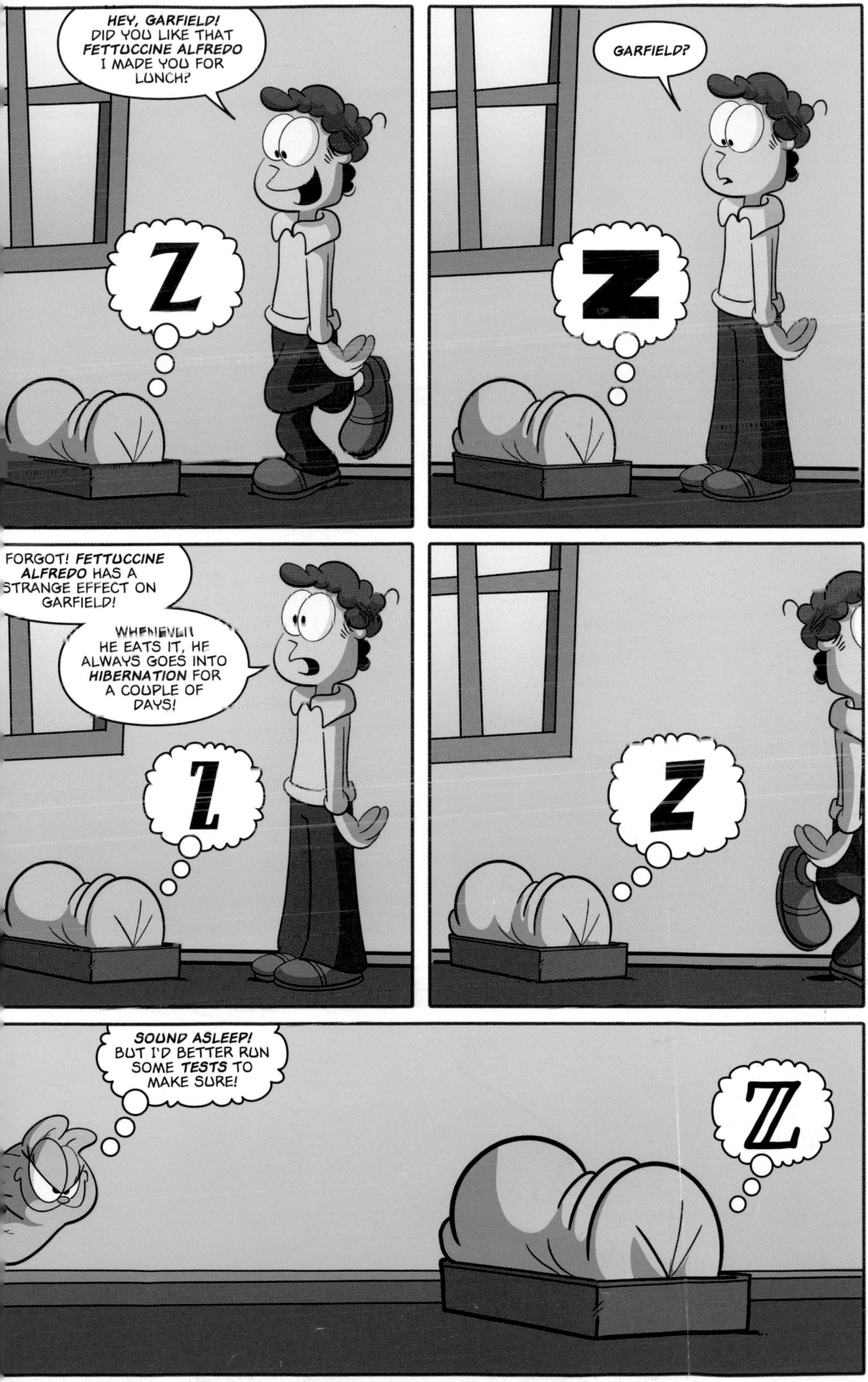
HEY, GARFIELD! DID YOU LIKE THAT FETTUCCINE ALFREDO I MADE YOU FOR LUNCH?
Z
GARFIELD?
Z
FORGOT! FETTUCCINE ALFREDO HAS A STRANGE EFFECT ON GARFIELD!
WHENEVER HE EATS IT, HE ALWAYS GOES INTO HIBERNATION FOR A COUPLE OF DAYS!
Z
Z
SOUND ASLEEP! BUT I'D BETTER RUN SOME TESTS TO MAKE SURE!
Z

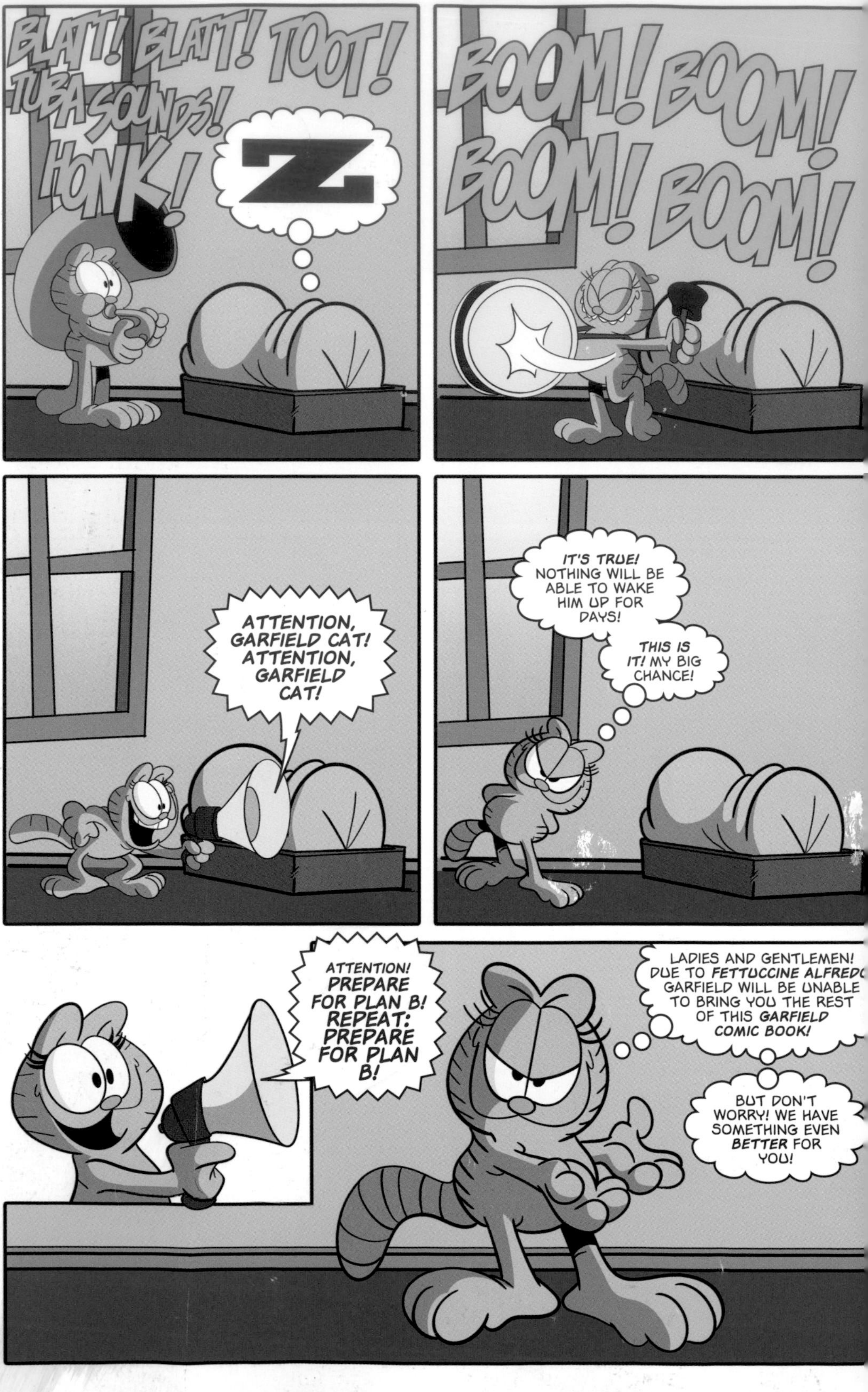
BLATT! BLATT! TOOT!
TUBA SOUNDS!
HONK!
Z
BOOM! BOOM!
BOOM! BOOM!
ATTENTION, GARFIELD CAT! ATTENTION, GARFIELD CAT!
IT'S TRUE! NOTHING WILL BE ABLE TO WAKE HIM UP FOR DAYS!
THIS IS IT! MY BIG CHANCE!
ATTENTION! PREPARE FOR PLAN B! REPEAT: PREPARE FOR PLAN B!
LADIES AND GENTLEMEN! DUE TO FETTUCCINE ALFREDO GARFIELD WILL BE UNABLE TO BRING YOU THE REST OF THIS GARFIELD COMIC BOOK!
BUT DON'T WORRY! WE HAVE SOMETHING EVEN BETTER FOR YOU!

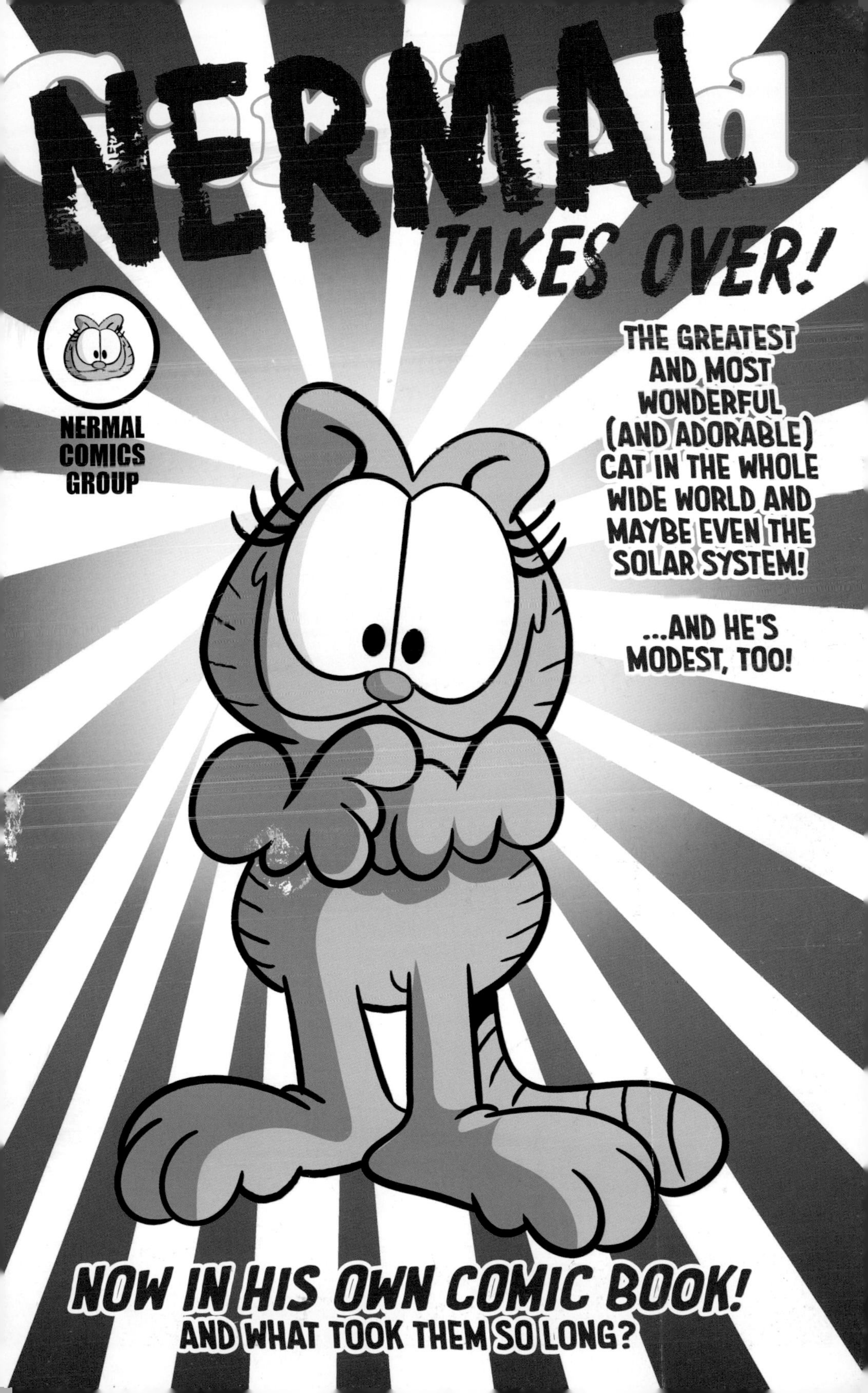
NERMAL
TAKES OVER!
NERMAL COMICS GROUP
THE GREATEST AND MOST WONDERFUL (AND ADORABLE) CAT IN THE WHOLE WIDE WORLD AND MAYBE EVEN THE SOLAR SYSTEM!
...AND HE'S MODEST, TOO!
NOW IN HIS OWN COMIC BOOK!
AND WHAT TOOK THEM SO LONG?

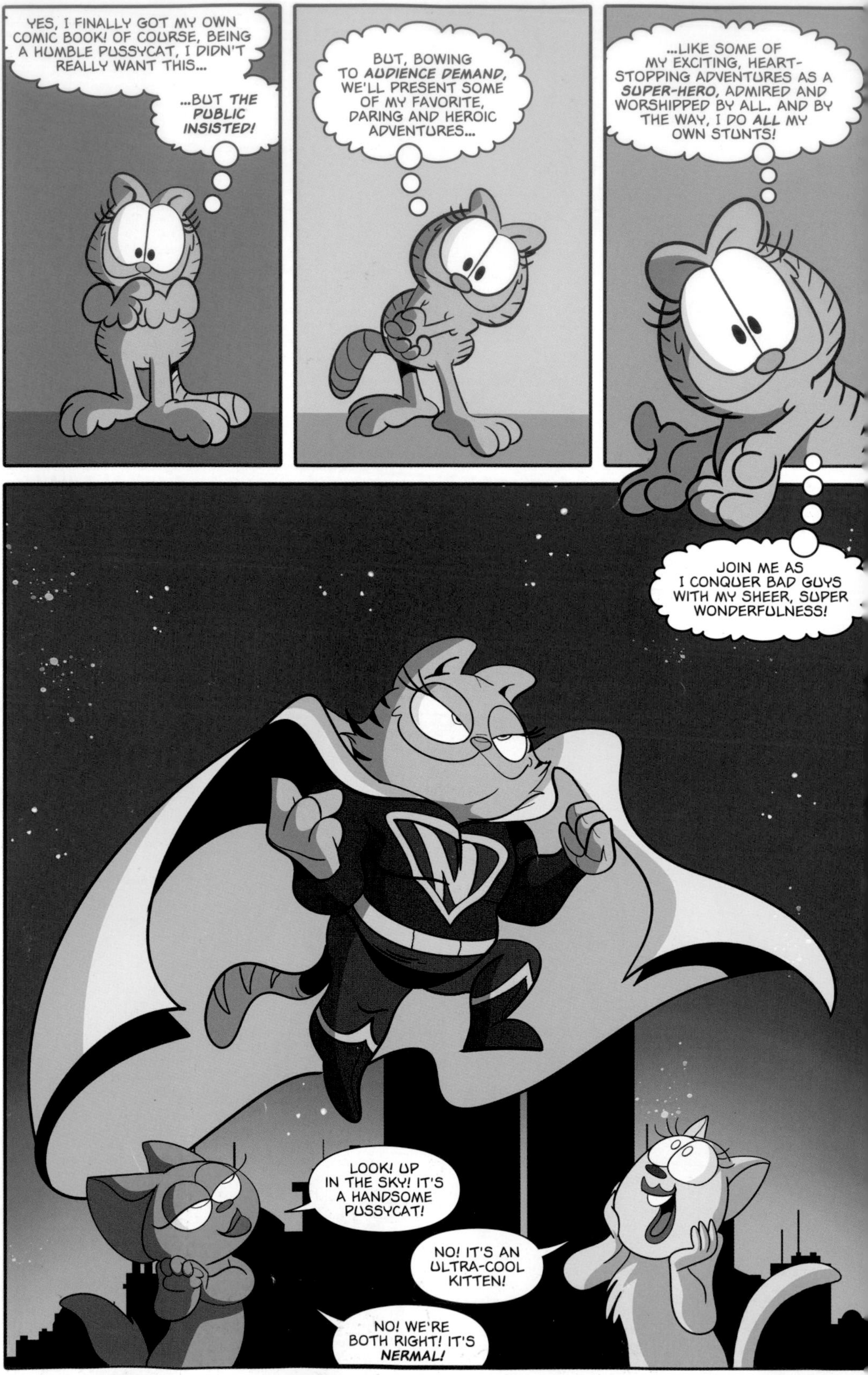
YES, I FINALLY GOT MY OWN COMIC BOOK! OF COURSE, BEING A HUMBLE PUSSYCAT, I DIDN'T REALLY WANT THIS...
...BUT THE PUBLIC INSISTED!
BUT, BOWING TO AUDIENCE DEMAND, WE'LL PRESENT SOME OF MY FAVORITE, DARING AND HEROIC ADVENTURES...
...LIKE SOME OF MY EXCITING, HEART-STOPPING ADVENTURES AS A SUPER-HERO, ADMIRED AND WORSHIPPED BY ALL. AND BY THE WAY, I DO ALL MY OWN STUNTS!
JOIN ME AS I CONQUER BAD GUYS WITH MY SHEER, SUPER WONDERFULNESS!
LOOK! UP IN THE SKY! IT'S A HANDSOME PUSSYCAT!
NO! IT'S AN ULTRA-COOL KITTEN!
NO! WE'RE BOTH RIGHT! IT'S NERMAL!

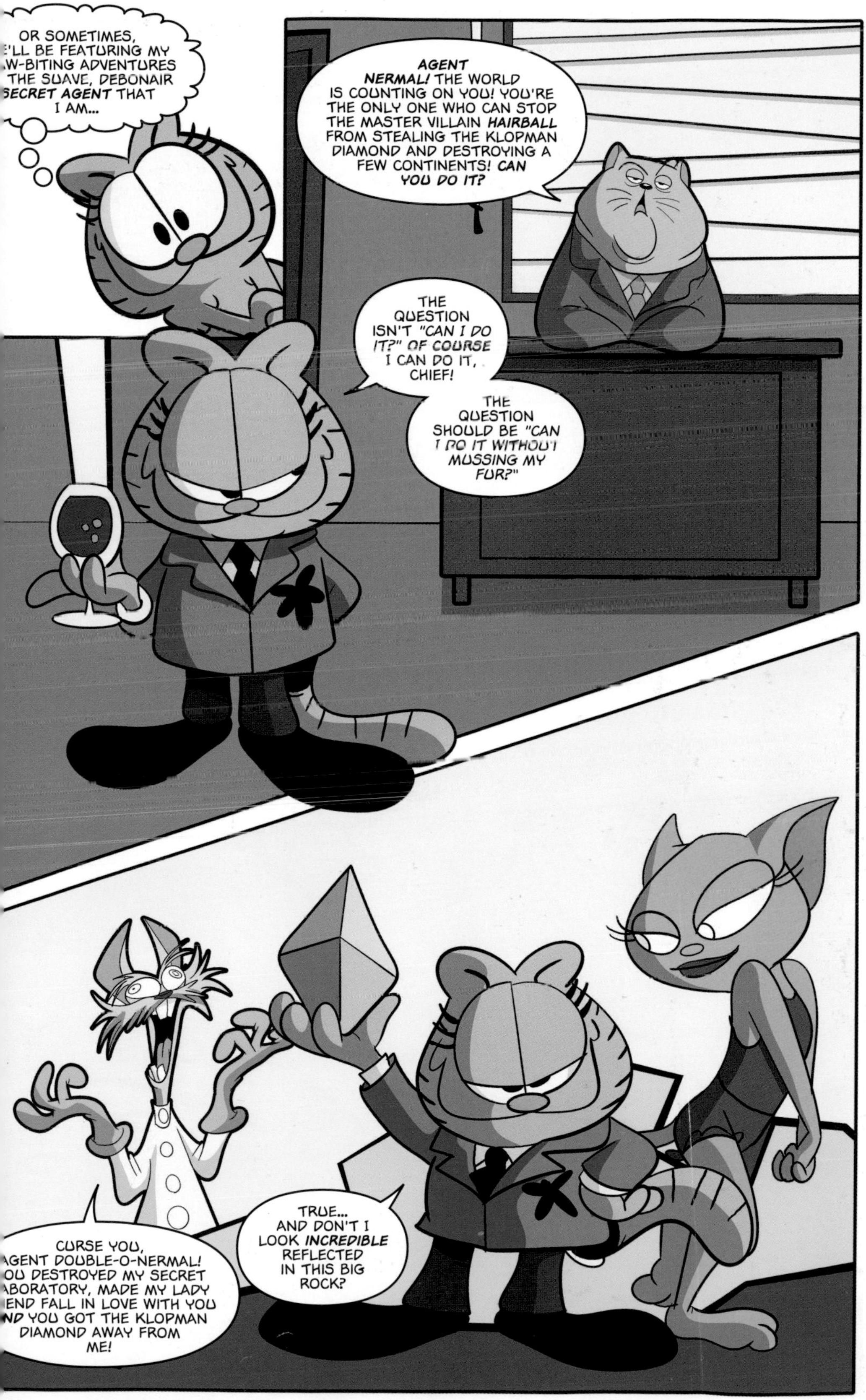
OR SOMETIMES, 'LL BE FEATURING MY W-BITING ADVENTURES THE SUAVE, DEBONAIR SECRET AGENT THAT I AM...
AGENT NERMAL! THE WORLD IS COUNTING ON YOU! YOU'RE THE ONLY ONE WHO CAN STOP THE MASTER VILLAIN HAIRBALL FROM STEALING THE KLOPMAN DIAMOND AND DESTROYING A FEW CONTINENTS! CAN YOU DO IT?
THE QUESTION ISN'T "CAN I DO IT?" OF COURSE I CAN DO IT, CHIEF!
THE QUESTION SHOULD BE "CAN I DO IT WITHOUT MUSSING MY FUR?"
CURSE YOU, AGENT DOUBLE-O-NERMAL! OU DESTROYED MY SECRET ABORATORY, MADE MY LADY END FALL IN LOVE WITH YOU ND YOU GOT THE KLOPMAN DIAMOND AWAY FROM ME!
TRUE... AND DON'T I LOOK INCREDIBLE REFLECTED IN THIS BIG ROCK?

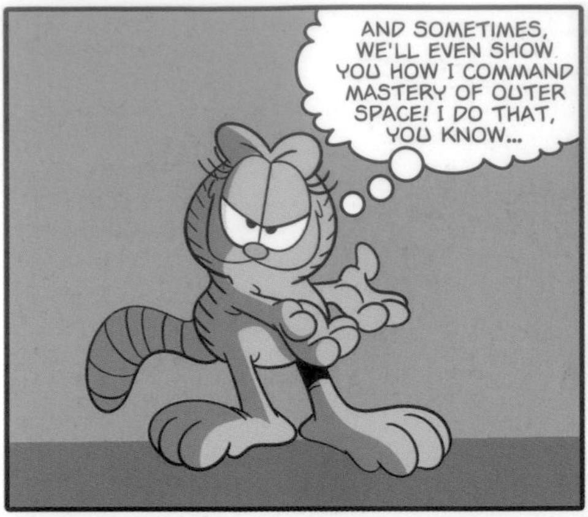
AND SOMETIMES, WE'LL EVEN SHOW YOU HOW I COMMAND MASTERY OF OUTER SPACE! I DO THAT, YOU KNOW...

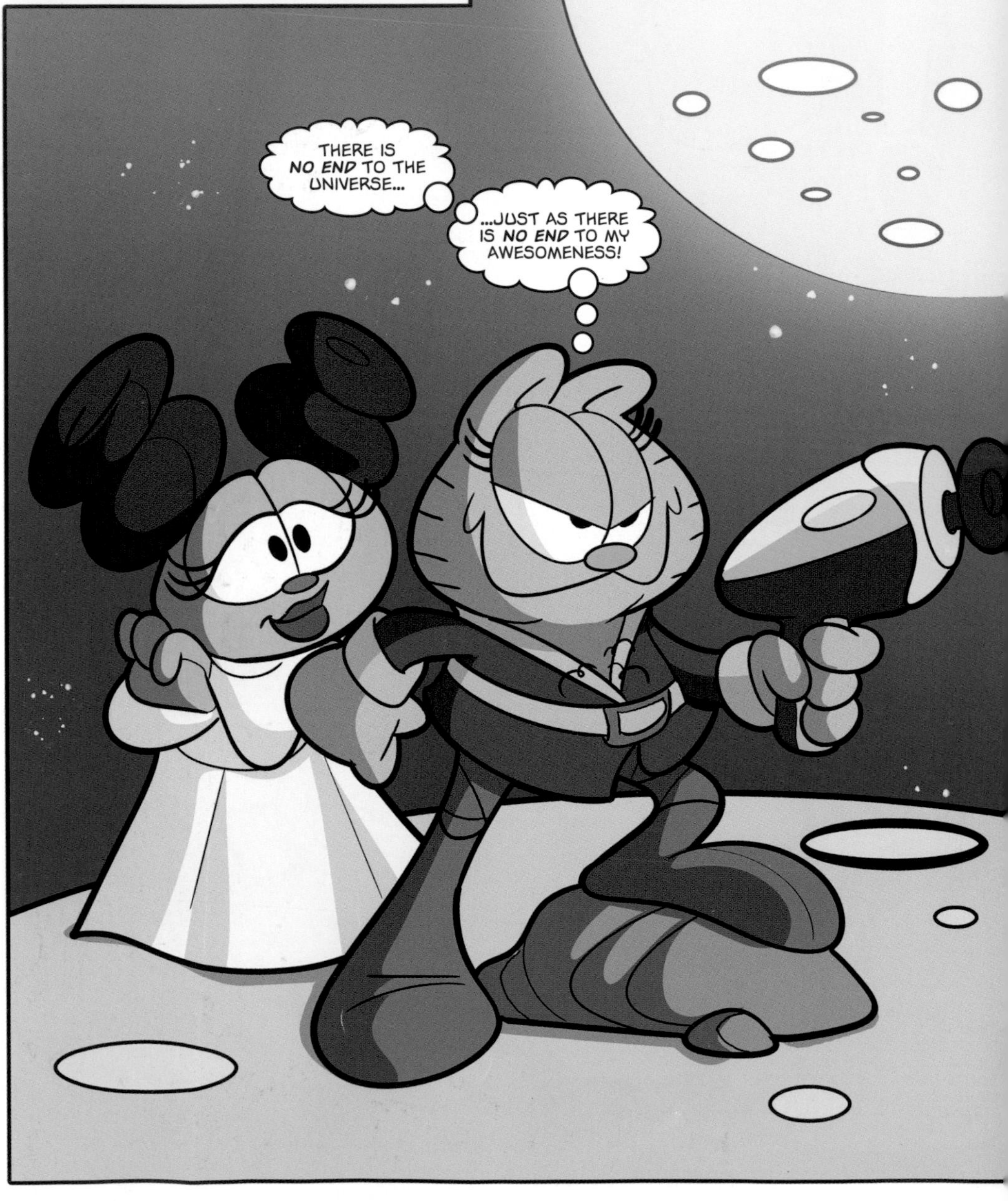
THERE IS **NO END** TO THE UNIVERSE...
...JUST AS THERE IS **NO END** TO MY AWESOMENESS!

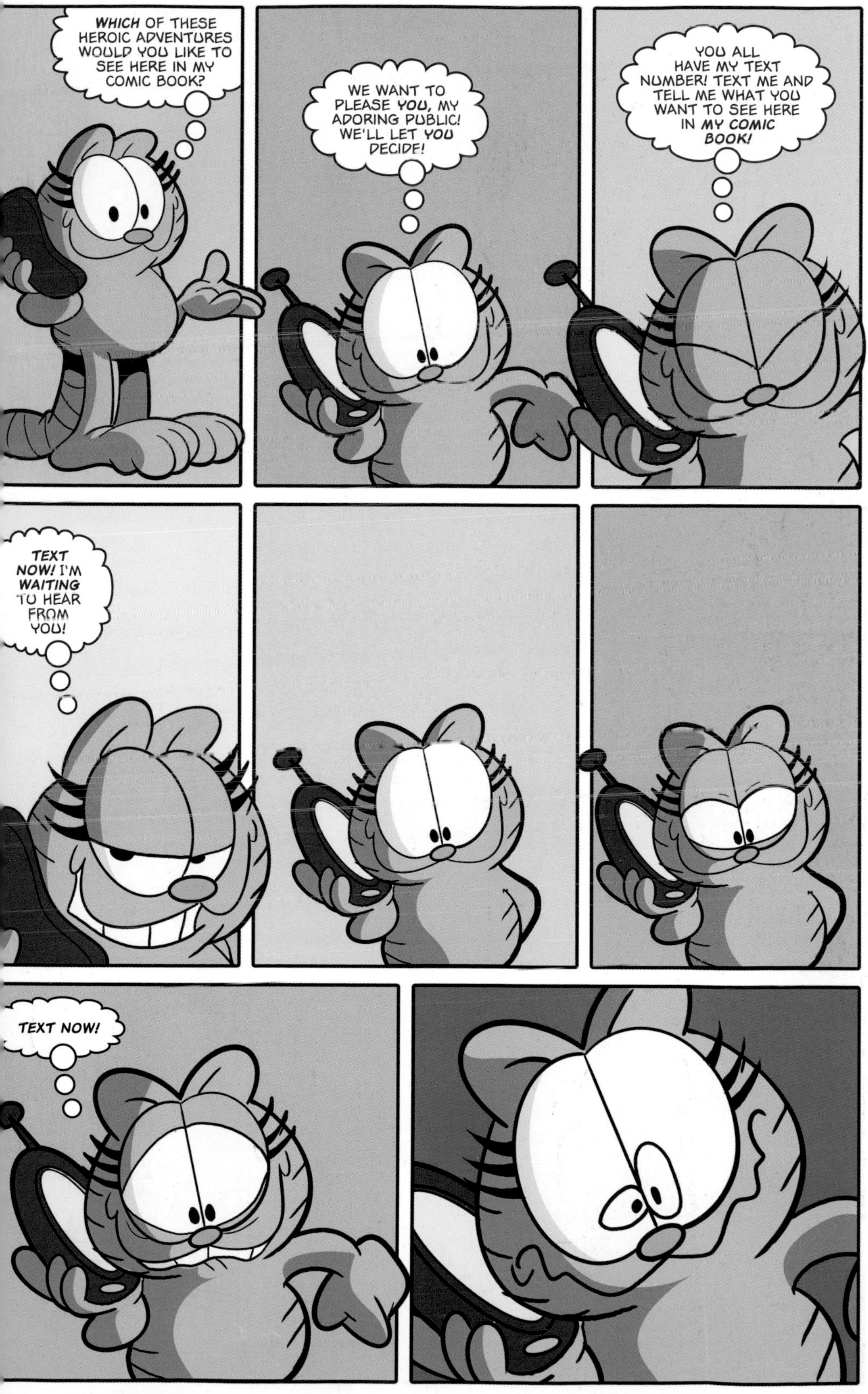
WHICH OF THESE HEROIC ADVENTURES WOULD YOU LIKE TO SEE HERE IN MY COMIC BOOK?
WE WANT TO PLEASE YOU, MY ADORING PUBLIC! WE'LL LET YOU DECIDE!
YOU ALL HAVE MY TEXT NUMBER! TEXT ME AND TELL ME WHAT YOU WANT TO SEE HERE IN MY COMIC BOOK!
TEXT NOW! I'M WAITING TO HEAR FROM YOU!
TEXT NOW!

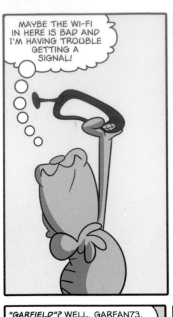

MAYBE THE WI-FI IN HERE IS BAD AND I'M HAVING TROUBLE GETTING A SIGNAL!

PING

AH! AT LAST, I HAVE A MESSAGE! LET'S SEE WHAT IT SAYS...

"WE DON'T WANT TO SEE YOU! WE WANT TO SEE GARFIELD!"

"GARFIELD"? WELL, GARFAN73, I'LL BET YOU'RE THE ONLY PERSON WHO WANTS TO SEE HIM IN MY COMIC BOOK!

PING PING PING PING PING PING PING PING PING PING PING PING PING PING PING PING PING

FINE! YOU WANT GARFIELD, I'LL GIVE YOU GARFIELD!

I'LL BE BACK IN A MINUTE!

GO READ SOME OTHER COMIC BOOK UNTIL THEN!

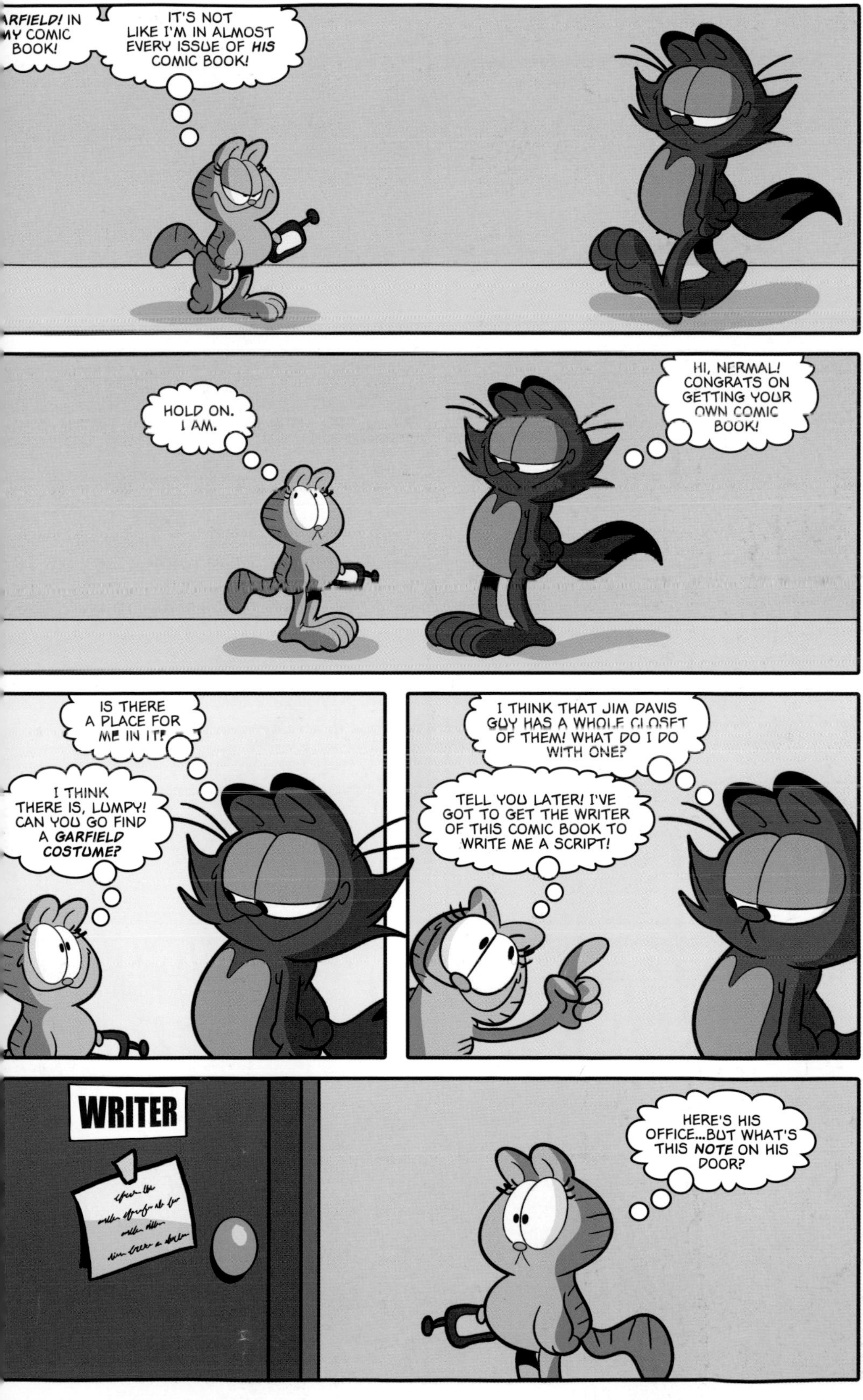
ARFIELD! IN MY COMIC BOOK!
IT'S NOT LIKE I'M IN ALMOST EVERY ISSUE OF HIS COMIC BOOK!
HOLD ON. I AM.
HI, NERMAL! CONGRATS ON GETTING YOUR OWN COMIC BOOK!
IS THERE A PLACE FOR ME IN IT?
I THINK THERE IS, LUMPY! CAN YOU GO FIND A GARFIELD COSTUME?
I THINK THAT JIM DAVIS GUY HAS A WHOLE CLOSET OF THEM! WHAT DO I DO WITH ONE?
TELL YOU LATER! I'VE GOT TO GET THE WRITER OF THIS COMIC BOOK TO WRITE ME A SCRIPT!
WRITER
HERE'S HIS OFFICE...BUT WHAT'S THIS NOTE ON HIS DOOR?

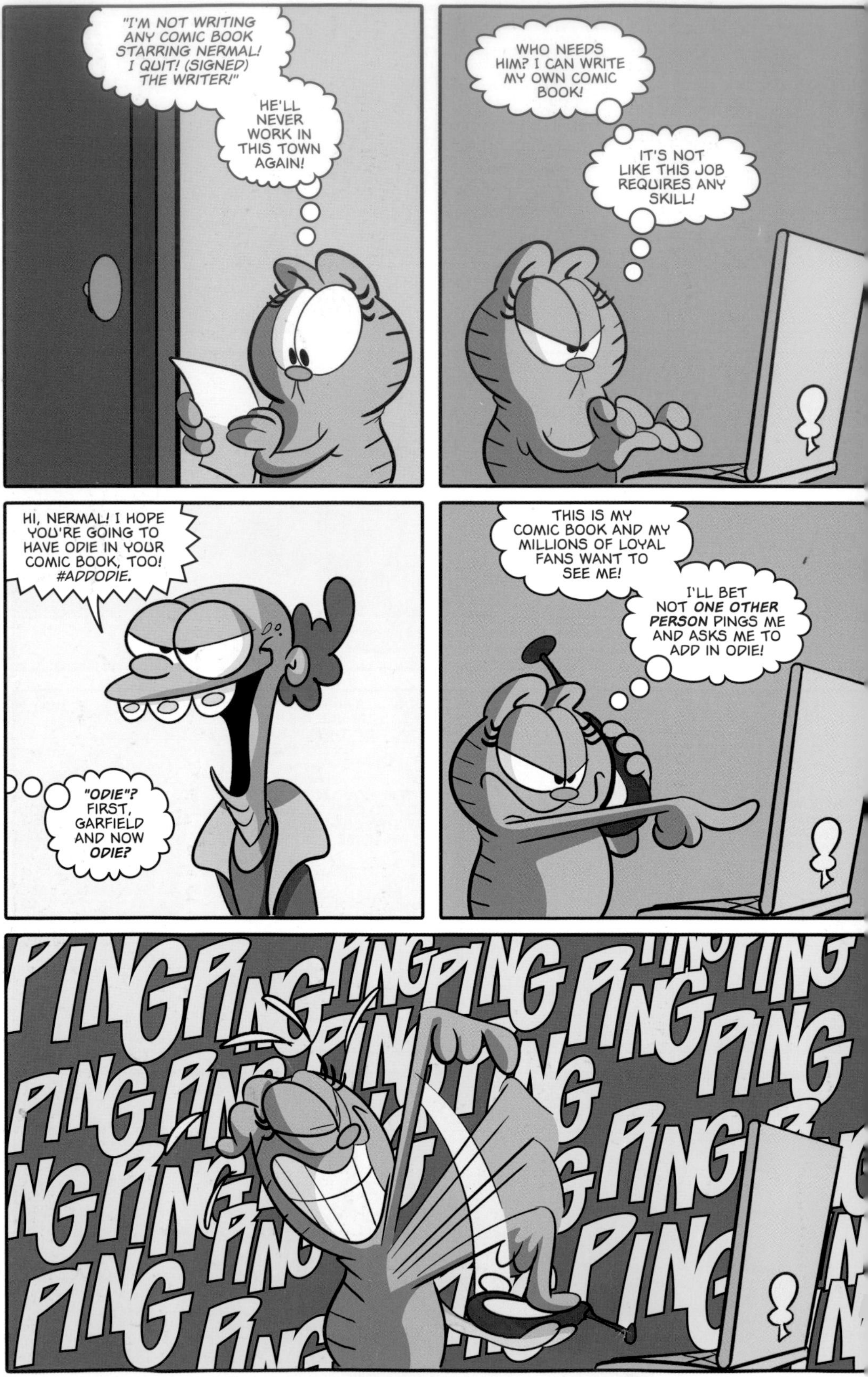
"I'M NOT WRITING ANY COMIC BOOK STARRING NERMAL! I QUIT! (SIGNED) THE WRITER!"
HE'LL NEVER WORK IN THIS TOWN AGAIN!
WHO NEEDS HIM? I CAN WRITE MY OWN COMIC BOOK!
IT'S NOT LIKE THIS JOB REQUIRES ANY SKILL!
HI, NERMAL! I HOPE YOU'RE GOING TO HAVE ODIE IN YOUR COMIC BOOK, TOO! #ADDODIE.
"ODIE"? FIRST, GARFIELD AND NOW ODIE?
THIS IS MY COMIC BOOK AND MY MILLIONS OF LOYAL FANS WANT TO SEE ME!
I'LL BET NOT ONE OTHER PERSON PINGS ME AND ASKS ME TO ADD IN ODIE!
PING PING PING PING PING PING PING PING PING PING PING PING PING PING

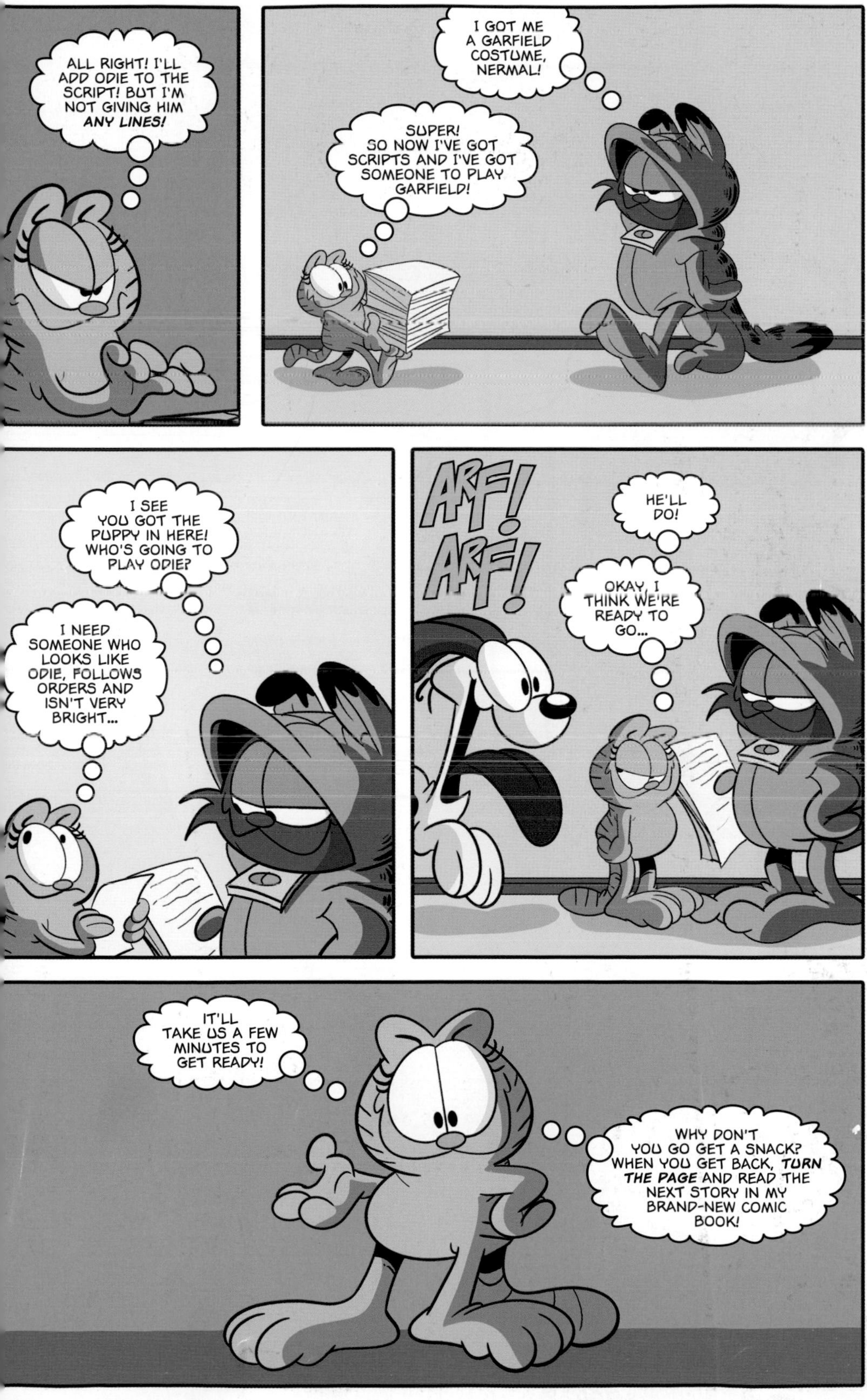
ALL RIGHT! I'LL ADD ODIE TO THE SCRIPT! BUT I'M NOT GIVING HIM *ANY LINES!*
I GOT ME A GARFIELD COSTUME, NERMAL!
SUPER! SO NOW I'VE GOT SCRIPTS AND I'VE GOT SOMEONE TO PLAY GARFIELD!
I SEE YOU GOT THE PUPPY IN HERE! WHO'S GOING TO PLAY ODIE?
I NEED SOMEONE WHO LOOKS LIKE ODIE, FOLLOWS ORDERS AND ISN'T VERY BRIGHT...
ARF! ARF!
HE'LL DO!
OKAY, I THINK WE'RE READY TO GO...
IT'LL TAKE US A FEW MINUTES TO GET READY!
WHY DON'T YOU GO GET A SNACK? WHEN YOU GET BACK, *TURN THE PAGE* AND READ THE NEXT STORY IN MY BRAND-NEW COMIC BOOK!

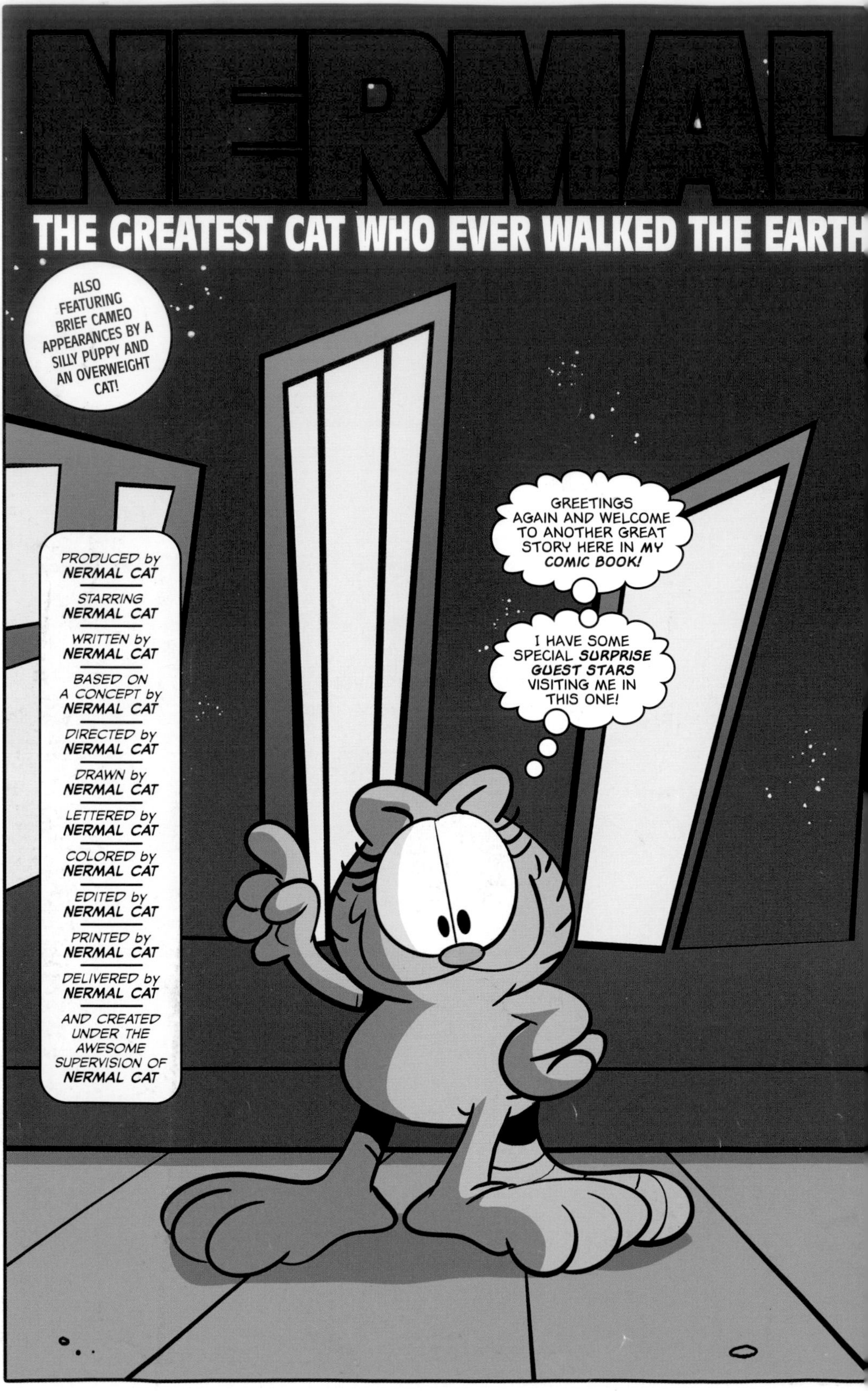
NERMAL
THE GREATEST CAT WHO EVER WALKED THE EARTH
ALSO FEATURING BRIEF CAMEO APPEARANCES BY A SILLY PUPPY AND AN OVERWEIGHT CAT!
PRODUCED by NERMAL CAT
STARRING NERMAL CAT
WRITTEN by NERMAL CAT
BASED ON A CONCEPT by NERMAL CAT
DIRECTED by NERMAL CAT
DRAWN by NERMAL CAT
LETTERED by NERMAL CAT
COLORED by NERMAL CAT
EDITED by NERMAL CAT
PRINTED by NERMAL CAT
DELIVERED by NERMAL CAT
AND CREATED UNDER THE AWESOME SUPERVISION OF NERMAL CAT
GREETINGS AGAIN AND WELCOME TO ANOTHER GREAT STORY HERE IN MY COMIC BOOK!
I HAVE SOME SPECIAL SURPRISE GUEST STARS VISITING ME IN THIS ONE!

OH, LOOK! HERE COMES ONE OF THEM NOW!

IT'S A PUPPY WHO'S ALMOST A *THIRD* AS ADORABLE AS I AM! *WELCOME,* ODIE!

AND NOW, WE'RE GOING TO BRING ON YOUR GOOD FRIEND, *GARFIELD!*

WANT TO SEE *GARFIELD,* ODIE?

YEAH! YEAH!

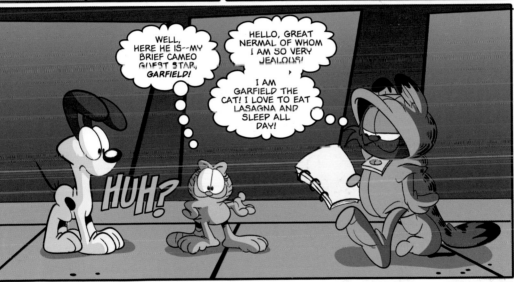

WELL, HERE HE IS--MY BRIEF CAMEO GUEST STAR, *GARFIELD!*

HELLO, GREAT NERMAL OF WHOM I AM SO VERY JEALOUS!

I AM GARFIELD THE CAT! I LOVE TO EAT LASAGNA AND SLEEP ALL DAY!

HUH?

OH, NERMAL! I WANT TO APOLOGIZE TO YOU FOR ALL THE HORRIBLE, BAD THINGS I HAVE DONE TO YOU!

GO ON...

LIKE THE 763 TIMES I HAVE STUFFED YOU IN A BOX AND MAILED YOU TO ABU DHABI...

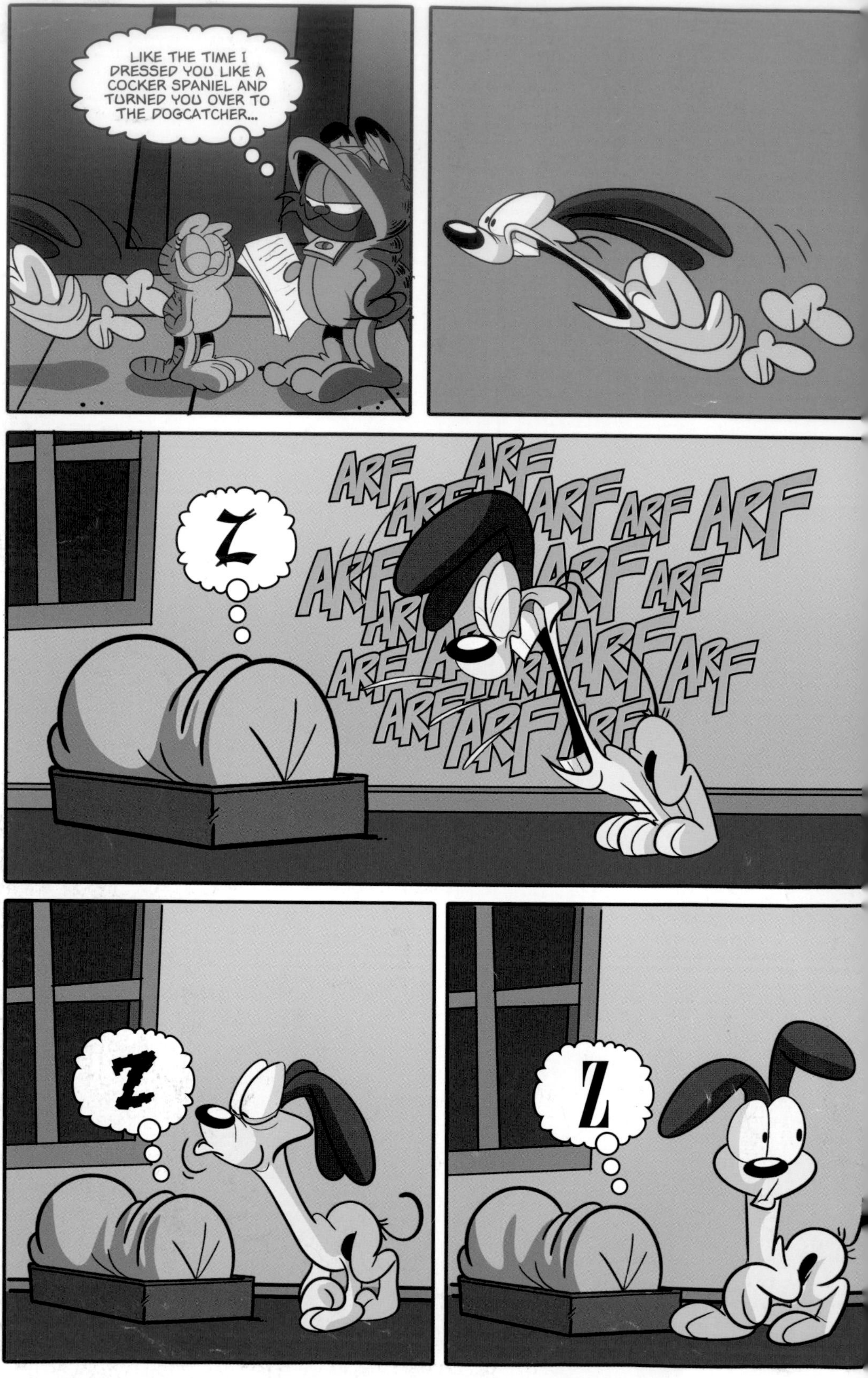
LIKE THE TIME I DRESSED YOU LIKE A COCKER SPANIEL AND TURNED YOU OVER TO THE DOGCATCHER...
Z
ARF ARF ARF ARF ARF ARF ARF ARF ARF ARF ARF ARF ARF ARF ARF ARF
Z
Z

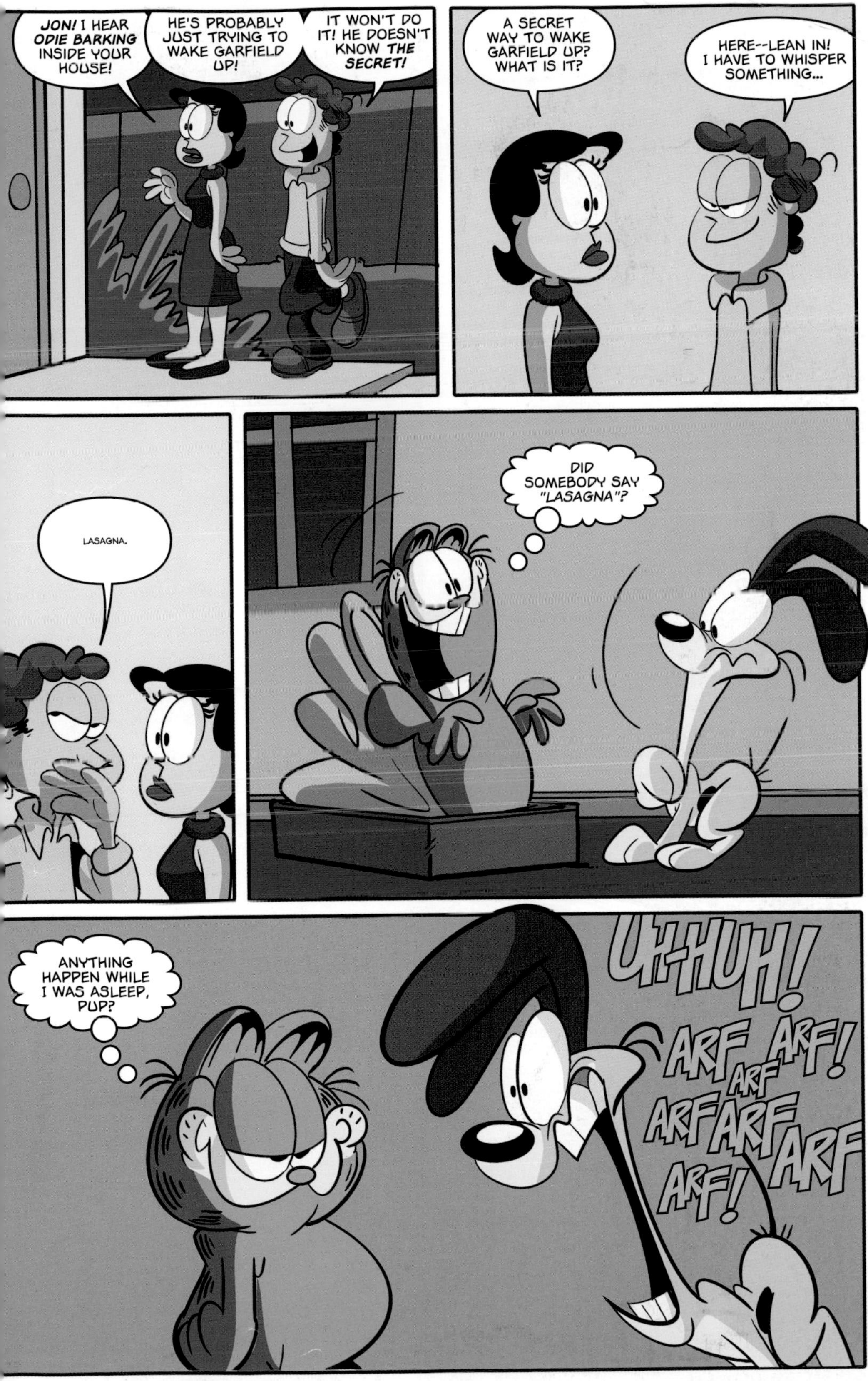

JON! I HEAR ODIE BARKING INSIDE YOUR HOUSE!
HE'S PROBABLY JUST TRYING TO WAKE GARFIELD UP!
IT WON'T DO IT! HE DOESN'T KNOW THE SECRET!
A SECRET WAY TO WAKE GARFIELD UP? WHAT IS IT?
HERE--LEAN IN! I HAVE TO WHISPER SOMETHING...
LASAGNA.
DID SOMEBODY SAY "LASAGNA"?
ANYTHING HAPPEN WHILE I WAS ASLEEP, PUP?
UH-HUH!
ARF ARF ARF!
ARF ARF ARF ARF
ARF!

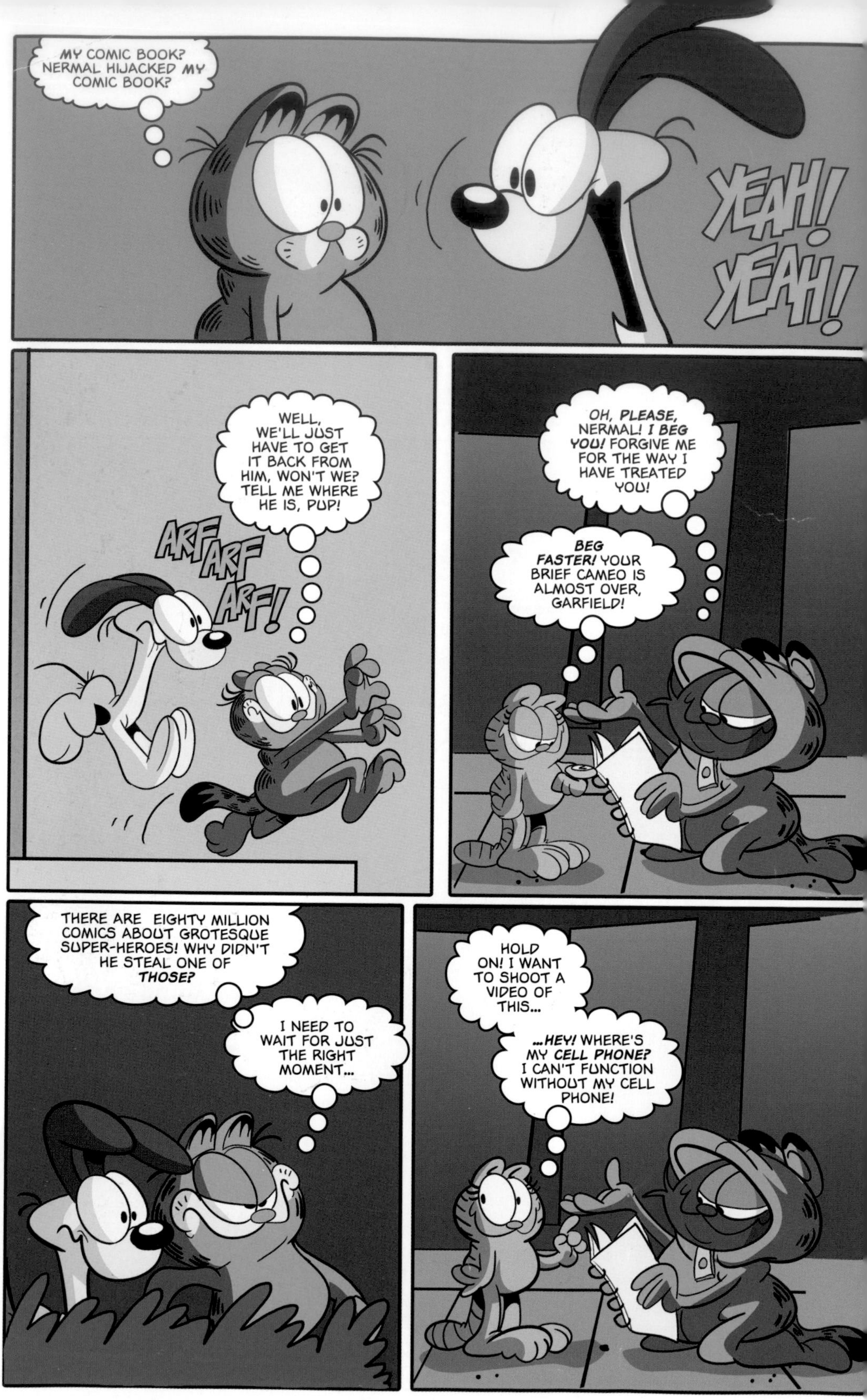
MY COMIC BOOK? NERMAL HIJACKED MY COMIC BOOK?
YEAH! YEAH!
WELL, WE'LL JUST HAVE TO GET IT BACK FROM HIM, WON'T WE? TELL ME WHERE HE IS, PUP!
ARF ARF ARF!
OH, PLEASE, NERMAL! I BEG YOU! FORGIVE ME FOR THE WAY I HAVE TREATED YOU!
BEG FASTER! YOUR BRIEF CAMEO IS ALMOST OVER, GARFIELD!
THERE ARE EIGHTY MILLION COMICS ABOUT GROTESQUE SUPER-HEROES! WHY DIDN'T HE STEAL ONE OF THOSE?
I NEED TO WAIT FOR JUST THE RIGHT MOMENT...
HOLD ON! I WANT TO SHOOT A VIDEO OF THIS...
...HEY! WHERE'S MY CELL PHONE? I CAN'T FUNCTION WITHOUT MY CELL PHONE!

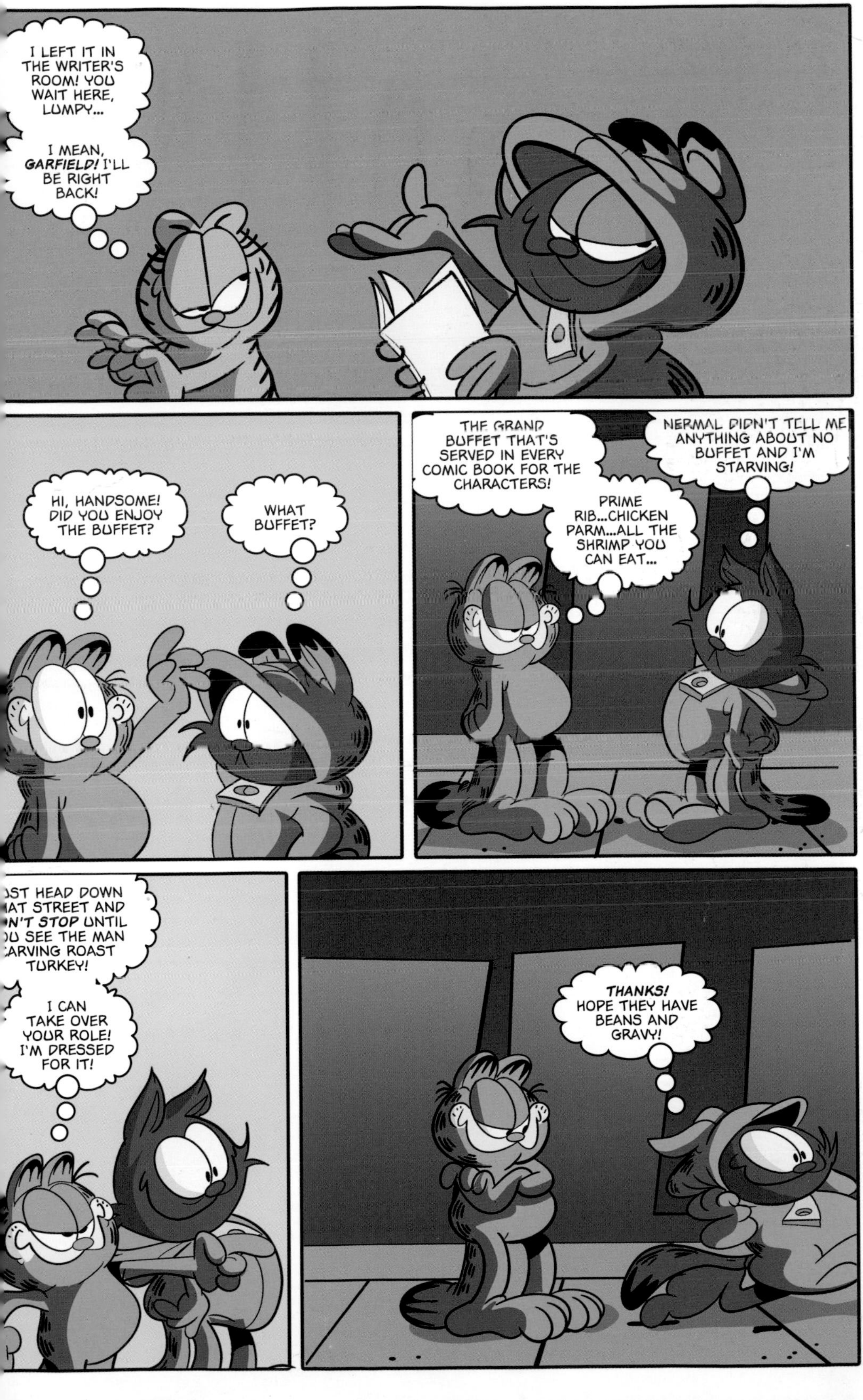
I LEFT IT IN THE WRITER'S ROOM! YOU WAIT HERE, LUMPY...
I MEAN, GARFIELD! I'LL BE RIGHT BACK!
HI, HANDSOME! DID YOU ENJOY THE BUFFET?
WHAT BUFFET?
THE GRAND BUFFET THAT'S SERVED IN EVERY COMIC BOOK FOR THE CHARACTERS!
PRIME RIB...CHICKEN PARM...ALL THE SHRIMP YOU CAN EAT...
NERMAL DIDN'T TELL ME ANYTHING ABOUT NO BUFFET AND I'M STARVING!
OST HEAD DOWN AT STREET AND N'T STOP UNTIL U SEE THE MAN ARVING ROAST TURKEY!
I CAN TAKE OVER YOUR ROLE! I'M DRESSED FOR IT!
THANKS! HOPE THEY HAVE BEANS AND GRAVY!

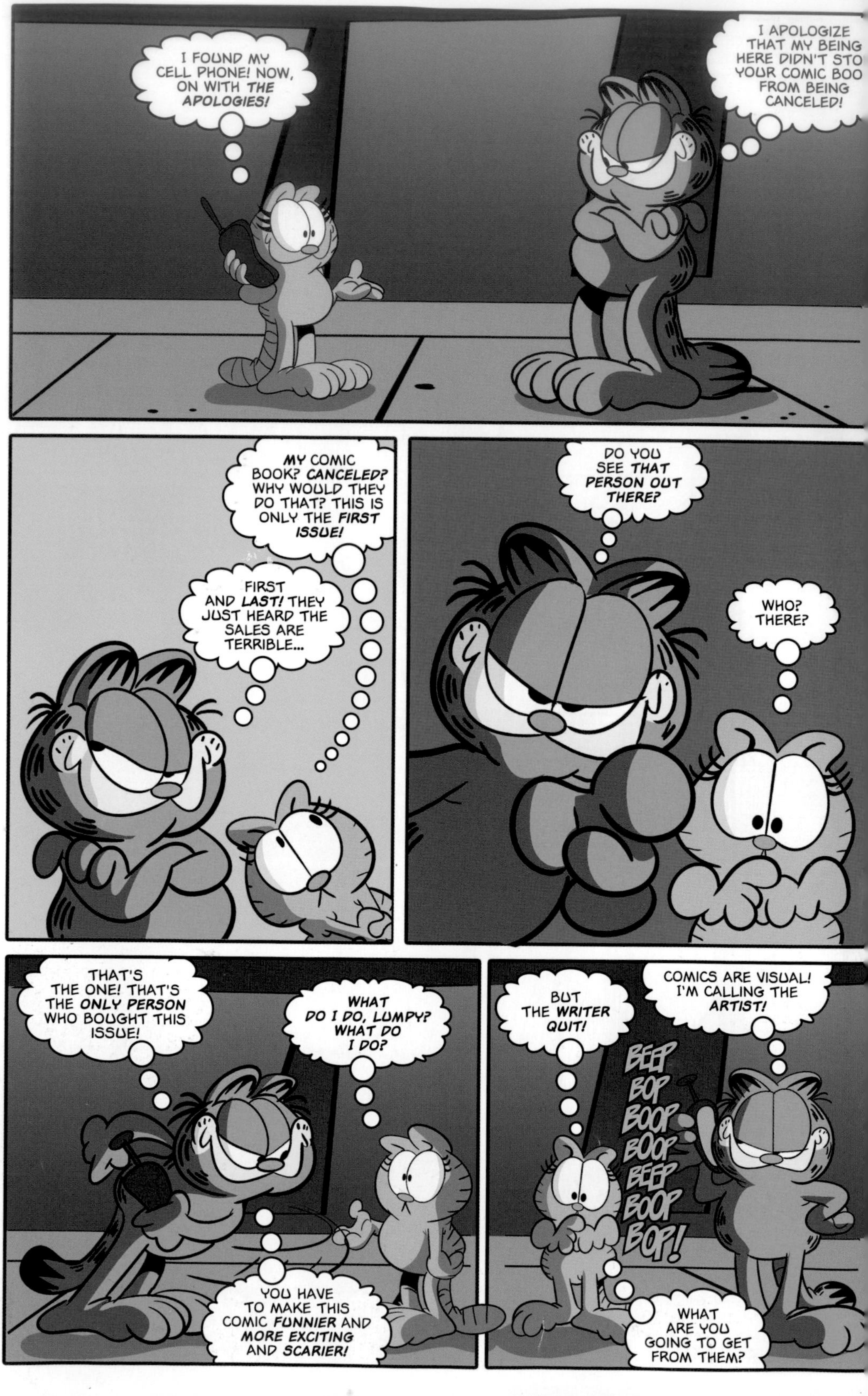
I FOUND MY CELL PHONE! NOW, ON WITH THE APOLOGIES!
I APOLOGIZE THAT MY BEING HERE DIDN'T STO YOUR COMIC BOO FROM BEING CANCELED!
MY COMIC BOOK? CANCELED? WHY WOULD THEY DO THAT? THIS IS ONLY THE FIRST ISSUE!
FIRST AND LAST! THEY JUST HEARD THE SALES ARE TERRIBLE...
DO YOU SEE THAT PERSON OUT THERE?
WHO? THERE?
THAT'S THE ONE! THAT'S THE ONLY PERSON WHO BOUGHT THIS ISSUE!
WHAT DO I DO, LUMPY? WHAT DO I DO?
YOU HAVE TO MAKE THIS COMIC FUNNIER AND MORE EXCITING AND SCARIER!
BUT THE WRITER QUIT!
COMICS ARE VISUAL! I'M CALLING THE ARTIST!
BEEP BOP BOOP BOOP BEEP BOOP BOP!
WHAT ARE YOU GOING TO GET FROM THEM?

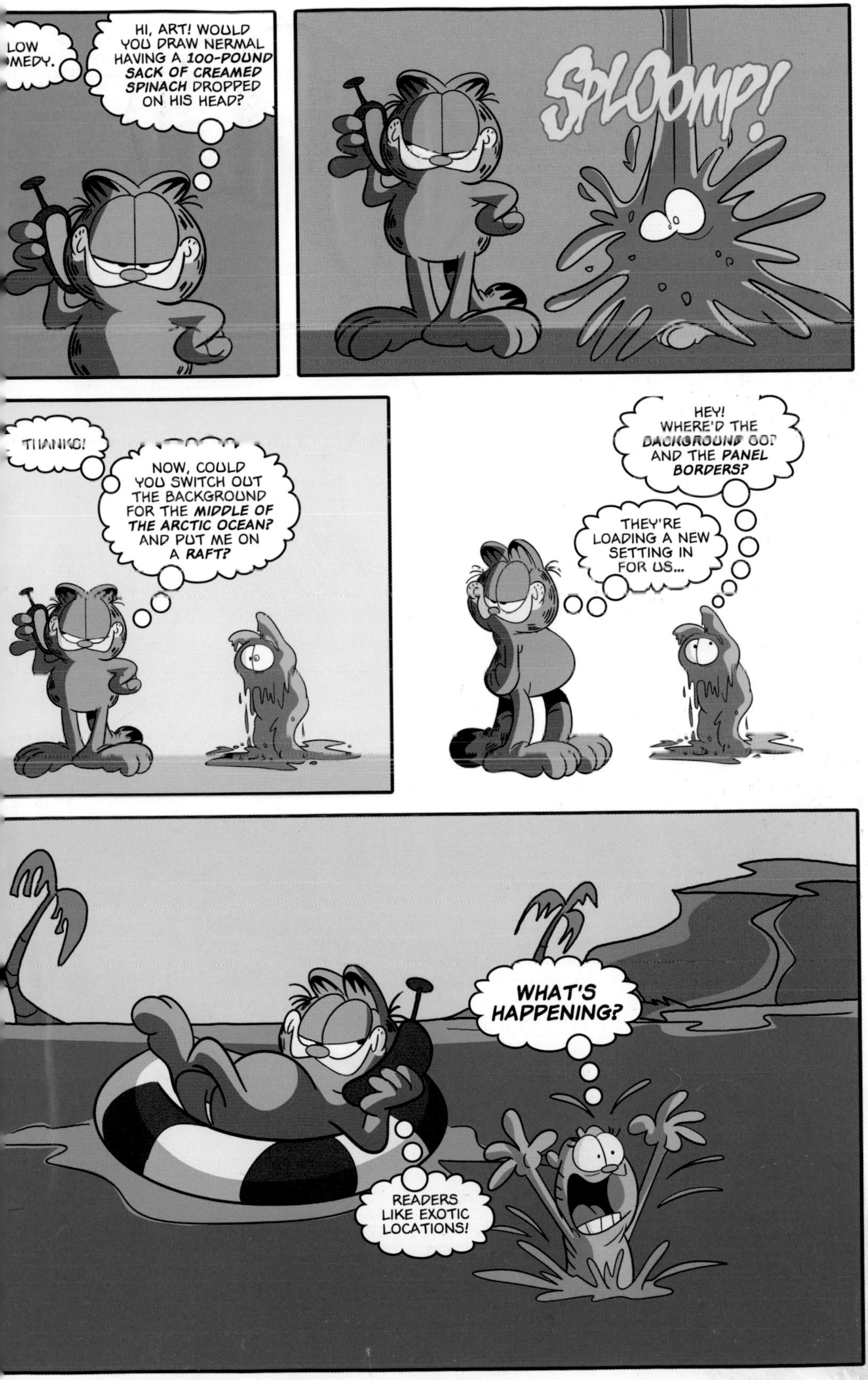

LOW
MEDY.
HI, ART! WOULD YOU DRAW NERMAL HAVING A 100-POUND SACK OF CREAMED SPINACH DROPPED ON HIS HEAD?
SPLOOMP!
THANKS!
NOW, COULD YOU SWITCH OUT THE BACKGROUND FOR THE MIDDLE OF THE ARCTIC OCEAN? AND PUT ME ON A RAFT?
HEY! WHERE'D THE BACKGROUND GO? AND THE PANEL BORDERS?
THEY'RE LOADING A NEW SETTING IN FOR US...
WHAT'S HAPPENING?
READERS LIKE EXOTIC LOCATIONS!

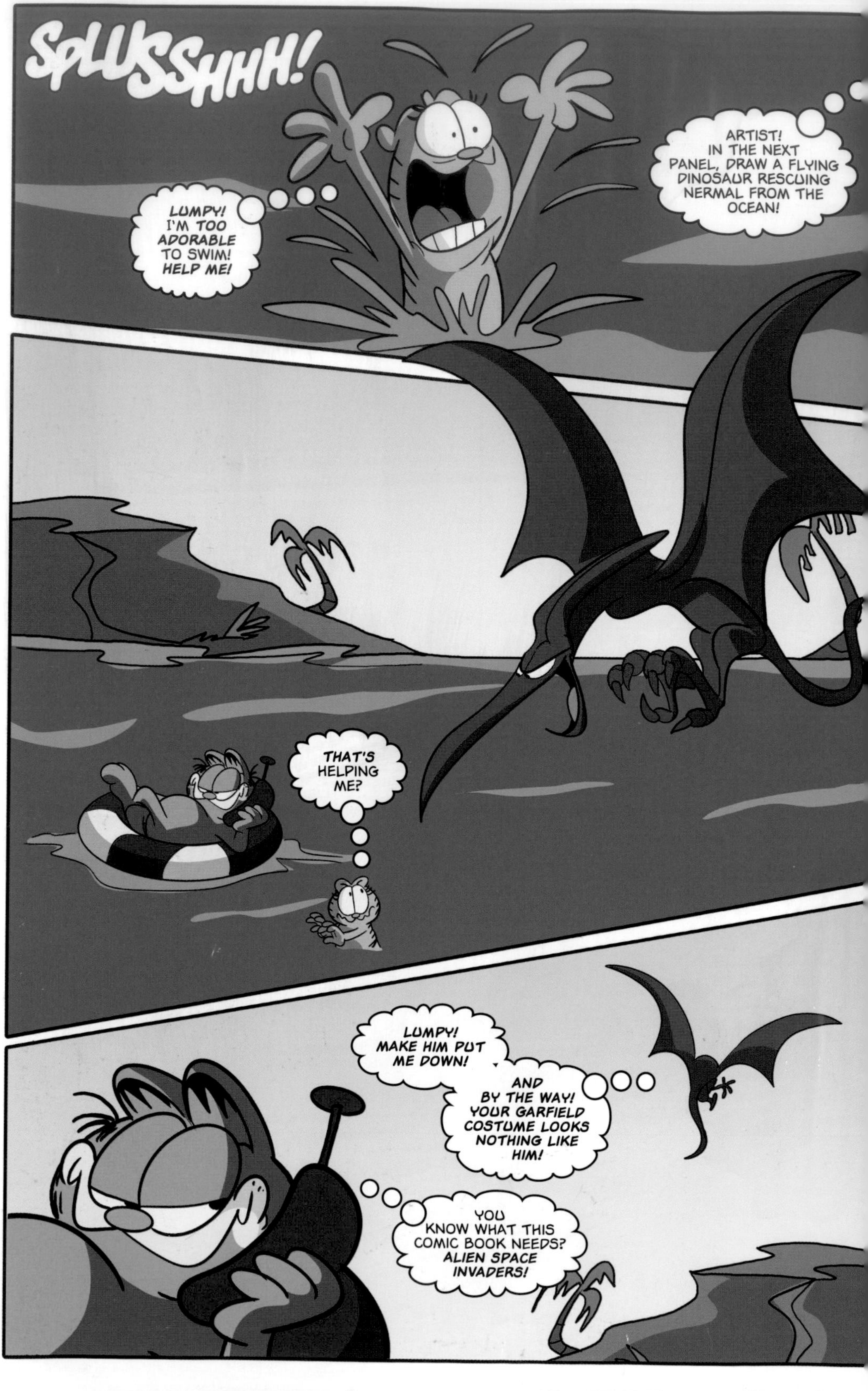
SPLUSSHHH!
LUMPY! I'M TOO ADORABLE TO SWIM! HELP ME!
ARTIST! IN THE NEXT PANEL, DRAW A FLYING DINOSAUR RESCUING NERMAL FROM THE OCEAN!
THAT'S HELPING ME?
LUMPY! MAKE HIM PUT ME DOWN!
AND BY THE WAY! YOUR GARFIELD COSTUME LOOKS NOTHING LIKE HIM!
YOU KNOW WHAT THIS COMIC BOOK NEEDS? ALIEN SPACE INVADERS!

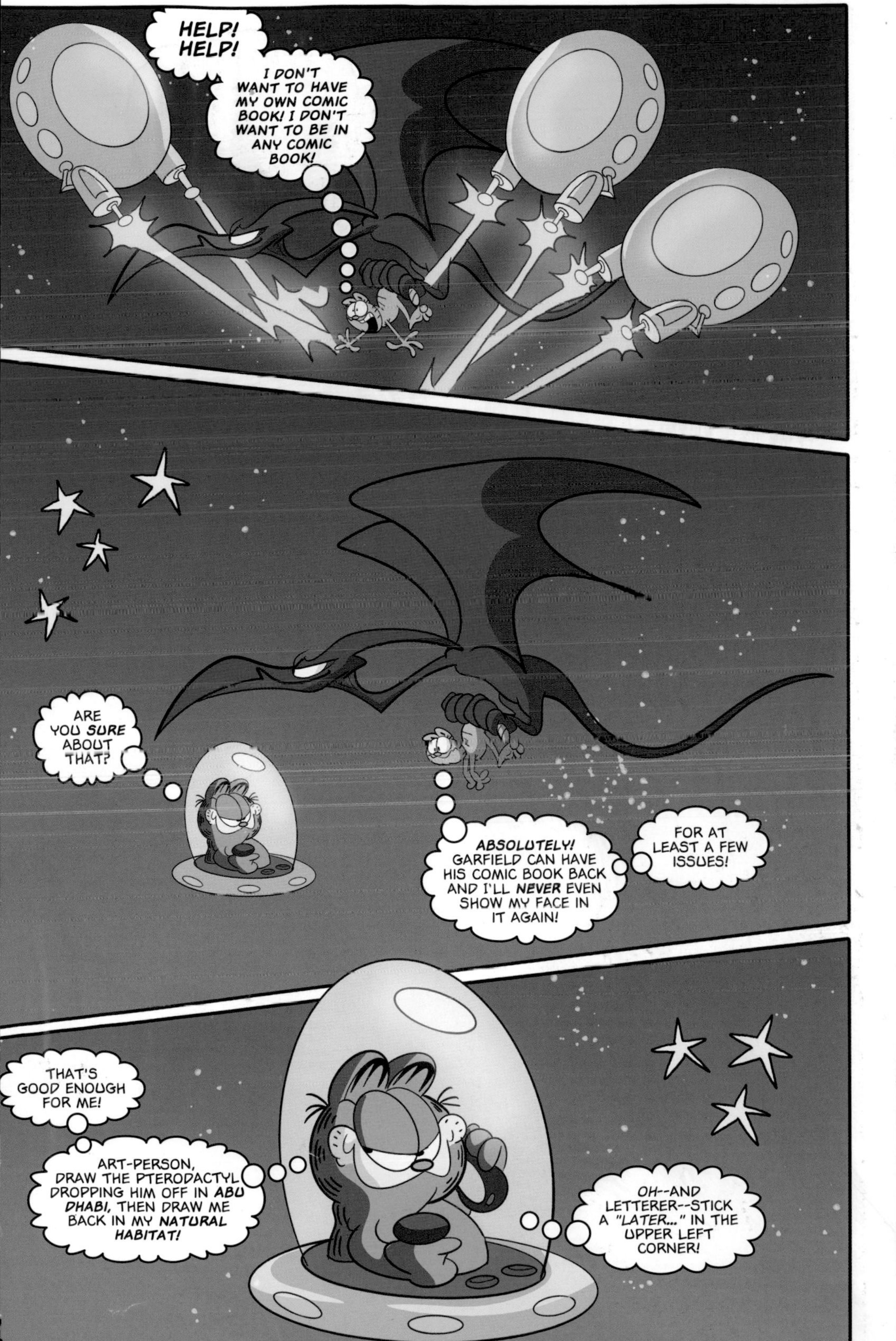
HELP! HELP!
I DON'T WANT TO HAVE MY OWN COMIC BOOK! I DON'T WANT TO BE IN ANY COMIC BOOK!
ARE YOU SURE ABOUT THAT?
ABSOLUTELY! GARFIELD CAN HAVE HIS COMIC BOOK BACK AND I'LL NEVER EVEN SHOW MY FACE IN IT AGAIN!
FOR AT LEAST A FEW ISSUES!
THAT'S GOOD ENOUGH FOR ME!
ART-PERSON, DRAW THE PTERODACTYL DROPPING HIM OFF IN ABU DHABI, THEN DRAW ME BACK IN MY NATURAL HABITAT!
OH--AND LETTERER--STICK A "LATER..." IN THE UPPER LEFT CORNER!

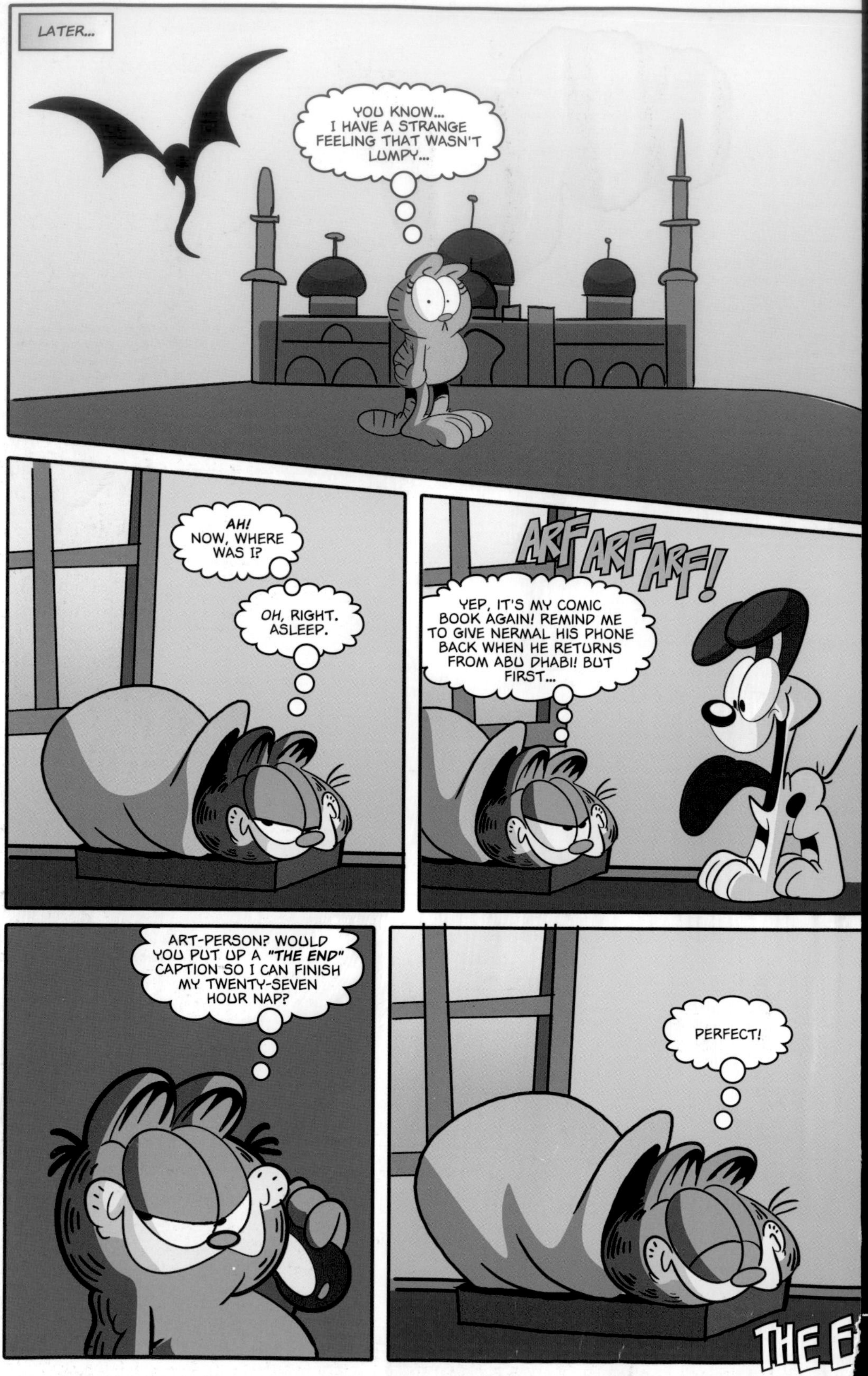
LATER...
YOU KNOW... I HAVE A STRANGE FEELING THAT WASN'T LUMPY...
AH! NOW, WHERE WAS I?
OH, RIGHT. ASLEEP.
ARF ARF ARF ARF!
YEP, IT'S MY COMIC BOOK AGAIN! REMIND ME TO GIVE NERMAL HIS PHONE BACK WHEN HE RETURNS FROM ABU DHABI! BUT FIRST...
ART-PERSON? WOULD YOU PUT UP A "THE END" CAPTION SO I CAN FINISH MY TWENTY-SEVEN HOUR NAP?
PERFECT!

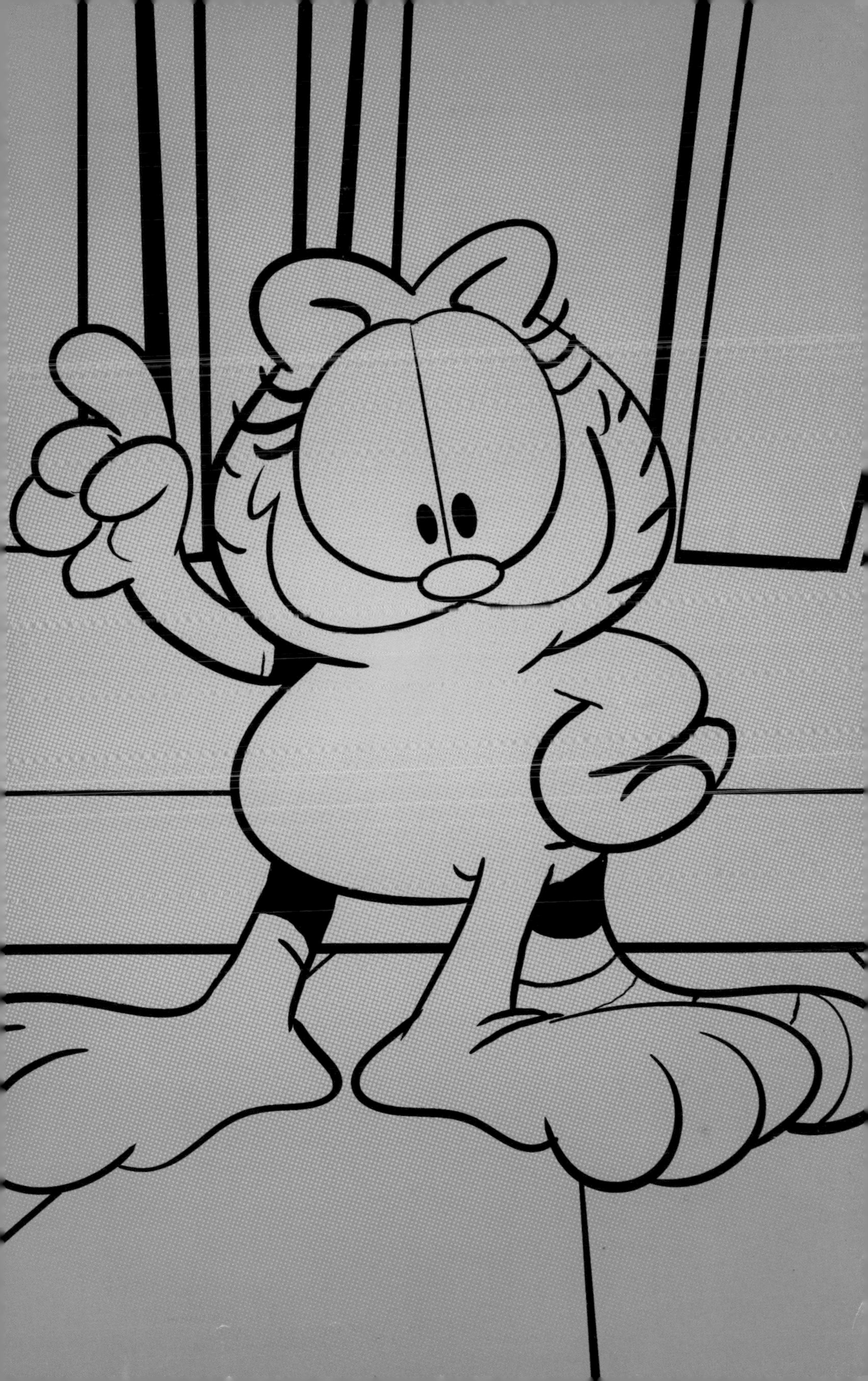

"THE UNDERSEA ADVENTURES OF JACQUES GARFEAU"

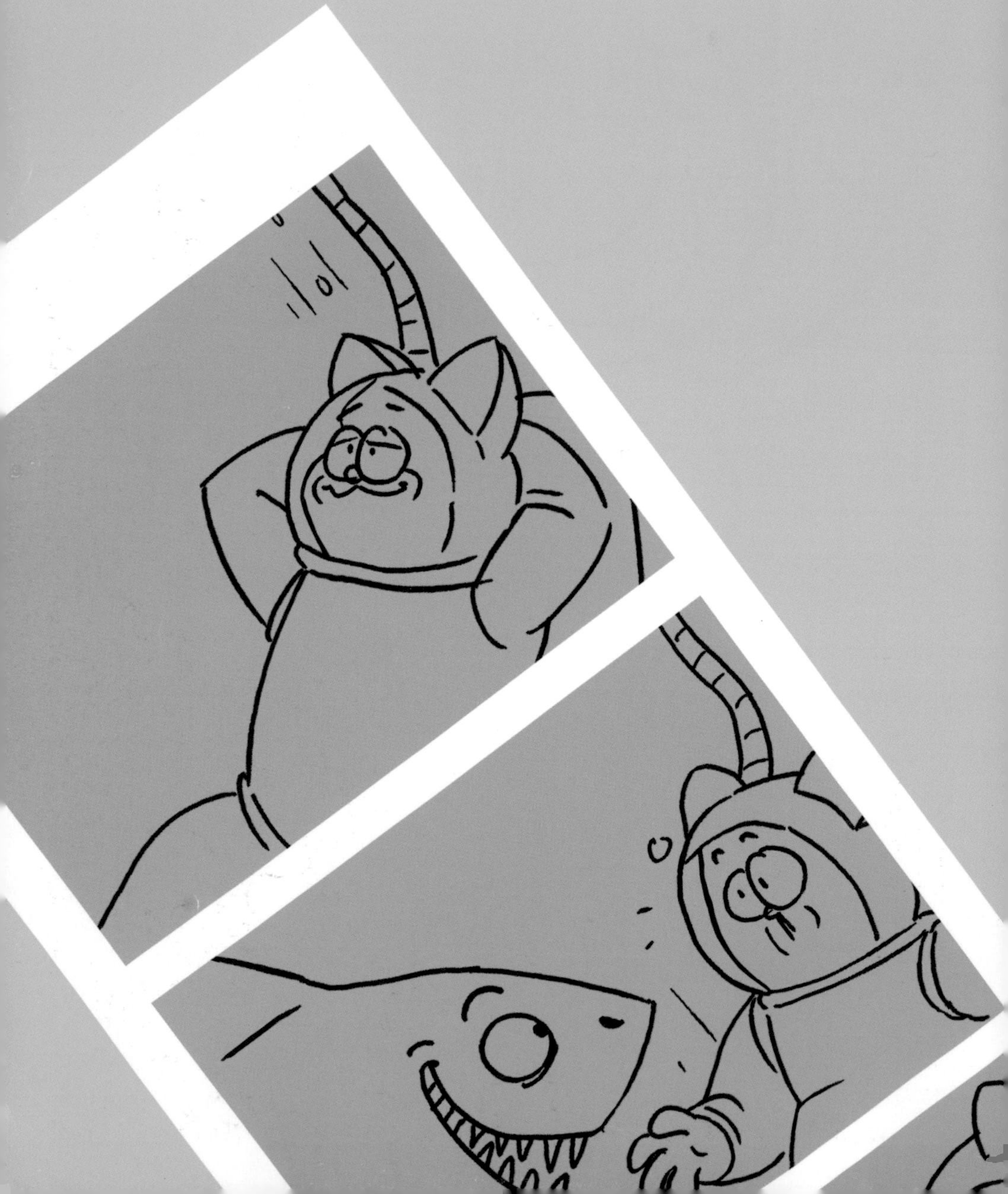

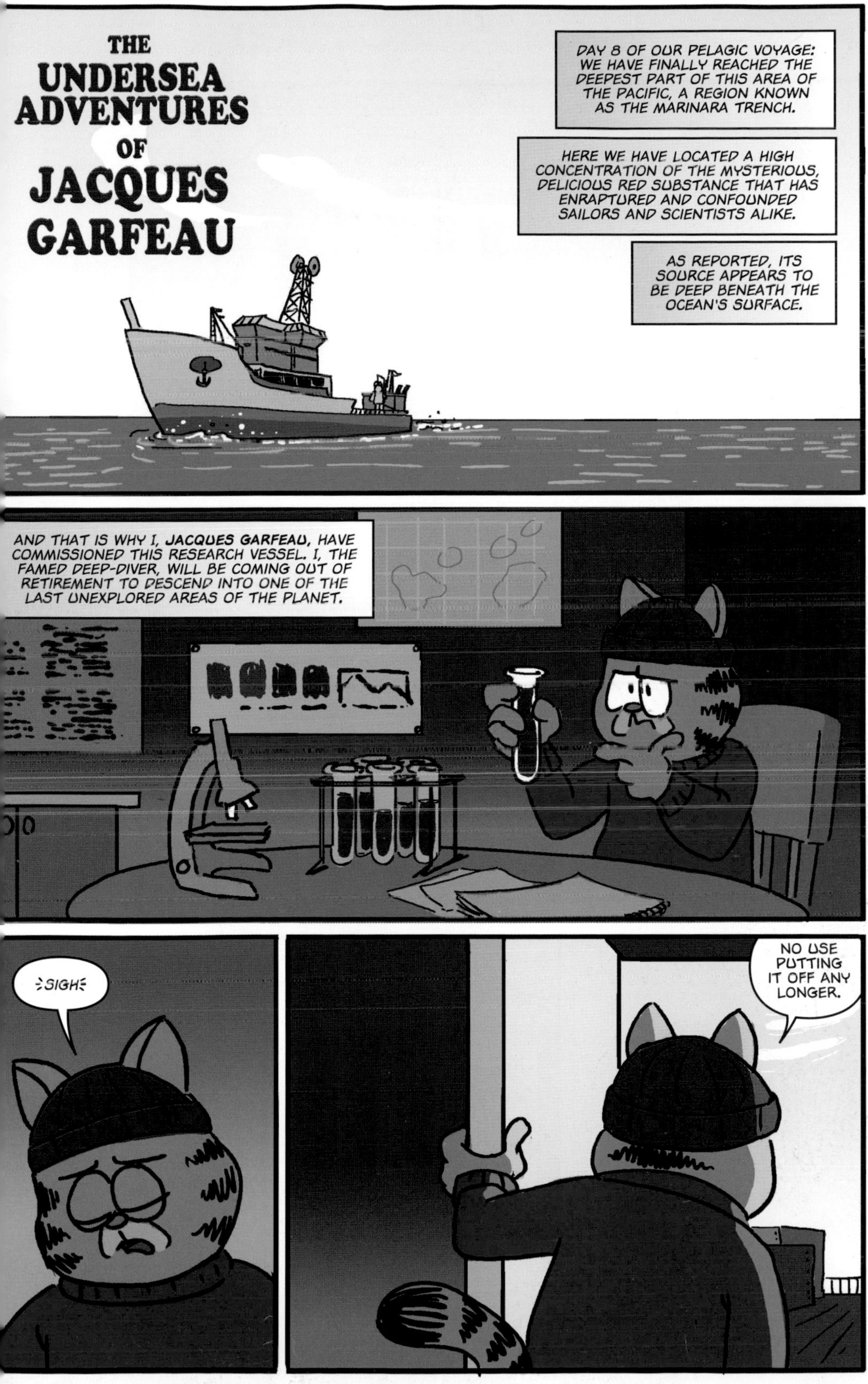
THE UNDERSEA ADVENTURES OF JACQUES GARFEAU
DAY 8 OF OUR PELAGIC VOYAGE: WE HAVE FINALLY REACHED THE DEEPEST PART OF THIS AREA OF THE PACIFIC, A REGION KNOWN AS THE MARINARA TRENCH.
HERE WE HAVE LOCATED A HIGH CONCENTRATION OF THE MYSTERIOUS, DELICIOUS RED SUBSTANCE THAT HAS ENRAPTURED AND CONFOUNDED SAILORS AND SCIENTISTS ALIKE.
AS REPORTED, ITS SOURCE APPEARS TO BE DEEP BENEATH THE OCEAN'S SURFACE.
AND THAT IS WHY I, JACQUES GARFEAU, HAVE COMMISSIONED THIS RESEARCH VESSEL. I, THE FAMED DEEP-DIVER, WILL BE COMING OUT OF RETIREMENT TO DESCEND INTO ONE OF THE LAST UNEXPLORED AREAS OF THE PLANET.
SIGH
NO USE PUTTING IT OFF ANY LONGER.

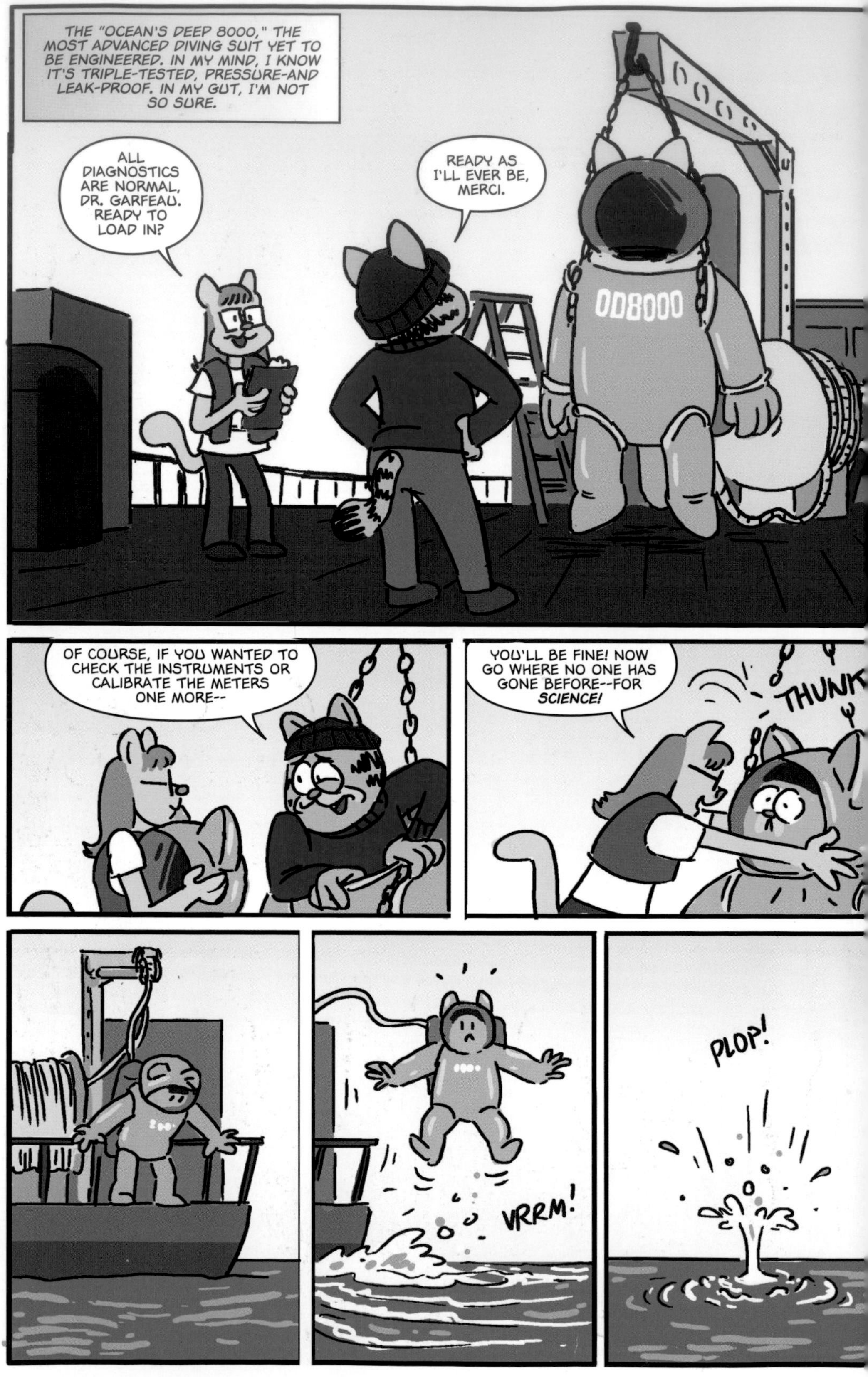
THE "OCEAN'S DEEP 8000," THE MOST ADVANCED DIVING SUIT YET TO BE ENGINEERED. IN MY MIND, I KNOW IT'S TRIPLE-TESTED, PRESSURE-AND LEAK-PROOF. IN MY GUT, I'M NOT SO SURE.
ALL DIAGNOSTICS ARE NORMAL, DR. GARFEAU. READY TO LOAD IN?
READY AS I'LL EVER BE, MERCI.
OD8000
OF COURSE, IF YOU WANTED TO CHECK THE INSTRUMENTS OR CALIBRATE THE METERS ONE MORE--
YOU'LL BE FINE! NOW GO WHERE NO ONE HAS GONE BEFORE--FOR *SCIENCE!*
THUNK
VRRM!
PLOP!

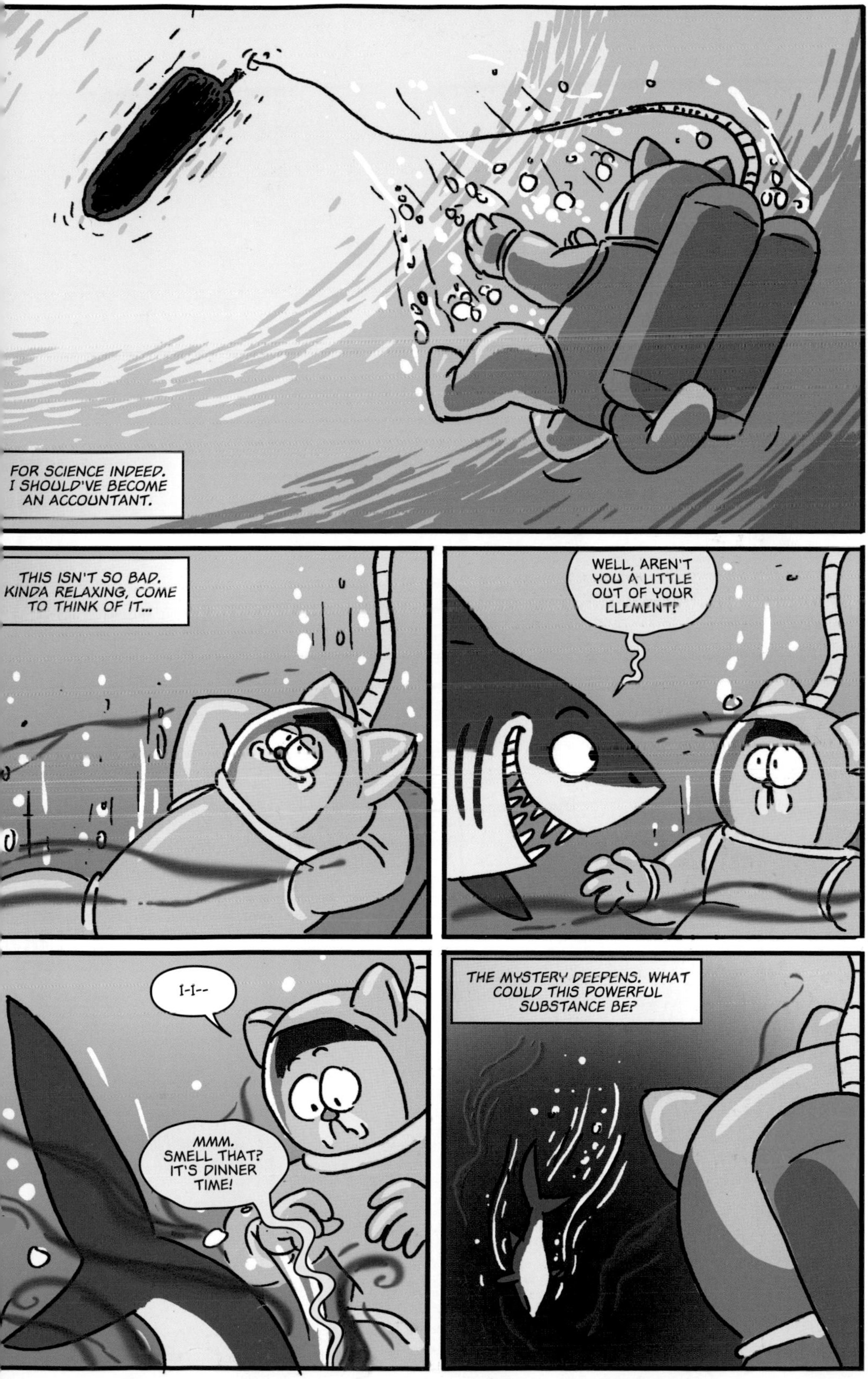
FOR SCIENCE INDEED. I SHOULD'VE BECOME AN ACCOUNTANT.
THIS ISN'T SO BAD. KINDA RELAXING, COME TO THINK OF IT...
WELL, AREN'T YOU A LITTLE OUT OF YOUR ELEMENT?
I-I--
MMM. SMELL THAT? IT'S DINNER TIME!
THE MYSTERY DEEPENS. WHAT COULD THIS POWERFUL SUBSTANCE BE?

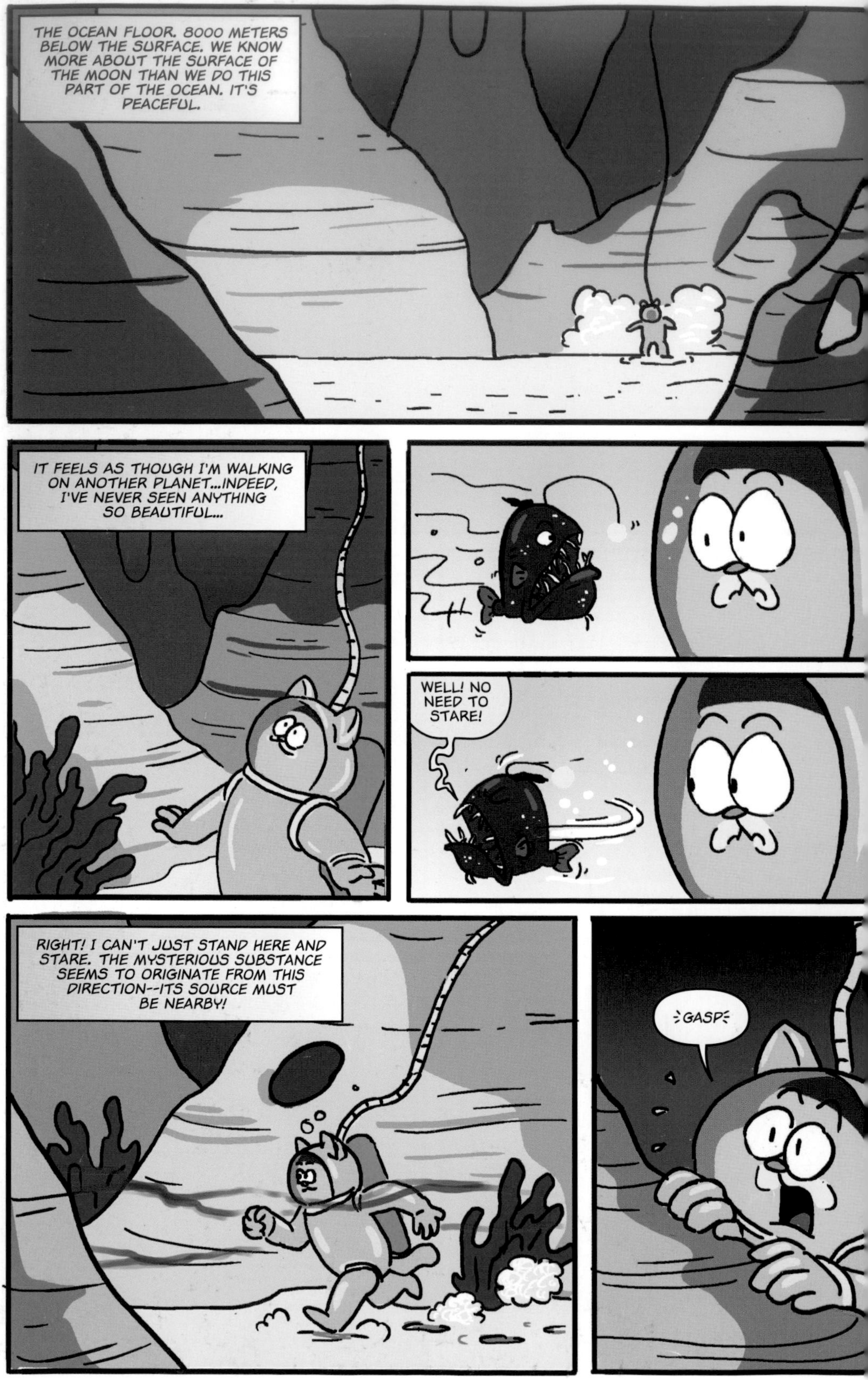

THE OCEAN FLOOR. 8000 METERS BELOW THE SURFACE. WE KNOW MORE ABOUT THE SURFACE OF THE MOON THAN WE DO THIS PART OF THE OCEAN. IT'S PEACEFUL.
IT FEELS AS THOUGH I'M WALKING ON ANOTHER PLANET...INDEED, I'VE NEVER SEEN ANYTHING SO BEAUTIFUL...
WELL! NO NEED TO STARE!
RIGHT! I CAN'T JUST STAND HERE AND STARE. THE MYSTERIOUS SUBSTANCE SEEMS TO ORIGINATE FROM THIS DIRECTION--ITS SOURCE MUST BE NEARBY!
GASP

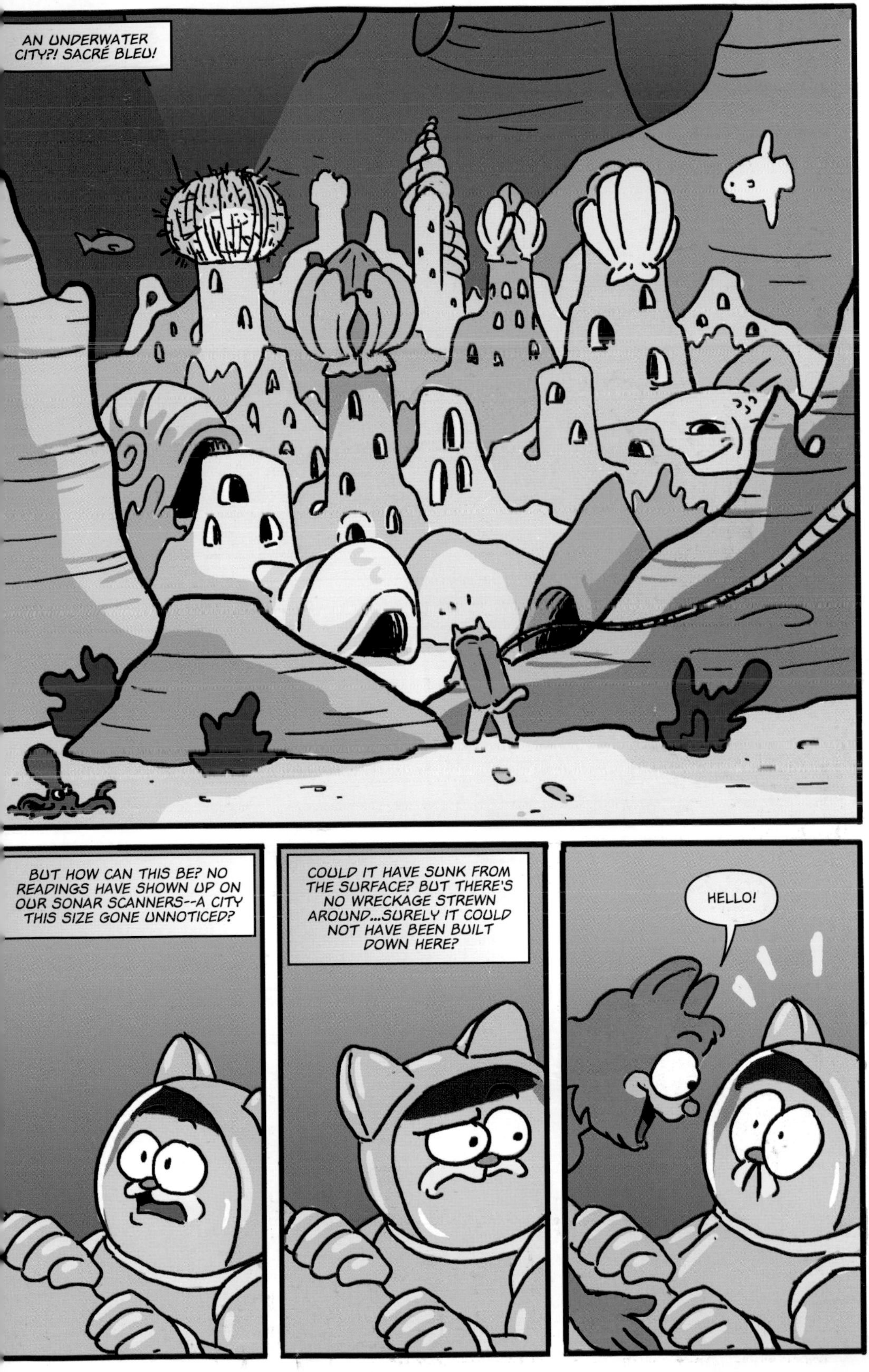
AN UNDERWATER CITY?! SACRÉ BLEU!
BUT HOW CAN THIS BE? NO READINGS HAVE SHOWN UP ON OUR SONAR SCANNERS--A CITY THIS SIZE GONE UNNOTICED?
COULD IT HAVE SUNK FROM THE SURFACE? BUT THERE'S NO WRECKAGE STREWN AROUND...SURELY IT COULD NOT HAVE BEEN BUILT DOWN HERE?
HELLO!

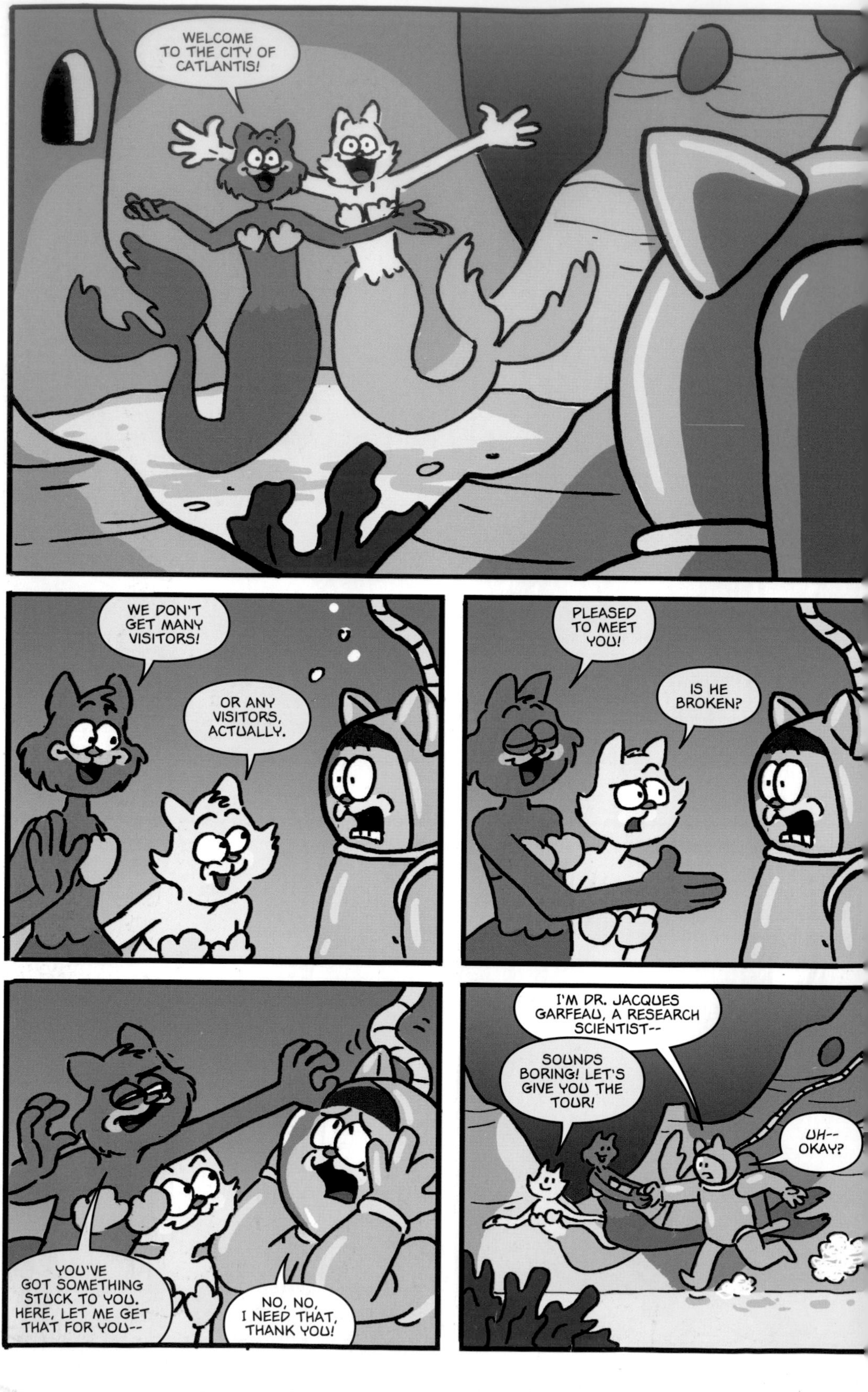
WELCOME TO THE CITY OF CATLANTIS!
WE DON'T GET MANY VISITORS!
OR ANY VISITORS, ACTUALLY.
PLEASED TO MEET YOU!
IS HE BROKEN?
YOU'VE GOT SOMETHING STUCK TO YOU. HERE, LET ME GET THAT FOR YOU--
NO, NO, I NEED THAT, THANK YOU!
I'M DR. JACQUES GARFEAU, A RESEARCH SCIENTIST--
SOUNDS BORING! LET'S GIVE YOU THE TOUR!
UH-- OKAY?

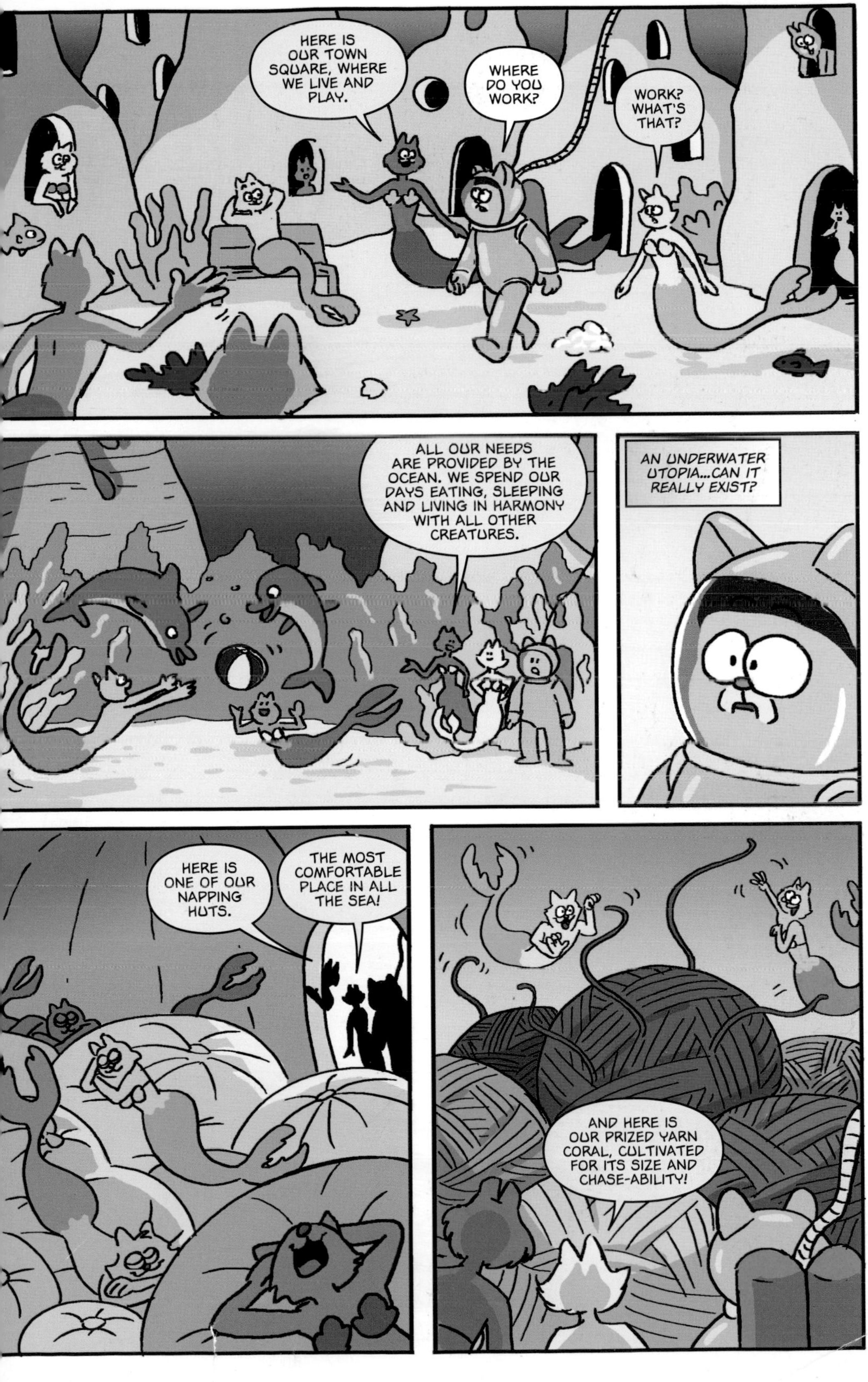
HERE IS OUR TOWN SQUARE, WHERE WE LIVE AND PLAY.
WHERE DO YOU WORK?
WORK? WHAT'S THAT?
ALL OUR NEEDS ARE PROVIDED BY THE OCEAN. WE SPEND OUR DAYS EATING, SLEEPING AND LIVING IN HARMONY WITH ALL OTHER CREATURES.
AN UNDERWATER UTOPIA...CAN IT REALLY EXIST?
HERE IS ONE OF OUR NAPPING HUTS.
THE MOST COMFORTABLE PLACE IN ALL THE SEA!
AND HERE IS OUR PRIZED YARN CORAL, CULTIVATED FOR ITS SIZE AND CHASE-ABILITY!

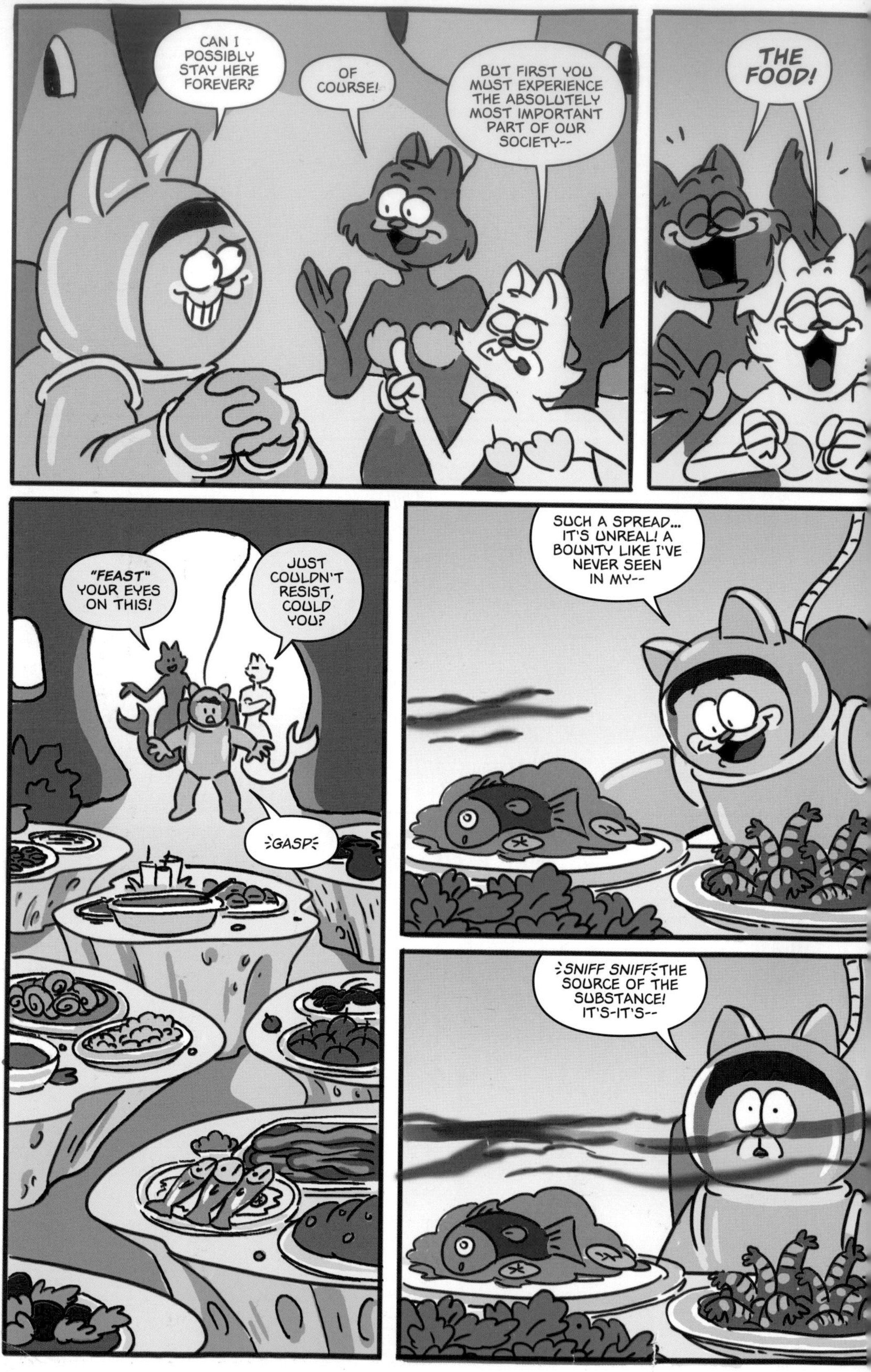
CAN I POSSIBLY STAY HERE FOREVER?
OF COURSE!
BUT FIRST YOU MUST EXPERIENCE THE ABSOLUTELY MOST IMPORTANT PART OF OUR SOCIETY--
THE FOOD!
"FEAST" YOUR EYES ON THIS!
JUST COULDN'T RESIST, COULD YOU?
GASP
SUCH A SPREAD... IT'S UNREAL! A BOUNTY LIKE I'VE NEVER SEEN IN MY--
SNIFF SNIFF THE SOURCE OF THE SUBSTANCE! IT'S-IT'S--

LASAGNA-OF-THE-SEA?!

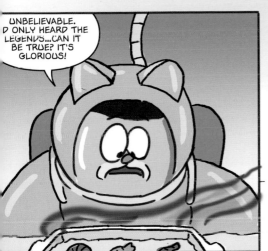

UNBELIEVABLE. D ONLY HEARD THE LEGENDS...CAN IT BE TRUE? IT'S GLORIOUS!

I VOW I WILL NEVER LEAVE THIS MAGICAL PLACE AS LONG AS I SHALL LIVE!

WELL, WHAT ARE YOU WAITING FOR? DIG IN!

JUST USE YOUR HANDS--WE ALL DO.

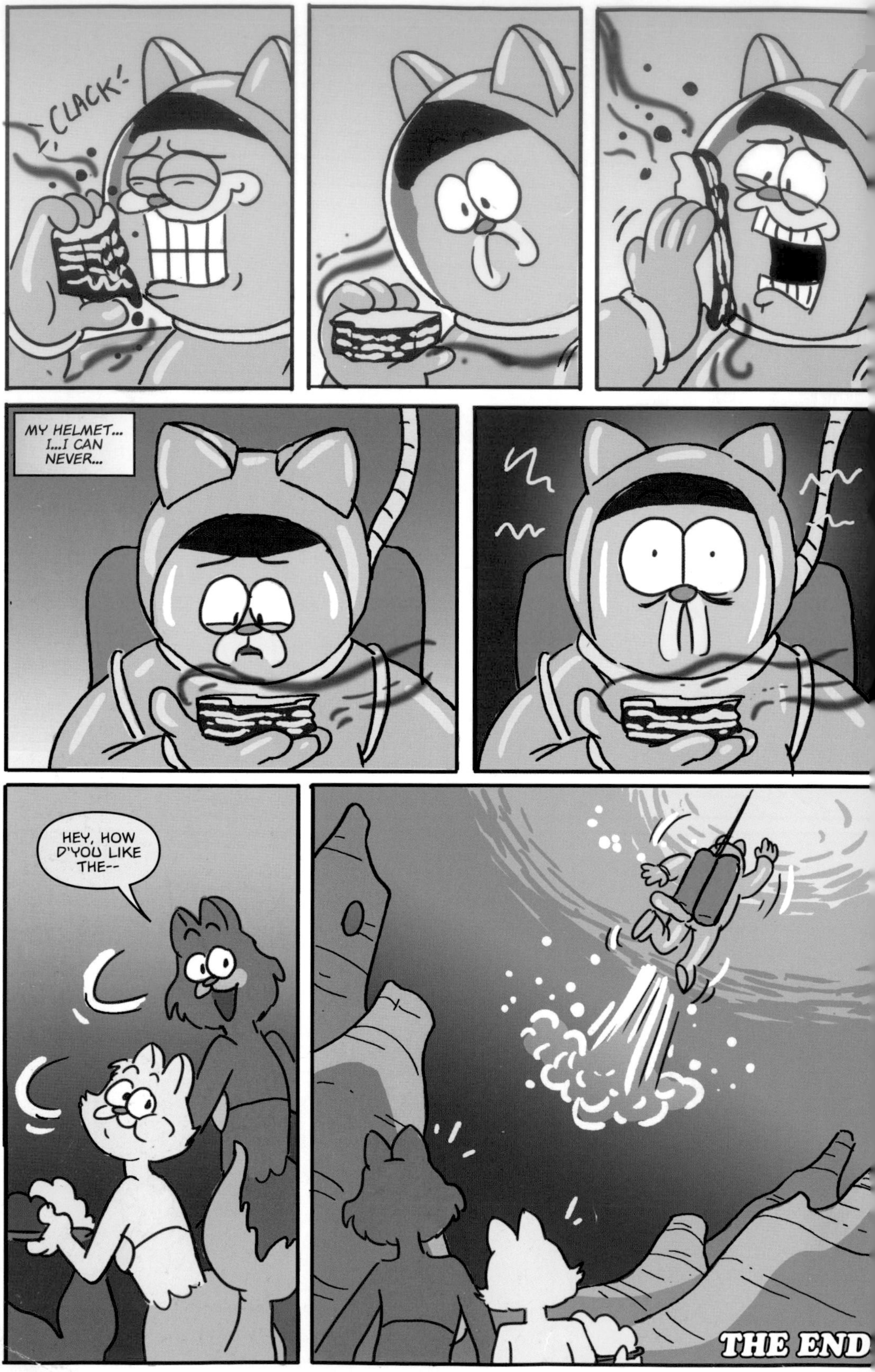
CLACK!
MY HELMET... I...I CAN NEVER...
HEY, HOW D'YOU LIKE THE--
THE END

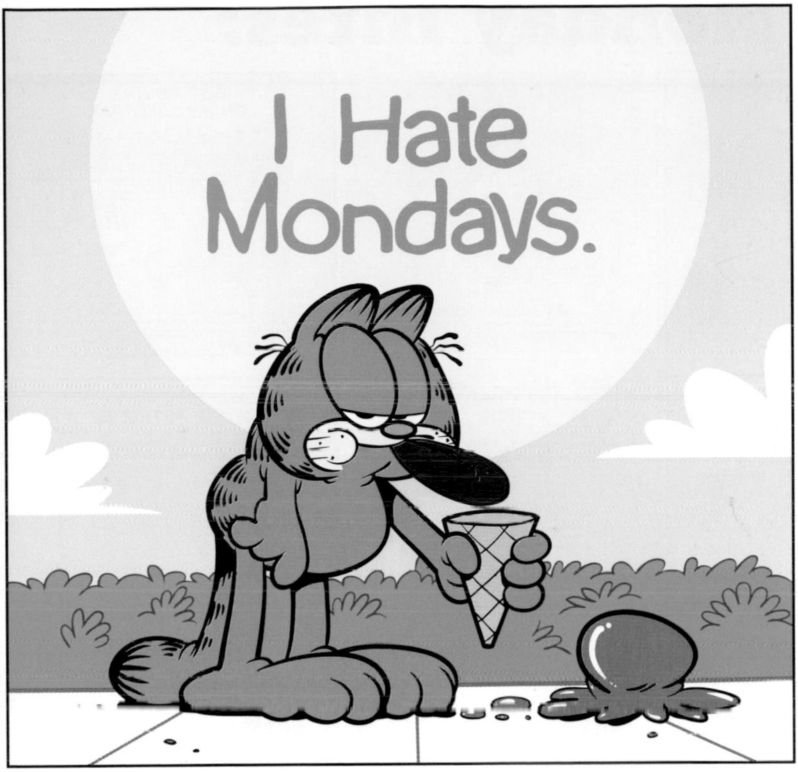
I Hate
Mondays.

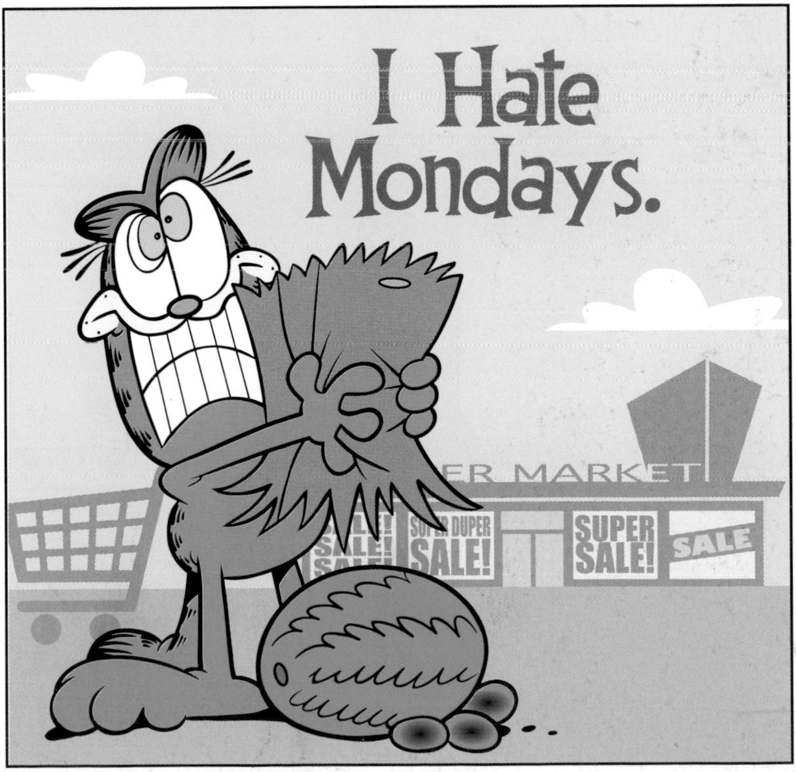
I Hate
Mondays.
SUPER
SALE!
SALE

Monday Bites!

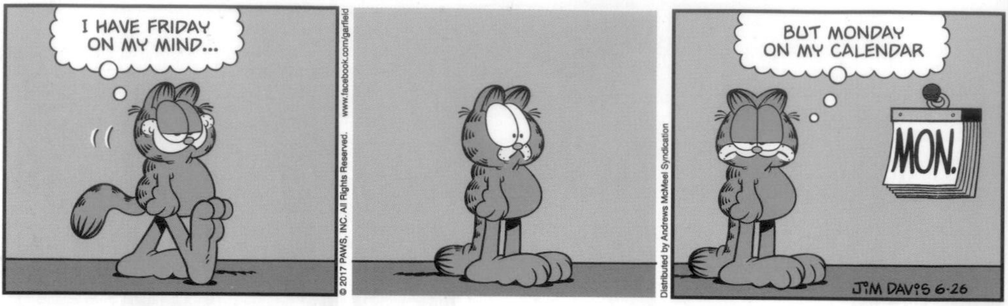
I HAVE FRIDAY ON MY MIND...
BUT MONDAY ON MY CALENDAR
MON.
JIM DAVIS 6-26
© 2017 PAWS, INC. All Rights Reserved. www.facebook.com/garfield
Distributed by Andrews McMeel Syndication

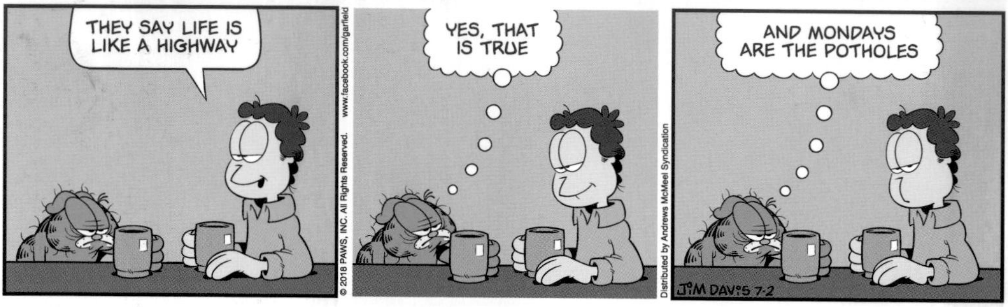
THEY SAY LIFE IS LIKE A HIGHWAY
YES, THAT IS TRUE
AND MONDAYS ARE THE POTHOLES
JIM DAVIS 7-2
© 2018 PAWS, INC. All Rights Reserved. www.facebook.com/garfield
Distributed by Andrews McMeel Syndication

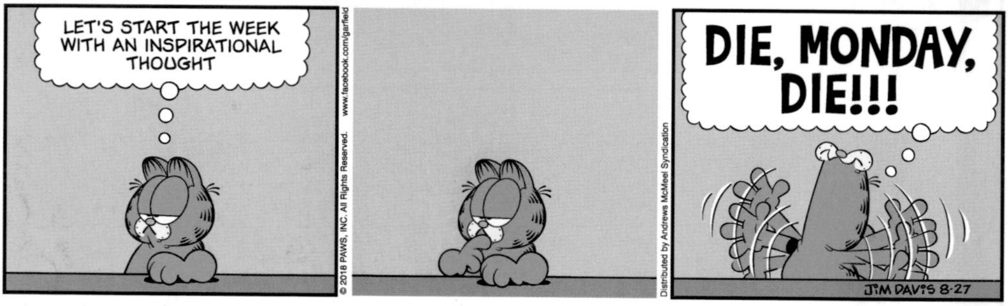
LET'S START THE WEEK WITH AN INSPIRATIONAL THOUGHT
DIE, MONDAY, DIE!!!
JIM DAVIS 8-27
© 2018 PAWS, INC. All Rights Reserved. www.facebook.com/garfield
Distributed by Andrews McMeel Syndication

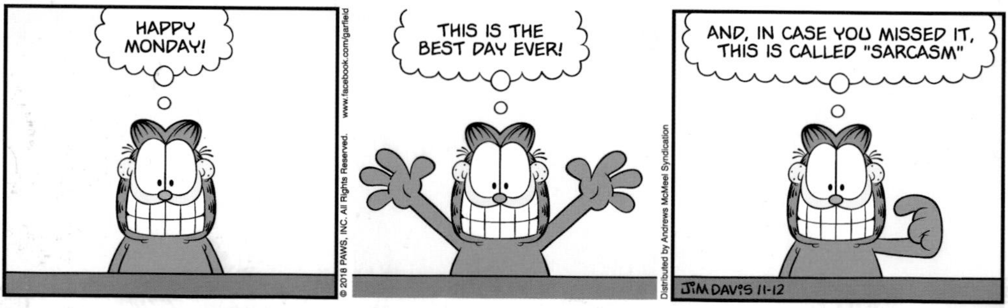
HAPPY MONDAY!
THIS IS THE BEST DAY EVER!
AND, IN CASE YOU MISSED IT, THIS IS CALLED "SARCASM"
JIM DAVIS 11-12
© 2018 PAWS, INC. All Rights Reserved. www.facebook.com/garfield
Distributed by Andrews McMeel Syndication

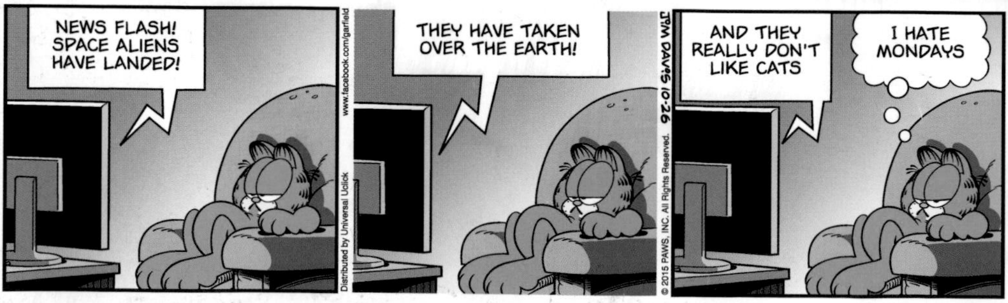
NEWS FLASH! SPACE ALIENS HAVE LANDED!
THEY HAVE TAKEN OVER THE EARTH!
AND THEY REALLY DON'T LIKE CATS
I HATE MONDAYS
JIM DAVIS 10-26
© 2015 PAWS, INC. All Rights Reserved. www.facebook.com/garfield
Distributed by Universal Uclick

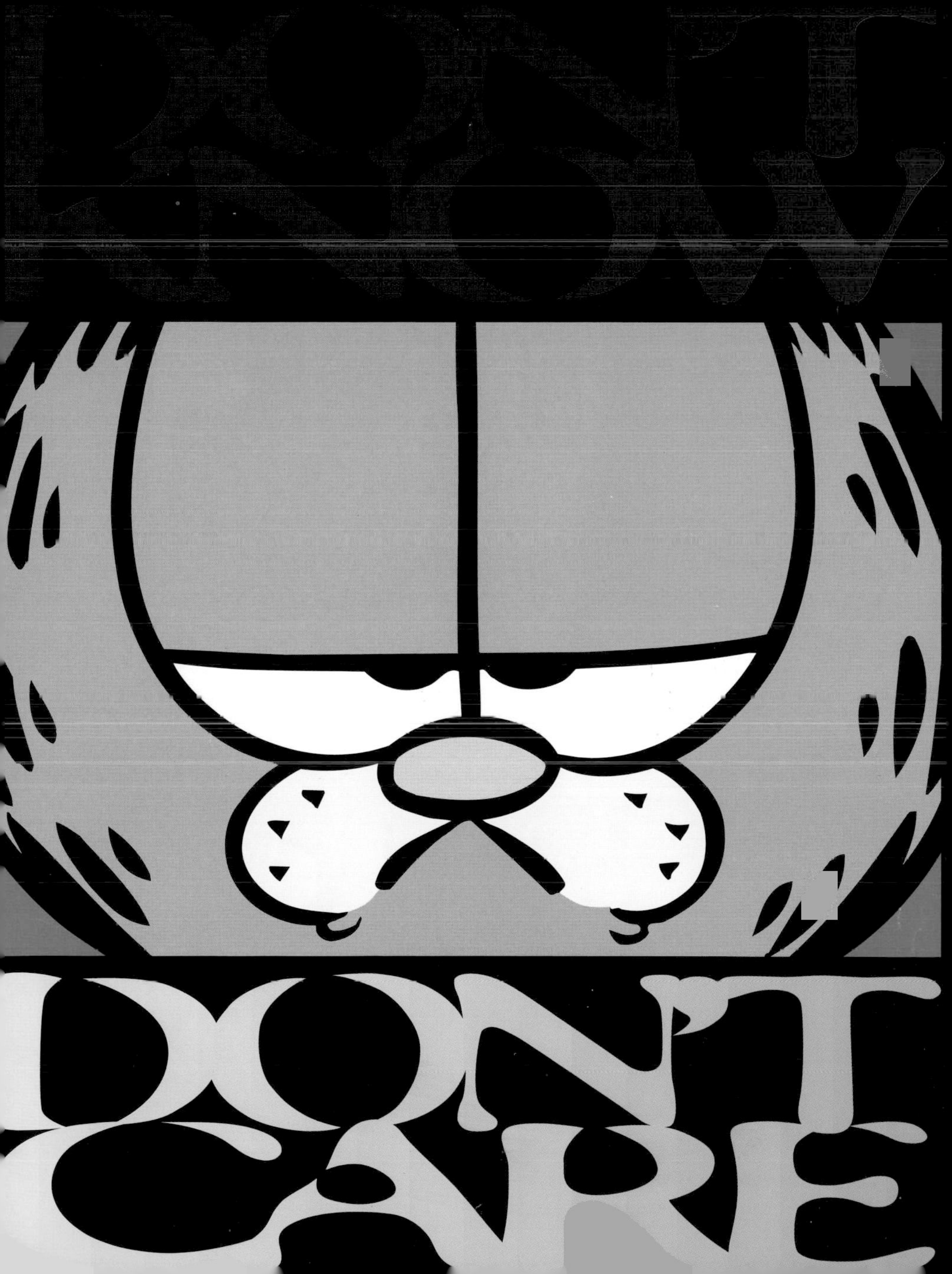
DON'T
KNOW
DON'T
CARE

NAP ATTACK

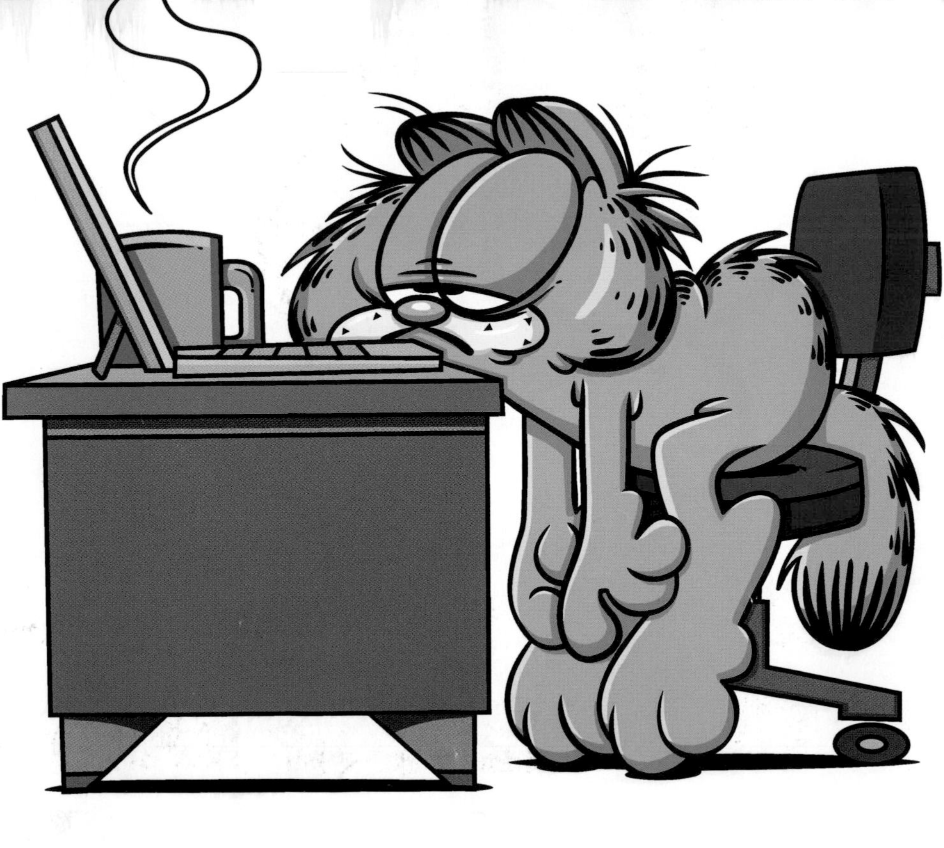

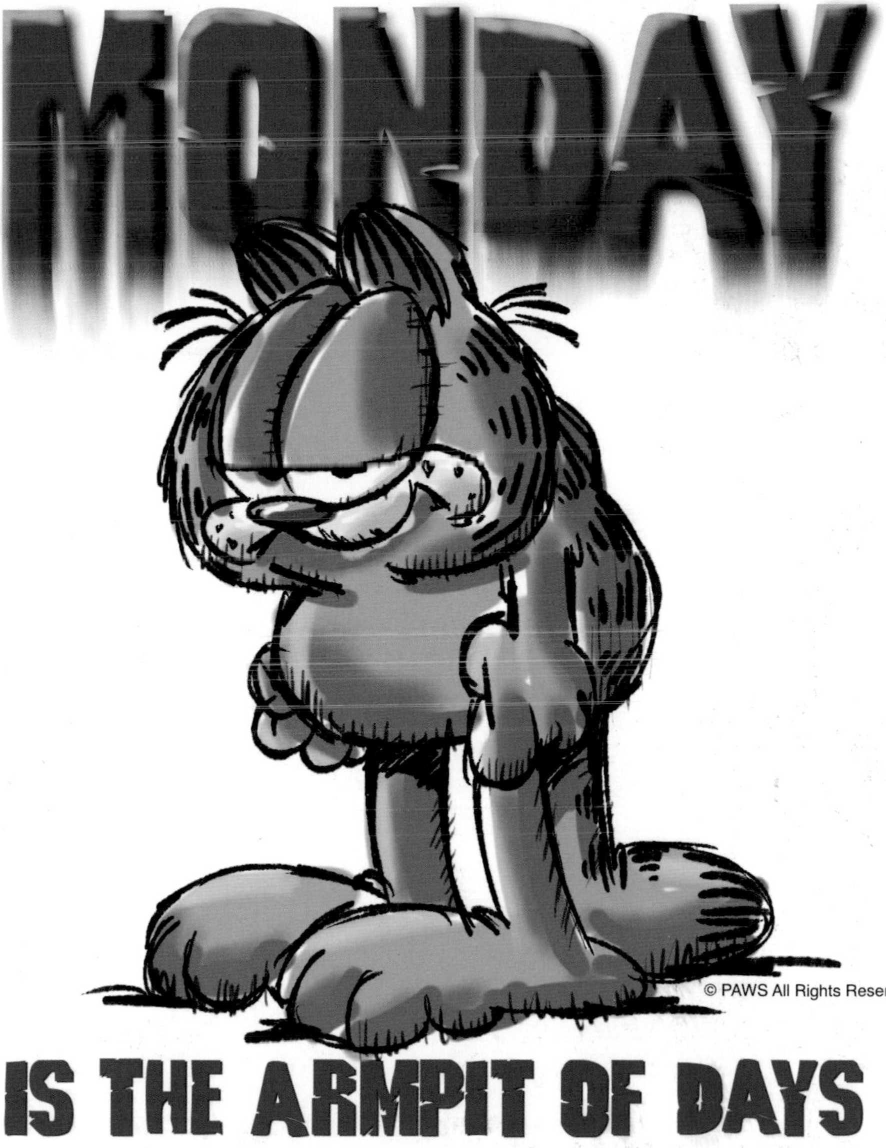
MONDAY
IS THE ARMPIT OF DAYS

Monday (Still) Bites!

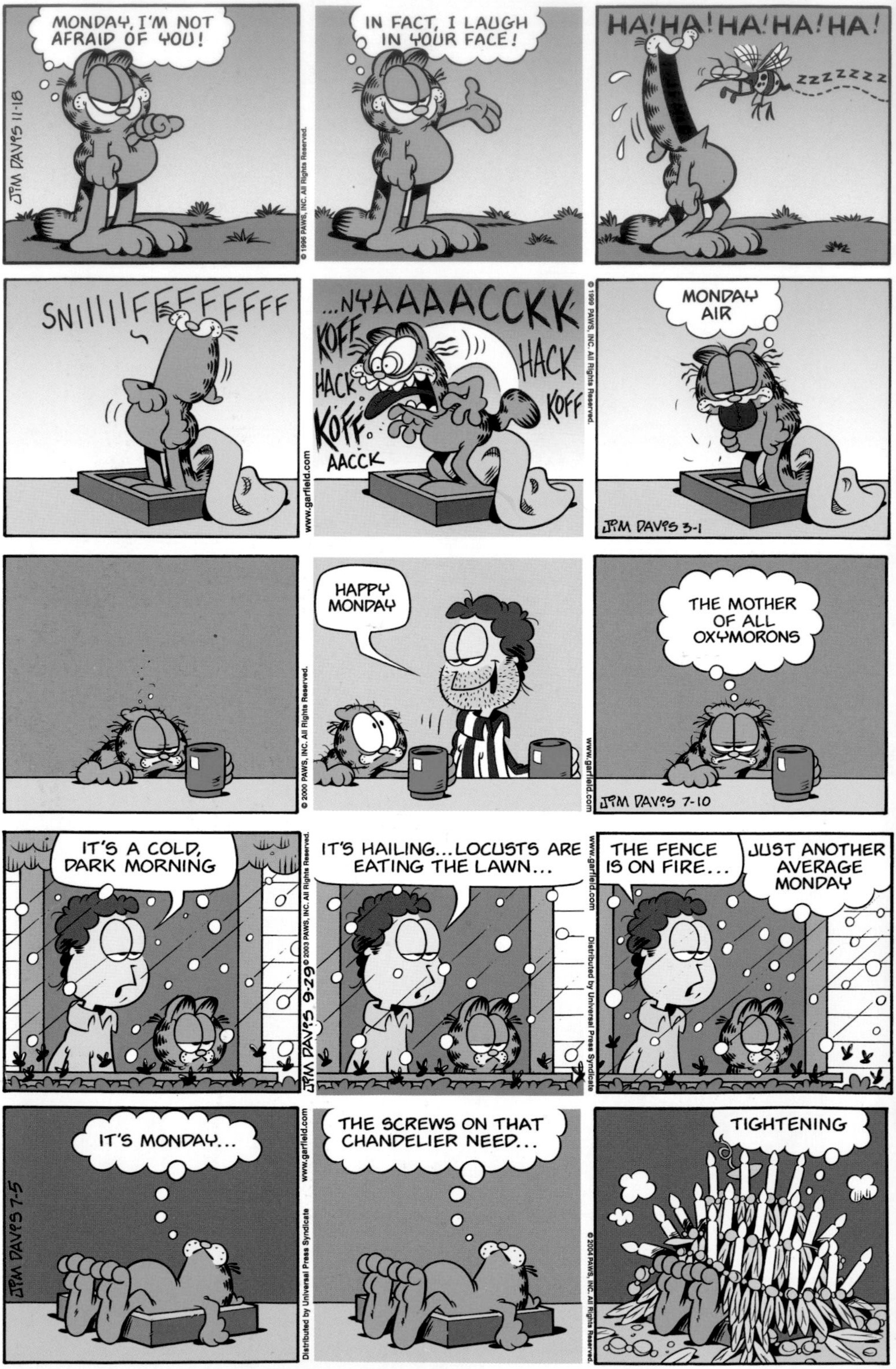

MONDAY, I'M NOT AFRAID OF YOU!
JIM DAVIS 11-18
IN FACT, I LAUGH IN YOUR FACE!
© 1996 PAWS, INC. All Rights Reserved.
HA! HA! HA! HA! HA!
ZZZZZZZ
SNIIIIIFFFFFFFFF
www.garfield.com
...NYAAAACCKK
KOFF
HACK
KOFF
AACCK
HACK
KOFF
© 1999 PAWS, INC. All Rights Reserved.
MONDAY AIR
JIM DAVIS 3-1
© 2000 PAWS, INC. All Rights Reserved.
HAPPY MONDAY
www.garfield.com
THE MOTHER OF ALL OXYMORONS
JIM DAVIS 7-10
IT'S A COLD, DARK MORNING
JIM DAVIS 9-29 © 2003 PAWS, INC. All Rights Reserved.
IT'S HAILING...LOCUSTS ARE EATING THE LAWN...
www.garfield.com Distributed by Universal Press Syndicate
THE FENCE IS ON FIRE...
JUST ANOTHER AVERAGE MONDAY
IT'S MONDAY...
JIM DAVIS 7-5
www.garfield.com Distributed by Universal Press Syndicate
THE SCREWS ON THAT CHANDELIER NEED...
© 2004 PAWS, INC. All Rights Reserved.
TIGHTENING

5 THINGS YOU DON'T KNOW ABOUT JON ARBUCKLE

Once recklessly washed darks and lights together

Secretly addicted to mayonnaise

Rooted for Kelsey on "The Bachelor"

Was second runner-up at Muncie Yodelfest 2017

Danced the polka with a rabid raccoon

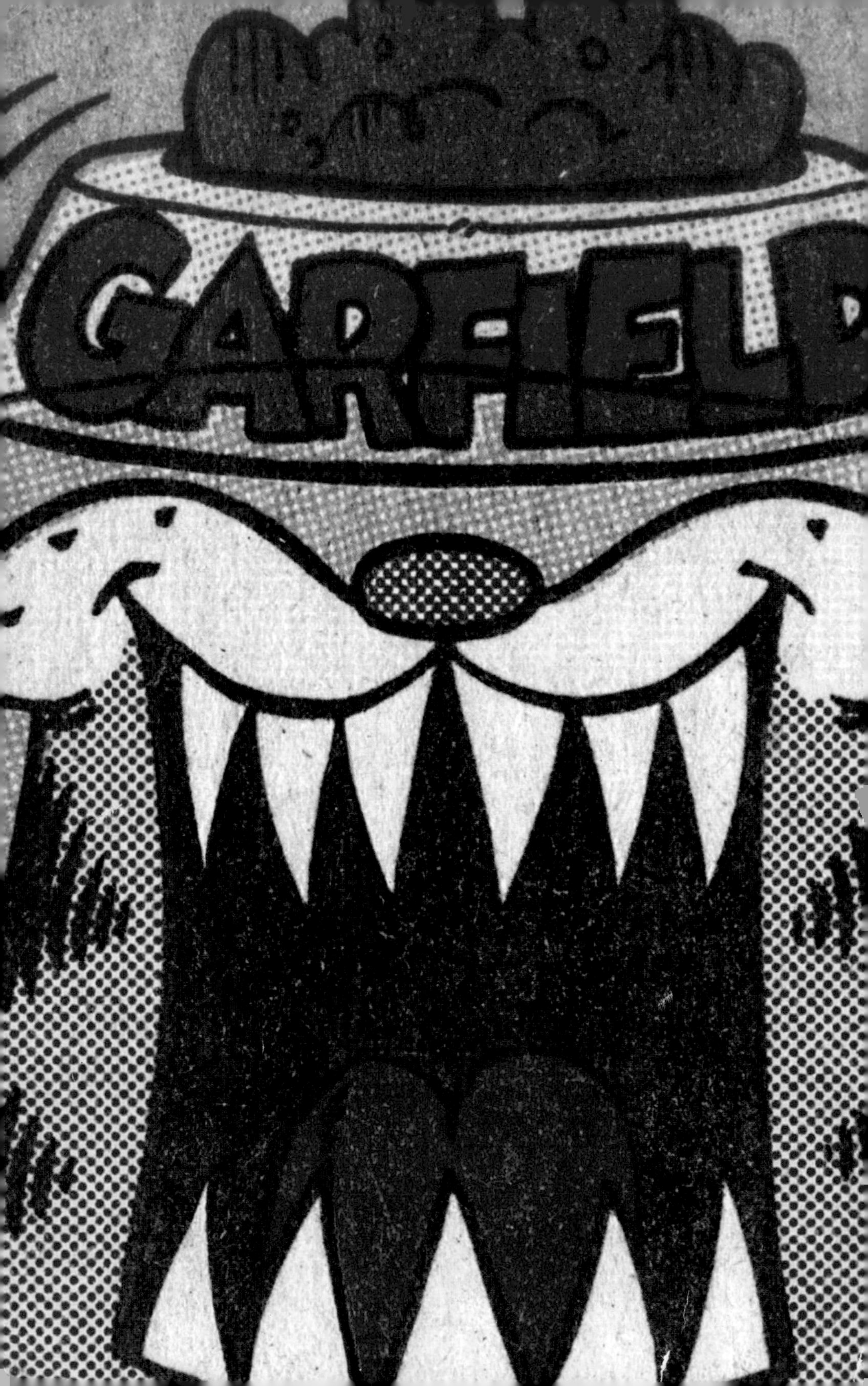
GARFIELD

Garfield Sunday Classics

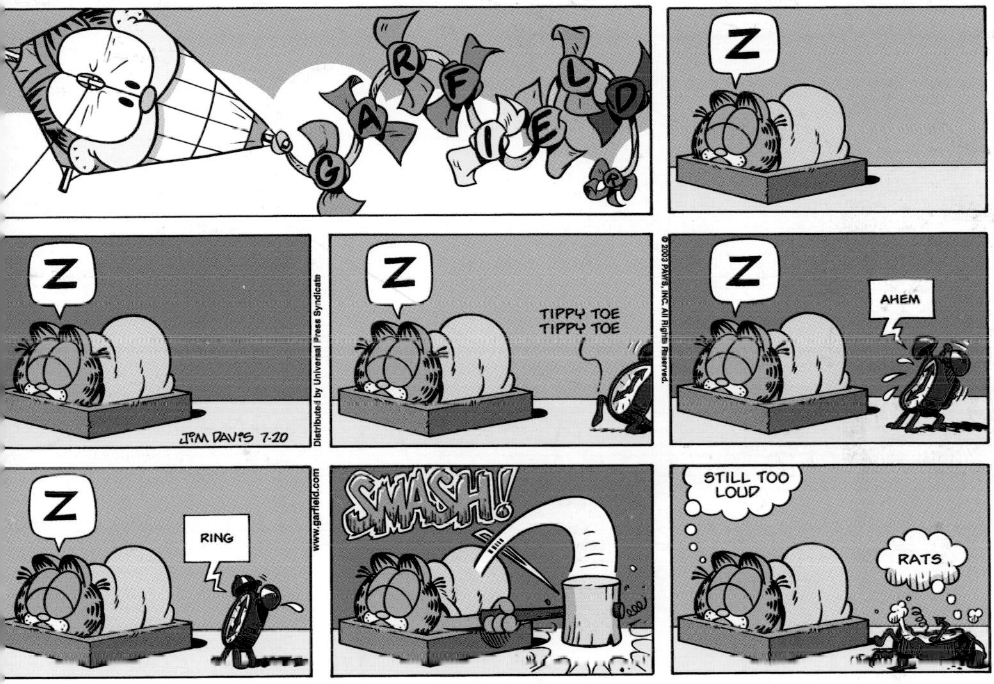
GARFIELD
Z
Z
JIM DAVIS 7-20
Distributed by Universal Press Syndicate
Z
TIPPY TOE
TIPPY TOE
© 2003 PAWS, INC. All Rights Reserved.
Z
AHEM
Z
RING
www.garfield.com
SMASH!
STILL TOO LOUD
RATS

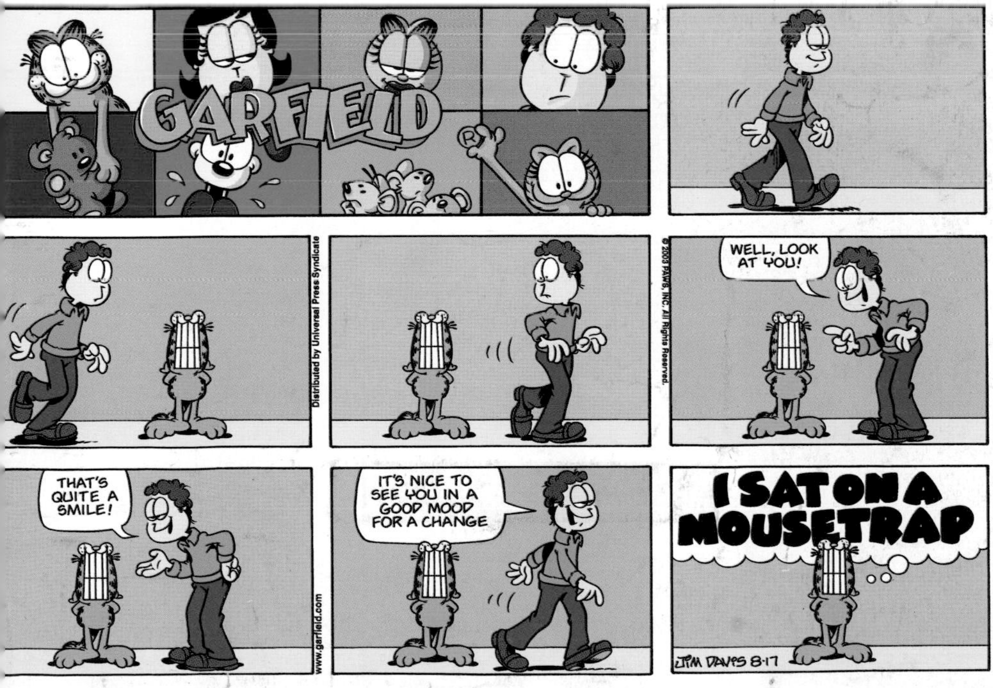
GARFIELD
Distributed by Universal Press Syndicate
© 2003 PAWS, INC. All Rights Reserved.
WELL, LOOK AT YOU!
THAT'S QUITE A SMILE!
www.garfield.com
IT'S NICE TO SEE YOU IN A GOOD MOOD FOR A CHANGE
I SAT ON A MOUSETRAP
JIM DAVIS 8-17

DISCOVER
EXPLOSIVE NEW WORLDS

ADVENTURE TIME

Brave Chef Brianna

KELLY THOMPSON BRIANNE DROUHARD M. VICTORIA ROBADO
MEGA PRINCESS

THE NOT-SO SECRET SOCIETY
DALEY · CRAFTS · CLARK · BRUNI

OVER THE GARDEN WALL

STEVEN UNIVERSE
VOLUME ONE

AVAILABLE AT YOUR LOCAL COMICS SHOP AND BOOKSTORE

To find a comics shop in your area, visit www.comicshoplocator.com

WWW.**BOOM-STUDIOS**.COM

kaboom!™

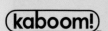

Adventure Time
Pendleton Ward and Others

Volume 1
ISBN: 978-1-60886-280-1 | $14.99 US

Volume 2
ISBN: 978-1-60886-323-5 | $14.99 US

Adventure Time: Islands
ISBN: 978-1-60886-972-5 | $9.99 US

The Amazing World of Gumball
Ben Bocquelet and Others

Volume 1
ISBN: 978-1-60886-488-1 | $14.99 US

Volume 2
ISBN: 978-1-60886-793-6 | $14.99 US

Brave Chef Brianna
Sam Sykes, Selina Espiritu
ISBN: 978-1-68415-050-2 | $14.99 US

Mega Princess
Kelly Thompson, Brianne Drouhard
ISBN: 978-1-68415-007-6 | $14.99 US

The Not-So Secret Society
Matthew Daley, Arlene Daley, Wook Jin Clark
ISBN: 978-1-60886-997-8 | $9.99 US

Over the Garden Wall
Patrick McHale, Jim Campbell and Others

Volume 1
ISBN: 978-1-60886-940-4 | $14.99 US

Volume 2
ISBN: 978-1-68415-006-9 | $14.99 US

Steven Universe
Rebecca Sugar and Others

Volume 1
ISBN: 978-1-60886-706-6 | $14.99 US

Volume 2
ISBN: 978-1-60886-796-7 | $14.99 US

Steven Universe & The Crystal Gems
ISBN: 978-1-60886-921-3 | $14.99 US

Steven Universe: Too Cool for School
ISBN: 978-1-60886-771-4 | $14.99 US